D1443527

SOUL SURVIVOR

ACKNOWLEDGMENTS

I'd like to thank my transplant surgeon, Dr. Daniel Murillo, for giving me a second chance at life with the success of the pancreas-kidney transplant he performed on me in 2006. My gratitude also goes out to my sister, Sarah Goodman, and my husband, Robert Glidewell, for their support and faith in me, and to my three grandchildren, Wyatt Zarda, Seth Reliford, and Marissa Vaughn, for keeping me young at heart. A special thanks goes out to Alice Duncan for her help in weeding out my dangling participles and doing such a terrific job at editing this novel, and to Evelyn Horan for her writing guidance.

Soul Survivor

Jeanne Glidewell

FIVE STAR

A part of Gale, Cengage Learning

Detroit • New York • San Francisco • New Haven, Conn • Waterville, Maine • London

GALE
CENGAGE Learning™

LIBRARY OF CONGRESS CATALOGING-IN-PUBLICATION DATA

Glidewell, Jeanne.
   Soul survivor / Jeanne Glidewell. — 1st ed.
    p. cm.
   ISBN-13: 978-1-59414-948-1 (hardcover)
   ISBN-10: 1-59414-948-8 (hardcover)
   1. Girls—Fiction. 2. Abduction—Fiction. 3. Reincarnation—Fiction. 4. Americans—India—Fiction. I. Title.
PS3607.L57S68 2011
813'.6—dc22   2010043413

Published in 2011 in conjunction with Tekno Books.

Printed in Mexico
2 3 4 5 6 7 15 14 13 12 11

Dedicated to Nikki Robbins, who gave me the inspiration for this novel by claiming, at five years old, to have once been known as Rachel, and also to her brother, Andy, who left us all too soon at the age of twenty-three. He will forever be loved and missed.

And last, but not least, I'd like to dedicate this book to my mother, Carol Van Sittert, who is fighting a courageous battle with breast cancer. She took me to many places around the world, including India, and taught me that anything is possible.

ONE

Is Skye having some kind of seizure? Zoe wondered as she watched the strange behavior of her five-year-old daughter who was sitting on the front steps of the farmhouse. Skye twitched uncontrollably from head to toe.

Zoe felt panic flooding through her. Just a few moments earlier, Skye had been peacefully drawing in her sketchbook while Zoe read a book and relaxed on the front porch swing. But now Skye's small body was rocking back and forth. Her head was bobbing up and down like that of a rooster strutting around a barnyard, and her tiny hands were clinched tightly into fists. Although she had a naturally pale complexion, Skye's face was almost devoid of color, now a translucent pearly white. Despite the bright sunshine, Skye's pupils were huge. Their light-blue irises were barely visible.

Zoe rushed to her daughter's side, and nearly tripped over the stubby pink crayon that had slipped from Skye's hand. "Skye? Are you all right?" Zoe asked. She gave Skye's shoulder a gentle shake as she crouched down beside her. She felt a fierce shudder ripple through the small child's body.

Looking into Skye's owlish pupils, Zoe saw that the child's eyes were vacant and unblinking. Skye seemed to be looking right through her, as if she were made of glass.

Skye gave a loud, piercing scream that almost knocked Zoe over in fright. Skye's entire torso began to tremble and quake.

9

Her long blond ponytail swished back and forth across her back like a pendulum. Zoe wanted to grab the ponytail to stop the eerie swaying motion.

"Skylar? Honey? Are you all right?" Zoe asked again, shaking her daughter in a more violent way.

Skye's body stopped twitching and rocking. Zoe watched with deep concern as the girl blinked several times in rapid succession. After a short pause her pupils began to recede and her labored breathing eased. Skye swallowed raggedly and responded. "Uh, yeah. Uh, I'm okay."

"You were shaking all over, punkin. What's wrong?"

"Nothing, Mommy. Uh, I'm okay now. I'm ready to go inside though. I feel kind of hot."

Zoe touched Skye's forehead with the palm of her hand. Skye didn't seem to have a fever. "Let's go inside then," Zoe said. "Let me hold on to you, sweetie. I think you should lie down for a little while after you have something cool to drink, just to be sure."

As Zoe leaned down to gather Skye's sketchbook and crayons, her shoulder-length brown hair fell across her face. With trembling fingers she brushed it back and anchored her long bangs behind her ears. "Punkin, are you sure that everything is okay with you? You had Mommy really worried. What were you drawing in your sketchbook?"

"I wasn't drawing anything. I was writing my name."

"Writing your name?" Zoe asked, glancing down at the opened page, expecting to see an array of letters in haphazard order. She was surprised instead to see precise block lettering in vivid pink, sprawled across the entire page. RADHA it read. "Honey, that's not how you spell Skylar."

"No, Mommy, I meant my old name," Skye explained. "When I was fifteen, they called me Radha."

★ ★ ★ ★ ★

Two hours later, Zoe's husband entered the yard. He'd been working in the north field. Afraid the old barn would collapse on his John Deere, Trey had begun parking the tractor in front of the garage, and that's where he was now. Zoe often wondered whether she could drive a bicycle through any of the gaps in the walls of the barn, for there was far more sunlight shining through them than through the plate glass window of their living room. The thought never failed to amuse her and annoy her at the same time.

Zoe knew that Trey was concerned about the fate of his wheat and milo crops. Due to the recent drought, the crops were at a critical stage, and he'd have to begin irrigating soon. If not, he might be forced to dip into Zoe's small inheritance account, and Zoe knew that Trey would sell every stick of furniture they owned before he'd resort to using her money. Zoe considered herself and Trey equal partners, but Trey behaved as if her inheritance was off-limits to him, and he was just stubborn enough to turn pride and independence into a self-destructive trait.

Zoe watched Trey climb down from the tractor and wondered if he'd gained an ounce of weight since their marriage in 1995. As an only child, Trey was extremely close to his parents and had kept busy helping his father farm the section of land they shared. The constant activity kept his figure lean and sinewy. Trey was lanky, standing over six feet tall. The top of Zoe's head just reached the bottom of his chin.

To Zoe, Trey seemed to grow more handsome as he grew older. She loved the way his broad shoulders tapered down to a slim waist and strong, narrow hips. He had what her generation referred to as "six-pack abs," acquired naturally from the physical labor required to manage a farm.

He had nice hands too, with unusually well-manicured nails

11

for a farmer. But she thought his eyes were his most attractive feature. Trey's eyes were the same cornflower blue as Skye's, framed by thick, dark lashes. His wavy hair was light brown with blond highlights, bleached from his many hours in the sun. His tanned face was just beginning to show subtle creases from the outdoor exposure. He would age gracefully, Zoe was certain. For some odd reason, that irritated her. If only she could be so lucky.

When Trey's father, Joseph Jackson Robbins, Jr., had built a new ranch home on the far edge of the property, the old farmhouse had been handed down to Trey. At Zoe's request, Trey had spent the last few winters remodeling it. He'd made it clear to Zoe that he'd never consider moving away from the family farm. Zoe was still trying to adapt to country living.

Zoe was tired of being cooped up on the farm, several miles away from her friends in town. She missed the hustle and bustle of city life. She even missed the sound of horns honking, sirens wailing, and people shouting. It was difficult to sleep at night with only the sound of crickets chirping outside the bedroom window. Zoe wasn't sure if she could ever become accustomed to living in the country, and not even certain she wanted to keep trying.

Zoe watched Trey disconnect a small harrow from the hitch of the tractor before calling out to him. "When are you going to start to work on rebuilding that barn?"

"When I feel like it," Trey replied sharply. "You know I don't have time to work on it right now, so quit harping on it. The barn is not a priority at this time, and it's not your problem anyway. Trust me. I'll get to it when I have time."

Zoe sighed. "It's my problem when I need to get my van out of the garage and you aren't around to move the tractor out of the way," she said. Zoe worried less about getting the van out of the garage than she did about the barn crashing down while

Skye was outside playing around it. It was as much of a hazard as it was an eyesore.

"Why would you need to get the van out? You have nowhere you really need to go." Trey's blue eyes darkened in anger.

Yes I do, Zoe thought. *I need to go back to the city where Skye and I can have real lives—lives that involve more than sitting on the porch watching milo grow.*

"Okay, whatever," she said. "Dinner will be ready in about five minutes." Zoe entered the house and slammed the door behind her. She wasn't going to argue about the barn tonight. It was becoming a tiresome subject. She patted Skye's head as she hurried past her on the way to the kitchen.

Skye was sitting on the sofa, talking in a soothing voice to her favorite doll. "I'll take care of you, little one," Zoe heard her whisper.

Zoe took the skinless chicken breasts out of the oven, thinking maybe she should take Skye to Dr. Milner's for a check-up. The episode on the porch had frightened her; it wasn't something she could ignore.

After dinner, Trey and Skye went to the den while Zoe cleaned up the kitchen. After loading the new dishwasher, Zoe picked up Skye's notebook and entered the den to show it to her husband. Those five vivid, pink letters looked like something out of the twilight zone to Zoe, but Trey seemed unaffected by them. Even Skye's shaking, twitching and screaming, which Zoe described, didn't seem to alarm him.

"Maybe she was playing with an imaginary friend again," Trey said. "She has no one else to play with, so she has to invent her own friends."

Zoe ignored the jab. Trey had tried to convince her to enroll Skye in preschool, but Zoe enjoyed having Skye around during the day to keep her company. "How would she know how to spell Radha, or even know what she'd spelled? She's just recently learned to spell her own name," Zoe reminded. "I know that Skye is highly intelligent, but you know, at her age she can't be expected to spell perfectly."

Skye had been an early bloomer. She had walked at the age of six months, and had spoken in full sentences before her first birthday. But despite her expansive vocabulary and ability to reason beyond her years, she'd never shown much interest in reading and writing. Skye was more of a verbal communicator and had only just recently, with great reluctance, begun to work on her writing skills.

"Don't worry about it, Zoe," Trey said with a shrug. "Five-year-olds are always doing things that are surprising or amazing for someone their age, and especially Skye. Maybe it's something she saw or heard on TV. You know how she picks things up instantly. She always has."

Zoe wasn't convinced, but neither was she in the mood to bicker with Trey tonight. When Trey was in one of his argumentative moods, it was better for her to let him talk, nod at appropriate intervals, and be quiet. Tonight Trey was more interested in talking about a new brand of fertilizer, a parcel of land the bank was foreclosing on up the road, and the drought that was threatening his crops. He wanted to talk about anything but the barn or why his young daughter would think that she was once fifteen and called Radha.

A week later it had still not rained, and Trey was even more concerned about his wheat and milo crops. Skye was in the garage with him that morning, watching him sharpen the blades on his tiller and chattering in her usual way.

"That ought to be good and sharp now. Huh, Daddy? Are you still worried about it not raining?"

"Yes, we need rain badly for our crops to do well. We can't

afford to have all our crops fail this year."

"You know I can get a job if I have to, Daddy. It would help with the family, uh, what do you call it? Budgie?"

"Budget?"

"Yeah, the budget. I could help with the budget."

"I think we can get by without you having to get a job, baby. But thanks for offering," Trey added, chuckling as he winked at his daughter. "One way or another, your daddy will take care of you and Mommy. I don't want you worrying about it, okay? I promise I won't let us starve."

"Okay, I won't worry. But it sure is dry, ain't it?"

"Isn't," Trey corrected out of habit. He tested the sharpness of the blade with his index finger.

"Isn't it, I meant," Skye replied automatically. "Boy, our grass sure is brown in the yard. There are cracks in the ground. Good thing you don't grow cotton like my other daddy did. I think it needs even more water than wheat and milo."

"Your other daddy?" Trey asked, nonplussed by Skye's statement. He knew she was precocious with an active imagination.

"Uh-huh. The one I had before you."

Trey looked at Skye's serious expression and shook his head. *Where does she get this stuff?* he wondered. Is this something new, or had he just not been listening to her closely enough? Maybe Zoe's right and he should pay more attention to both of them.

He looked at Skye and stroked his chin in a thoughtful manner. "Well, I hope your other daddy had better luck than I seem to be having with the weather," he said softly.

The next morning, Zoe stood at the stove and stirred the scrambled eggs as she watched Skye, who was sitting at the table turning soggy Fruit Loops into a finger food. Zoe looked up as Trey walked into the room. She took a coffee cup out from the cabinet and set it on the kitchen counter for him.

"*Shubha prabhata Pitaji,*" Skye said to her father. Trey had awakened with a headache and was later than usual in getting his day started. Bewildered, he glanced at Skye and reached for the coffee carafe on the counter.

Zoe stopped stirring the scrambled eggs and stared at Skye. A shiver ran up her spine.

"What did you say, Skye?" Trey asked, pouring himself a cup of steaming hot coffee. He reached for the sugar decanter.

"*Shubha prabhata Pitaji. Kya hamlog aaj bark ja kar batako ko dana chuga sakate hai,*" she said without glancing up from her cereal bowl.

Trey turned to Zoe with a questioning look. "Did you hear that, Zoe? What did Skye say?"

Zoe shrugged. Thoughts of a previous day ran through her mind, and the word *Radha* stuck in her thoughts. "One of those surprising and amazing things that five-year-olds say, I guess." She couldn't help feeling smug now and a little sarcastic because Trey hadn't paid attention to her concern the week before.

"My God, is our daughter being possessed by the devil?" Trey muttered to himself, barely loud enough for Zoe to hear. "It sounds like she was speaking in a foreign language, or speaking in tongues or something. It even sounded like she spoke with a foreign accent."

Zoe had no idea what speaking in tongues meant, but she found herself hoping that Skye was doing exactly that. Anything would be an improvement over Skye being possessed by the devil. Zoe was beginning to see scenes from the movie *The Exorcist* flash before her eyes. She looked at Skye as if expecting green stuff to begin spewing from her mouth at any moment.

"Has she been around any foreigners?" Trey asked.

"No, none at all."

"Has she been sick? Does she have a fever?"

"No."

"Has she been watching TV?"

"I haven't turned on the television in weeks," Zoe replied. She'd always been a reader, unlike Trey who enjoyed watching action movies with lots of car crashes and flying bullets. *If Trey paid more attention to his family,* Zoe thought, *maybe he wouldn't have to ask all these questions regarding his own daughter.* "Should I call her pediatrician?"

"No. Absolutely not."

"Why?"

"Skye spends too much time at the doctor's office as it is. Hauling her over there every time she sneezes is bad enough, without taking her there just because she babbles some nonsense. I think I'll give Charlie a call."

Charlie Davis was one of Trey's golfing buddies. Charlie was director of the language department at a nearby university. He was fluent in a number of languages and familiar with many others. Zoe knew that Charlie wasn't much of a golfer, but he was a brilliant linguist.

Trey put on a pair of reading glasses, picked up the cordless handset, and punched out a number. "Charlie, this is Trey. Got a question to ask you. Does *Shubha prabhata Pitaji* mean anything to you?"

After listening a few moments, Trey asked, "Are you sure?" There was astonishment in his voice.

Several minutes later, Trey hung up the phone and turned to Zoe who was twisting the ends of her hair between her fingers. "I don't know what to think now," Trey said softly, "but I am starting to get a little concerned."

"What did Charlie say?"

"He said that he's pretty sure that *Shubha prabhata Pitaji* means 'Good morning, Father' in Hindi. That's the closest interpretation or translation that Charlie could make."

Zoe had heard of Hindi, but she couldn't really recall what it was. Perplexity clearly shown on her face, as Trey continued.

"Hindi is the primary language of India, from the Hinduism sect, according to Charlie. Why would our daughter be speaking in Hindi all of a sudden?"

"I have no idea, Trey," Zoe whispered. "Why would our daughter ever be speaking in Hindi, or any other foreign language? She's smart, but she's not that smart!" She shook her head and pushed her bangs back behind her ears. "Could it just be an odd coincidence? Maybe she was just babbling and it sounded like she told you 'Good morning' in Hindi. You know, she did have food in her mouth at the time."

"That could be."

"Must be."

"Had to be," Trey told Zoe, although there was obvious skepticism in his voice.

"Had to be. Guess we should just ignore it," Zoe said.

Trey nodded. "Yeah, I think so too, but just for the heck of it, take her to see Dr. Milner tomorrow."

Two

Wyoming, 1929

Juan Torres was restless and anxious. With the short legs of his stocky body he paced across the floor of the small log cabin built by his father many years ago. The cabin was nestled in the Great Divide Basin of central Wyoming. Now the stock market had plunged and placed the entire country into turmoil.

Juan frowned and scratched the side of his head. He was worried about the repercussions the dismal state of the nation's economy would have on his family, and the Torres cattle ranch. The ranch had been struggling to survive since the onset of the Depression.

Beads of sweat formed on Juan's upper lip, giving his oily complexion a shiny look. His wife, Maria, entered the room with a disdainful look on her flushed face. She threw a threadbare dishtowel down on an old wooden box that served as a coffee table.

Juan steeled himself for an outburst of anger and contempt. He couldn't remember the last time that Maria had made a pleasant remark to him about anything or anybody. She was like a black cloud following him, ready to lash out in fury at any given moment. He felt the urge to escape.

With a hand on each hip and a scornful expression, Maria turned to Juan, "Have you thought about what you're going to do with this good-for-nothing piece of land you call a ranch?"

she asked. "It's becoming worse than useless. It's more of a hindrance than a help."

Weary of her non-stop complaining, Juan sighed and said, "This good-for-nothing ranch has kept this family fed and clothed, which is more than some area ranchers can say about their properties. These are tough times, Maria."

Well-to-do parents had reared Maria and had spoiled her to excess. Over the years since her marriage to Juan, she'd become more and more discontented. Now that the economy had taken its turn for the worse, she was almost unbearable in her unhappiness.

There will be no satisfying her now, Juan thought. He couldn't foresee himself ever being able to supply her with the fancy clothes and impressive home she felt she deserved. He'd be lucky to be able to continue to feed the family if the ranch kept up its steady rate of decline.

"Juan, can't you do something, *anything,* about our financial situation? Get a real job in town perhaps?" Maria asked. "This is the third night in a row for pinto beans and bread. You know I can hardly stomach beans, and I can't possibly be seen in public in this raggedy old dress. It's humiliating. This shack of a home is embarrassing as well. Surely there is something you can do. We can't continue on this way. At least I know I can't!"

"I'm doing the best I can, Maria," Juan said with a grimace as he struggled to remain calm. "We're not the only family in financial straits, my dear. The entire country is suffering and trying to survive. You'll just have to try to be patient. Surely the economy will eventually turn around. I had hoped that you would be happier once we had children for you to raise. Now I see I was wrong."

"If you remember right, you are the one who wanted children, Juan. Not me," Maria reminded him with a toss of her head. "Eduardo is always underfoot, tugging on my skirt, wanting one thing or the other, and I am sick to death of Rafael's constant whining and fussing. I am just sick and tired—period!"

Juan knew that taking care of a sickly infant was a monumental task, but he'd assumed that any mother would have enough maternal instincts to accept that kind of responsibility without hesitation or complaint. Rafael José had been born premature after a shortened, but difficult, pregnancy. He had precariously clung to life for several months and was just now beginning to show promise of surviving. At least their three-year-old son, Eduardo José, was healthy, robust, and full of life. But Juan knew it was Eduardo's lively and spirited nature that seemed to aggravate his mother.

Juan prayed that Maria's temperament would mellow as the boys matured and became more independent. Perhaps her mood would even lighten once she had recovered from the afflictions of childbirth. Afflictions he felt sure were exaggerated to make him feel guilt and despair. Maria seemed to go out of her way to make him feel miserable. She wore his misery like a badge and showed little regard for his feelings of pride and self-worth.

Juan sighed. He scraped his thumb across the stubble of his short beard. "I'm sorry, Maria. I'll do what I can to help you with the boys," he murmured, as Maria left the room without replying.

Juan slipped out the back door and strode with a brisk gait to the chicken coop where he kept a bottle of cheap Scotch hidden beneath an old wooden crate.

Three

Kansas, 2001

"Mrs. Robbins, I really don't know what to make of all this, but I'm quite certain that the problem's not related to a physical condition," Dr. Milner told Zoe. "I've performed a complete examination of your daughter and found nothing out of the ordinary. I would suggest you have Skylar evaluated by a child psychologist. I can refer you to Dr. Karem Azzam, who works well with children. He's had tremendous success treating schizophrenia, post-traumatic stress, and conditions of that nature."

Zoe listened in shocked silence. She couldn't believe that Dr. Milner felt there was a possibility her child could be a schizophrenic or possess any other mental disorder. She watched as he removed a penlight from his shirt pocket and directed it into Skye's right eye as if searching for proof of other aberrant personalities lurking within her head.

Dr. Milner frowned and placed the penlight back in his pocket. "Would you like my receptionist to set up an appointment with Dr. Azzam?" he asked.

Zoe hesitated. She didn't want to know what a child psychologist might tell her about her daughter. But she glanced at Skye, took a deep breath, and with great reluctance nodded her agreement.

Ten minutes later, Skye was redressed and frisking about the room when Dr. Milner returned.

"Dr. Azzam will be able to work you in this afternoon due to a cancellation." He gave Zoe a piece of paper with the pertinent information.

"Thank you, Doctor."

"I wish you well," he said before hurrying off to see his next patient.

Dr. Azzam's office was located in the same medical complex as Dr. Milner's, and Zoe and Skye had over an hour's wait before their next appointment. Zoe held Skye's hand as they walked across the street to McDonald's for lunch. Next to the fast-food restaurant was the local Wal-Mart. Outside the discount store was a mechanical, coin-operated wooden horse. Seeing the child-sized black stallion, Skye pointed to it as she looked up at Zoe excitedly. "Look, Mommy, it's Thunder," she cried excitedly.

"Thunder? Why do you call him that?"

"Because it looks just like a horse I used to have named Thunder. Can I ride him?"

Zoe knew Skye had a toy box full of stuffed animals, but she couldn't recall a black horse being one of them. "Sure honey, why not? We still have plenty of time to spare."

Skye broke away from Zoe's clasp and raced toward the mechanical horse. By the time Zoe caught up with her and dug a quarter out of her purse, Skye had climbed astride the horse she had dubbed Thunder.

Zoe was amused to see how much pleasure Skye seemed to derive from riding the toy horse. Skye was more animated and cheerful than Zoe had seen her in weeks. This was a quarter well spent, she decided. It served not only as a reward for Skye's patient endurance during the painstaking inspection by Dr. Milner but also to help fill time before the session with the shrink. A shrink, for goodness sake! While they were at Wal-Mart, she'd better pick up a couple bottles of Excedrin, Zoe thought. She had a feeling she was going to need them.

Zoe was relieved to see how well Skye related to Dr. Azzam. An Egyptian, Dr. Azzam had received his training in Cairo, and on his office wall were certificates to prove he was well schooled in the field of psychology. Zoe explained the situation to him as best she could, including Dr. Milner's remarks earlier that day. Her distress must have been apparent, because the doctor was quick to assure her schizophrenia was out of the question. "I think a mental ailment of any kind is unlikely," Dr. Azzam told her. "Highly unlikely, in fact."

Zoe's relief was almost overwhelming. She sighed and sank down in the chair the doctor offered. She wasn't sure if she could remain standing anyway. She felt as if the bone and cartilage in her knees had turned into silly putty.

"Let's not panic at this point," Dr. Azzam said. "There is no reason to put Skylar through costly and unnecessary tests."

"So what could be causing Skye's odd behavior recently?" Zoe asked. She swiped the palms of her damp hands up and down the sides of her faded denim jeans.

"I can't be certain. I have an idea that what's transpired is more indicative of something unrelated to a health issue, but I don't want to make any assumptions quite yet. At this juncture, a wait-and-see game is called for, in my opinion."

Zoe nodded. She was content to play the "wait-and-see" game. She'd be happy to play any game that didn't involve schizophrenia or any other mental disorder. She thought she'd be glad to go back to Wal-Mart and ride Thunder herself if that was the game she had to play to ensure that Skye was a perfectly normal, healthy little girl. She had enough on her plate right now, just keeping her marriage intact, without the added challenge of a daughter with a mental problem.

Walking back through the parking lot to the van, Zoe felt relieved and encouraged. Or at least she felt that way until Skye looked up at her and stated, "I need to go home and visit my family."

Alarmed, Zoe stopped and crouched down in front of Skye. "What family are you talking about, honey? I'm your mommy. I am your family! Are you talking about Daddy, or Grandma and Grandpa Robbins?"

"No Mommy, I mean my family in Bombay. The family I had when I was Radha. I haven't seen them in many years."

Zoe gasped, plucked Skye up off the pavement, and sprinted back to the building they had just exited. The "wait-and-see" game was over.

Trey had spent the better part of three hours replacing the chaffer sieve on his combine. He had just reattached the grain pan when he looked up and saw the mini-van pulling down the driveway. He shaded his eyes with his hand and waited while the van approached.

"What's up?" Trey asked Zoe when he saw the panicked look on her face as she approached. Zoe looked as if she were on the verge of tears, and a feeling of dread settled over Trey. The last time she'd looked that way she'd just been told of her father's cancer diagnosis.

Zoe patted Skye on the back. "Go on in the house, honey. I'll be in there in just a couple of minutes."

After Skye had left, Zoe turned back to Trey. "Dr. Milner said Skye did not have any kind of physical problem and referred us to Dr. Azzam, a child psychologist. Dr. Azzam was convinced the whole thing was just a fluke and there was nothing to worry about. He said a mental problem was highly unlikely."

"Yeah, that's what I figured. I knew it'd be a waste of time and money to take her to the doctor," Trey said, turning back to resume working on his tractor. He didn't want Zoe to see the relief that was evident on his face. He, too, was concerned about his daughter's unusual behavior recently, more concerned than he wanted Zoe to know.

"But wait, Trey, there's more. After we left his office the oddest thing happened." Zoe explained the incident in the parking lot. "Dr. Azzam wants to meet with all three of us tomorrow morning."

Trey shook his head in exaggerated disgust. "I think he was right the first time. There's nothing to worry about. I think Skye is just trying to get attention, maybe assert a little independence."

He didn't have to add "from you" to make his point. He knew Zoe was well aware of his concern about her tendency to be overprotective and smother their daughter with love. Since Skye's birth, Trey felt as if he were slowly becoming invisible. *We're drifting farther and farther apart,* he thought, *and I've no idea what to do about it.* Zoe spent so much time doting on Skye, there was no time left for Trey. Skye might be happier and better adjusted too, if he could just convince Zoe to enroll her in preschool. If she had the opportunity to interact with other children, they wouldn't even be having this conversation about meeting with a child psychologist.

Trey married Zoe in 1995 after an on-again, off-again relationship. Even though he'd felt he had very little in common with Zoe, he'd loved her and wanted her to be a part of his life. He knew she was a city girl through and through. But he'd hoped she'd enjoy country living once she'd become accustomed to it. He'd renovated the farmhouse in a desperate attempt to make Zoe happy, but even that didn't seem to help. Trey knew Zoe would still prefer to live in one of the cookie-cutter housing developments in town where several of her friends lived. *What would I do in the city?* Trey asked himself.

Farming's all he knew how to do. He was too old to start sacking groceries or asking people if they wanted fries with their burgers.

Although Trey and Zoe didn't seem to agree on much, one thing they did agree on was having a child right away. Four days after their first anniversary, Skylar Rae Robbins was welcomed into the world. She was a perfect specimen, except for two small purplish birthmarks. One was below her right hip. The other one was in the middle at the back of her neck, which would be totally obscure once her hair grew out.

From the beginning, Zoe was obsessed with the baby, and Trey began to feel like an intrusion to the point of being jealous of his small daughter and resentful of the time Zoe spent with her. He knew it was an immature reaction, but he missed the time Zoe had once spent with him, when he, instead of Skye, was the center of her universe. He still loved Zoe, but could feel her slipping away from him and he didn't know how to discuss his feelings with her.

Skye would be turning six in the fall and enrolling in kindergarten. Trey hoped it would be a beneficial thing for all three of them. School would allow Skye to have a social life of her own, and he and his wife could spend more time together. Allowing their child to attend school four hours a day would be a major adjustment for Zoe, but he thought that day couldn't come soon enough.

"So, are you going to go with us tomorrow or not?" Zoe asked, somewhat impatiently.

Coming out of his reverie, Trey said, "Oh, I suppose." He felt it was an unnecessary expense, but he couldn't deny his child medical care, no matter how trivial it might seem.

Zoe thought about what the session with Dr. Azzam would entail as her family gathered in the kitchen the next morning.

Skye played with her Ariel the Mermaid doll, Trey drank his coffee and read the morning paper, and Zoe prepared Belgian waffles. It wasn't a typical morning scene at the Robbins house, because Trey would usually have already been out working in the field before Skye and Zoe had come down for breakfast.

"Look here," Trey said to Zoe. He placed the entertainment section on the counter before her. "A special package to Disney World, including airfare, hotel accommodations, and two full-day passes to the park. Are you still thinking about taking Skye there this summer?"

Zoe wasn't certain if Trey's question meant he wasn't planning to accompany them. She was also not certain whether she wanted to know. Turning to Skye, she asked, "Would you like to go see Mickey Mouse and Donald Duck, punkin?"

"Oh, I suppose," Skye replied absentmindedly. To Zoe she sounded just like her father. Skye seemed more interested in Ariel than Mickey and Donald at the moment.

Zoe sighed, turned to Trey, and said, "Well, let's discuss it later." She would inquire about Trey's intentions then. She didn't want to initiate a discussion before Skye that might turn into a heated argument.

"Whatever," Trey said, folding the newspaper.

"Breakfast is ready," Zoe said. "We need to eat and get dressed so we can make it on time to our ten o'clock appointment with Dr. Azzam."

Zoe sat nervously twirling her hair between her fingers as Trey wheeled the mini-van into the parking lot of the medical building at one minute before ten. Fortunately, Dr. Azzam was running behind schedule, so she and Trey sifted through magazines while Skye played in the activity center designed for children in a corner of the small waiting room. They entered the doctor's office some twenty minutes later.

Dr. Azzam greeted them and apologized for the delay as he lifted Skye and put her down onto a metal table. Skye giggled and said, "Hi, Mister Doctor."

The doctor patted his young patient's head and responded. "Hi yourself, Miss Skylar," he said with a smile. "How are you today?"

"Fine," Skye replied. "Are you going to listen to my heart like the other doctor did?"

"No, not today, sweetie. Today I'm more concerned about what's going on in here, than here," he said, pointing to her head and then her chest. "Do you know why?"

Skye shrugged in an exaggerated manner and shook her head, as if she'd just been asked to explain the laws of gravity. She had no idea why she was being shuttled from one doctor to another.

"Because I already know you have a very good heart. Dr. Milner told me so," Dr. Azzam said. "He told me you were just as physically healthy and sweet as a little girl could be. But he's concerned there might be something bothering you. Maybe something in your thoughts that frightens you. I don't really think so, myself, but we're going to find out if it's okay with you, Skylar." Dr. Azzam's voice was cheerful and warm.

Skye giggled and nodded at the doctor. Zoe was surprised at the affinity Skye seemed to have with the doctor she had only met once before, and even then it had been for a few scant minutes. Skye had always shied away from strangers, older male strangers in particular.

Dr. Azzam chatted with Zoe and Trey for a few minutes, asking general questions about their daughter's demeanor and behavior. Then he turned back to Skye and began to ask her a few personal questions.

"Are you happy, Skye?"

"Yes." She nodded, looking down at her feet, which were

swinging back and forth below the metal table.

"Do you love your mommy and daddy and feel like they love you just as much?"

"Yes."

"Are you upset or sad about anything?" he asked.

"No." Skye gave short responses without elaborating or making eye contact with anyone.

Then to Zoe's surprise, Dr. Azzam changed his tack and asked, "Can you tell me what you remember from when you were big?" There was no response. The room was in absolute silence as Zoe held her breath in anticipation.

"Tell me about when you were a big girl, Skylar."

Zoe could hear the clock on the wall ticking. Tick-tock, tick-tock. It sounded incredibly loud and eerie.

Skye stared at her lap in silence, a thoughtful expression on her face. *What's going through her mind?* Zoe wondered. Still Skye sat silent and motionless.

"Do you still want to go to Bombay and visit your family, the family from when you were called Radha?"

Skye jerked her head up in perfect unison with Zoe's. Then Zoe heard Trey gasp, as Skye looked the doctor squarely in the eyes and replied, *"Han. Unlogon ki yaden mere pas hain, aur main unki kami mahsoos karta hoon."*

Trey gasped again, louder this time, and rose from his chair. Zoe pressed on his shoulder, forcing him back down. She stared at her daughter in astonishment.

"Can you speak in English, please?" Dr. Azzam asked Skye. "I can speak Arabic, but not Hindi," he said.

"Okay," Skye hesitated a moment and then went on to say, "I remember my family there. I miss them and want to visit them."

"What do you remember about your family in Bombay? Where did you live?"

"We lived on Little Gibbs Road on Malabar Hill. We could

see Chowpatty Beach from our window. My mother's name was Asha, and I loved her very much. She worked at the Bal Anand Community Center at the bottom of the hill, and I went with her and played with the other children," Skye explained.

Zoe glanced at Trey. He looked as perplexed as she felt. Trey's brow was knitted and his mouth was hanging open.

"What was your father's name when you were Radha?"

"Nirav."

"Do you think he might still be alive? When did you last see him?"

"I think it was 1966. I don't know if he or my mother are still alive," Skye answered with a touch of melancholy in her voice. Her voice sounded lower and more mature. "I haven't spoken to them since then."

"What did your father do?" the doctor inquired.

"He picked cotton."

"He picked cotton? Did she say cotton? Oh, my God . . ." Zoe heard Trey's mutter. Skye had stopped swinging her feet. She was concentrating intently on her conversation with Dr. Azzam. Zoe's eyes darted from Skye to the doctor as if she were watching a tennis match. She felt as if she was witnessing a tragic accident about to happen, but she could do nothing to prevent it. She fought the urge to snatch her child and run from the room.

Zoe's glance swung back to the doctor as he continued.

"How old were you when you last saw or spoke to Asha and Nirav?"

"Fifteen," Skye replied.

"What happened to you? Why did you leave?" Dr. Azzam probed.

Skye began to squirm and grow visibly upset, refusing to or unable to respond. Zoe reached in an awkward motion, intent

31

on comforting her troubled daughter. "Please stop!" Zoe pleaded.

Dr. Azzam nodded without taking his eyes from Skye, and said, "Skylar, it is okay. You are Skylar now, and everything's fine. You are happy and healthy and with people who love you."

Wrapped in Zoe's arms, Skye grew calm again. Dr. Azzam opened the door and called out to his assistant. He spoke in hushed tones as Zoe tried to regain her composure. Trey's mouth was still hanging open, as it had been since the dialogue between physician and patient had begun. He stared at his daughter as if she were some unimaginable thing that had just slithered out of a storm sewer. Zoe shivered from head to toe, wondering what he was thinking.

Dr. Azzam held out his hand toward Skye and said, "Skylar, Nurse Becky tells me she has some gummy bears for you in her desk. Would you like to go with her to her office for a few minutes?"

When Skye responded with a wooden nod, the doctor lifted her down from the table and handed her over to his assistant. He turned back to Zoe and Trey. "I don't want to alarm you folks, but this conversation has convinced me that a thought I had yesterday is correct," he said thoughtfully, rubbing his chin and then folding his arms across his chest.

Zoe was worried. She struggled to remain calm as she listened to the doctor. "Are either of you familiar with the theory of reincarnation and past life regression?"

Zoe shook her head in unison with Trey as they both stared at the doctor in stunned silence. Her stomach roiled in reaction to the overwhelming dread she felt at not knowing what was happening to Skye. Zoe forced herself to concentrate on Dr. Azzam, and ignore the queasiness in her belly. She fought to keep the saliva building in her throat from spilling out over her bottom lip. "I know of both, but not much about either," Zoe managed to murmur, as Trey nodded in agreement.

"The theory of reincarnation," Dr. Azzam said, "is based on the belief that when we die our souls are later reborn into new bodies. We may've all lived many different lifetimes in vastly different bodies, places, and times. Many famous people throughout history have held strong beliefs in reincarnation and felt they'd lived previous lifetimes: Ben Franklin, Socrates, Mark Twain, George S. Patton, Henry Ford, and Walt Whitman—just to name a few.

"Unlike many physicians, I believe in this theory. I have a good friend, Jutta Meyer, who's a certified regression therapist. She practices past life regression therapy. She helps patients overcome phobias and maladies in their current lives by taking them back to former lives through meditative hypnosis. She's been able to significantly help a number of patients I've referred to her over the last few years."

"And?" Zoe asked, feeling anxious and impatient.

"I know this is a lot to absorb, but bear with me," Dr. Azzam said. "Jutta explained to me that when our soul leaves our physical body at the time of death, it enters our spiritual body. At a time and place of our own choosing, our soul returns to physical form in a new body on a quest to learn new lessons. Our souls are forever striving to improve our spiritual knowledge and awareness.

"When we're young, we're not that far removed from the memories of our former lives, and many children are able to retain these memories. Under normal circumstances, they begin to fade after a few years, when the child reaches the age to attend school. However, some children retain these memories for many, many years. Dr. Ian Stevenson has impeccable credentials and is the Director of Personality Studies at the University of Virginia. He has researched several thousand case studies of children with past-life memories, and the results are most convincing. His findings are not unlike what we are experiencing with Skylar."

During Dr. Azzam's speech, Trey had reached over and clasped Zoe's hand. It had been trembling on her lap as if afflicted with palsy. He released it now, cleared his throat noisily, and asked, "So you think Skye's having memories from a past life?"

To Zoe, Trey sounded unconvinced, skeptical of the doctor's ability to come to a conclusion of this magnitude. Zoe knew reincarnation wasn't likely something Trey's Catholic parents would've ever discussed during Trey's childhood. And if they had discussed it, it wouldn't have been in glowing, positive terms, but rather as something completely beyond the realm of possibility.

Dr. Azzam nodded and shifted position before responding. "Yes, I believe Skylar's remembering a former incarnation. This would explain why she could speak about things she's never heard about in this lifetime. It's rare for an individual to retain knowledge of the native language from a past life, an ability known as *xenoglossy,* and this is an incredible validation for the existence of reincarnation. What's also unusual, but less so in children, is that she's spontaneously remembering details from a past life without being regressed through hypnosis. Judging from her reaction, I'd guess something happened to Radha at the age of fifteen that caused her to be separated from her family, perhaps death or something else traumatic. Even in another lifetime, Skylar seems to be unable to deal with the emotions of that memory."

Zoe's mind felt fragmented; she was experiencing a vast array of emotions, from fear and apprehension, to confusion, to out-and-out excitement. She had so many questions she wanted to ask Dr. Azzam. She started with a simple one. "Skye sounded so much older, more mature, while she was in that—that—well, that trance, I guess you'd call it."

"Yes," Dr. Azzam said. "That's very common, Mrs. Robbins. She was speaking from the perception of Radha, an older personality than the one we recognize as Skylar. And although it's not exactly like being in a trance state, it's similar. Your daughter's in a very pliable stage right now, and I was able to manipulate her and tap into her past-life persona. I have to say, it was a remarkable experience for me, as well. The most clear-cut example of past-life retentiveness I've ever witnessed."

Trey cleared his throat again and asked the doctor a question of his own. "So what do we do now? Perform an exorcism?" he asked, somewhat sarcastically.

"Not hardly. It's not a negative thing at all. Just realize that Skylar is an exceptional child, and when she speaks of her life as Radha, she's not crazy, nor is she pretending. Her past life is very real to her. These memories should fade in time, but for now I would encourage her to discuss them. It may well be therapeutic for Skye if there are circumstances from that incarnation that will affect her emotional or physical well-being in this lifetime."

"And how's that, Dr. Azzam?" Zoe asked.

"Once one understands the root of a phobia or physical ailment, stored in what's often called cell memory, he's able to release it and is no longer inhibited by it," Dr. Azzam explained. "All living matter's just a mass of cells, after all, and it's the belief of many that these cells have memory, and this cell memory retains everything that a soul's ever experienced, in both physical and spiritual form."

"Fascinating stuff," Trey said, still unconvinced, "but I am finding it hard to accept that it relates to our daughter."

"Yes," Dr. Azzam agreed, "it's a fascinating phenomenon. And I understand how it would be difficult for you to accept. It's always hard to accept something new to us, something with which we are not familiar. I'd suggest you read up on the subject and give my friend, Jutta, a call. She can explain it all much more clearly and in greater detail," Dr. Azzam said.

To Zoe, the doctor seemed very comfortable with the subject of people recalling previous lives. She felt calmer as he continued. "Reincarnation is not my area of expertise, even though I'm quite interested in the subject. Jutta can help you understand it better and be of great assistance to you in understanding the situation with Skylar."

With Jutta Meyer's address and phone number, and a daughter who was stuffed full of gummy bears, they left Dr. Azzam's office. Skye was fast asleep almost before Trey had driven the van out of the parking lot.

"So what do you think now?" Zoe asked in a hushed tone, trying not to awaken Skye.

"Well, I don't know what to think," Trey said after a few moments, "but I'd like to do as Dr. Azzam suggested and read more about it. As much as I'd like to reject the possibility altogether, it's difficult to do after watching that unbelievable exchange between Skye and the doctor." Trey cleared his throat as he concentrated on driving. "I don't want to jump to conclusions, and I know how you tend to overreact to anything that has to do with Skye."

Zoe shot a sharp glance at Trey. "I am not going to apologize or feel guilty for being concerned about our daughter's emotional stability," Zoe said, gritting her teeth and clenching her fists tightly.

"I didn't say you should."

"Well, you implied it!"

"Don't put words in my mouth, Zoe, or assume I'm implying something I'm not. I'm only saying we need to be calm and approach this rationally," Trey reasoned.

"Well, I want to approach it rationally too, but we can't risk causing permanent damage to her psyche. I think we should consider going to Bombay this summer, try to verify her memories, maybe even locate this family she said she remembers and misses."

Trey tried not to shout. "Oh, yeah, now that is really being rational. Do you have any idea what a trip like that would cost?" Trey asked Zoe, in the sarcastic manner he had adopted in Dr. Azzam's office.

"We can use some of the money I inherited when Dad died," Zoe suggested.

"We'd have to, and I'm not wild about the idea of spending your inheritance money," Trey said. "Besides, everyone would think we're plum crazy to go off on a trip like that, searching for Skye's other parents, for God's sake."

"We don't have to tell them why we're going to Bombay. We can just tell them we wanted to take a trip to see India, as tourists. People do it all the time," Zoe said.

"People who are wheat farmers in Kansas don't do it all the time," he countered. "Who's going to take care of the crops while we're gone?"

"We shouldn't have to stay over there so long that your dad couldn't take care of things without you while we're away. After all, you covered for him last summer when he had his appendectomy."

"That was unpreventable. A trip to India in the middle of the growing season would be a different matter altogether. We can't just walk away from the farm and risk our wheat and milo crops. Those crops are our livelihood."

"I understand that, Trey. But I'm afraid these memories are going to take a terrible toll on Skye if we don't do something proactive about this situation. She woke me up crying in her sleep last night. I think it's important to try to resolve what happened to Radha if Skye really is recalling memories of a past life, one that may have ended in violence."

Trey shook his head. "I don't know, Zoe. I understand what you're saying, but I'm not sure my father will. I guess I'll call Dad tonight and run it by him. I can just imagine what he's going to think about it though—and Mom too! I guess if he's okay with it," Trey said, shaking his head. "Well, we'll see. Just don't get your hopes up. Okay?"

Zoe fidgeted as she eavesdropped on Trey's phone call to his father. Listening to the one-sided conversation, Zoe knew Joe Junior was very skeptical about the doctor's diagnosis. His approval seemed doubtful to her. She could only imagine his disbelief at Trey's words.

"But—yeah, I know, but—yes, but," Trey said into the phone. "You had to be there, Dad. It was unbelievable."

Zoe twisted her hair nervously, and was surprised a few minutes later to hear Trey say, "Thanks, Dad. I'll let you know what we decide."

Trey hung up the phone and turned to Zoe. He told her his dad had said it was their decision whether or not to go to Bombay. If they wanted to waste money on a foolhardy venture like that, it was their business. He had no problem with taking care of the crops while they were away if they decided to make the trip.

Zoe breathed a relieved sigh, even though her in-laws thought she was a fool. She'd been called worse things, and this time it couldn't be helped. Her in-laws' opinion of her was something she'd have to deal with later.

The next morning she and Trey drove over to the travel agency they'd used to book flights to Paris for their honeymoon six years earlier. Mickey and Donald would have to wait; they would not be going to Disney World this summer. In ten days' time they would be flying to Bombay, or what was now renamed Mumbai, India, since 1996.

FOUR

Wyoming, 1936

The summer of 1936 was one of the hottest on record. People in food lines were dropping like flies from heat exhaustion and dehydration. *The heat wave couldn't have come at a worse time,* Juan thought. *By the end of this winter the boys and I'll probably be in food lines, too.*

The Great Depression, now in its eighth year, had caused financial ruin for many Americans, including Juan and the Torres cattle ranch. As Juan surveyed his property, he saw his livestock decaying in the fields. The stench was almost overwhelming. The fields had all dried up, most of them scorched from the rampant wildfires that seemed to take nothing more than the flicker of a firefly to ignite.

"Rafael!" Juan called out to his youngest son. "Come help me with this steer. I need to get him to the barn, and he's too weak to walk there by himself."

"Why're you taking him to the barn, Papa?" Rafael asked. "Is he dying too?"

"Yeah, gotta slaughter him, son. He ain't got no chance to make it, and I need the beef to trade with in town anyway."

"Oh, all right, Papa. I'll be right there," Rafael said, running toward his father.

Rafael ran everywhere, even when walking would serve his purpose just as well. Although almost eight years old, Rafael

40

was still small, but strong, unlike during his early years when he was frail and lethargic. And he was intelligent. Juan considered Rafael to be a sharper and quicker thinker than even Rafael's older brother, Eduardo. That was saying a lot; Eduardo was considered by many as a child prodigy. With great remorse, Juan had pulled the boys out of school. He could no longer afford them even the luxury of an education. He was a failure as both a husband and a father.

"Wish we could move away from this ranch, Papa. It's getting awfully depressing. We're spending more time burying cattle than we are feeding them. Sometimes I think we should just leave here and never look back."

Juan nodded as Rafael's words brought back memories from three years prior, when his wife, Maria, had run off with Herman DeWalt. DeWalt, the local banker, had amassed a small fortune by foreclosing on farms and ranches as the Depression took its toll. He'd quickly bought up other properties also, for pennies on the dollar of their previous value. DeWalt was shrewd and merciless, and one of the few to capitalize on the horrific financial situation sweeping the country.

Juan knew one of Herman DeWalt's most appealing qualities, in Maria's eyes, at least, was the girth of his wallet. The girth of his abdomen was less appealing, Juan thought, but he was sure Maria could overlook DeWalt's body as long as she could wrap her arms around his bank account. Maria had wanted a lot more than Juan could ever hope to give her, and Juan knew she'd revel in her role as the wife of a wealthy landowner. As long as he could keep a few cattle alive and grow enough vegetables in the garden to feed the boys, he'd never turn the deed to his land over to the likes of any self-serving banker, Juan vowed. The land had been in his family for generations, and he was lucky to not have a mortgage to maintain. There was no money available to pay bank notes, no money for anything, other than an occasional bottle of Scotch. Juan's drinking bothered his sons almost as much as it had bothered Maria, so he still kept his Scotch hidden in the chicken coop. The boys might smell it on his breath, but at least he could enjoy it without being scowled at every time he took a swallow. That was worth a lot in itself. Juan wasn't proud of his need to drown his sorrows in alcohol.

Juan still found it odd that neither Rafael nor Eduardo ever asked about their mother's abandonment. It was as if she were just another heifer who'd been taken off to market. Here today, gone tomorrow. *Maybe they couldn't blame her for wanting to leave the ranch behind. Hadn't Rafael just said he wished the three of us could do the same?* Juan asked himself. More likely, though, the reason was that Maria never showed much maternal interest in her sons to begin with. It was her loss. She couldn't have asked for smarter or sweeter sons than the two she was blessed with. Juan felt very fortunate to have them.

As he thought about the boys, Juan considered his elder son. Eduardo, at nearly eleven, was stout and mature, and developing into a handsome young man. He was zealous in his protection of his younger brother, Rafael. Eduardo's facial features were much firmer and more pronounced than Rafael's. He wore his dark brown hair long and slicked down, while Rafael had numerous cowlicks, causing tufts of his shorter and darker hair to stick out wildly in all directions. Rafael always looked as if he'd just walked through a wind tunnel. Juan chuckled at the thought.

Eduardo often wore a serious, thoughtful expression, as if he bore the weight of the world's problems on his shoulders. Rafael, on the other hand, had a more casual demeanor. A smile nearly always graced his face, despite the family's current circumstances. Juan admired this quality in Rafael. He wished he could honestly say that it was a trait he had passed on to his son.

Other than their skin, which was the color of coffee laden with cream, there weren't many physical similarities in Eduardo and Rafael, yet they seemed to resemble each other more the older they got. And they were as close-knit as two brothers could be.

Juan wondered what would become of his two sons. Would there be anything left of the ranch for them once he was gone? He sighed as he surveyed his ranch land. No, it didn't look very promising, but he guessed he'd have to keep trying.

"Eduardo, Rafael, I need the two of you to cut some firewood while I'm gone," Juan said as he crawled up onto the seat of his old wagon. The ailing steer had been butchered and wrapped, and Juan was heading into town with the packages of beef to barter for other commodities. Their stock at the ranch was meager, and inclement weather would soon be setting in. Aside from a few onions, turnips, and potatoes, their supply of fresh vegetables was depleted, and the garden was through producing for the year. Juan knew if he and his sons didn't freeze to death during the oncoming winter, they'd need some nonperishable food items to sustain them.

After loading his purchases into the wagon in Rawlins, most of which he was able to get in exchange for a side of beef, Juan counted out his change. Deciding he had just enough coins left to pay for two drinks, he stopped at his favorite watering hole, the Rawhide Saloon.

"I'll take a Scotch and water, Bart," he told the bartender. "Go easy on the water."

Juan gulped the first drink down and nursed the second, glancing through a week-old newspaper someone had left lying on the bar. An article about factories in India producing cotton and coir caught his attention. "You read this, Bart?" he asked. "They're hiring people in India to work in cotton factories to keep the production lines moving."

"Yeah, I read it, Juan," Bart replied, pouring a drink for a cowboy who'd just sauntered into the saloon. "Don't pay much though."

Bart was right, the pay was nominal—measly to be more precise—but a job was a job, and there were few jobs to be had in remote central Wyoming.

Like Rafael, Juan was ready for a change. The monotony and loneliness was getting to him. Never having a spare dime to spend was no picnic either. He was tired of having to turn a nickel over three times before daring to spend it.

Juan knew child labor was common in India, and his sons were smarter than most kids their ages. If the three of them could all procure jobs in a factory, maybe they could earn enough to get a fresh start once things were back to normal in the country. If and when the nation's economy did turn around, they could return to Wyoming, buy a good bull and a few good calf-producing cows, and rebuild the Torres cattle ranch in no time at all.

It was probably just a pipe dream, Juan realized, but it was the first time he'd felt any optimism since Maria had walked out on him. *A pipe dream is better than no dream at all,* Juan told himself.

With new purpose, Juan tucked the paper under his arm and stood up to leave. "Going already?" Bart asked. "You just got here. Why don't you sit a spell?"

"Can't do it, pardner. Got a lot to do," Juan said with a rare gleam in his eyes. He waved at Bart with the newspaper in his hand. *"Adios, mi amigo."*

Before heading home to the ranch, Juan quickly made arrangements to sell the few remaining cattle he owned, along with three sow hogs, a temperamental rooster, and a dozen chickens. It would bring in just enough, he hoped, to arrange passage for him and the boys to Bombay, India. *With any luck at all, we'll be gone before the snow flies,* Juan thought, whistling as he folded up the newspaper and shoved it into the front pocket of his tattered denim overalls.

FIVE

Kansas, 2001

Zoe spent the next week looking for material for her and Trey to read, anything she could find about reincarnation and other psychic sciences. Like Trey, Zoe had always assumed when you died, you died, and that was the end of it. Now she was discovering this was not necessarily the case. The more Zoe read, the more she began to believe death was just a shedding of the physical body as the soul moved on to a higher sphere of spiritual awareness.

She and Trey read books by James van Praagh and Sylvia Browne, both famous mediums who seemed to be able to see and communicate with spirits of the deceased. They watched John Edward's program on CBS called *Crossing Over.* Edward communicated with spirits that would come through for members of the audience, called the gallery, who would in turn validate the information he received. Zoe also found books and articles about reincarnation by Dr. Ian Stevenson, the physician Dr. Azzam had spoken about, and a book about the psychic readings of Edgar Cayce, perhaps the most famous medium of modern times.

Zoe knew Trey was far more skeptical than she. Still, he was trying to read the literature with an open mind. "Zoe," he said to her one evening. "What I don't understand is how the world's population keeps increasing if there's a limited number of souls continually reincarnating."

"Maybe God creates new souls," she said.

"Maybe so. And then again, maybe this is all a crock of crap. But still, you should ask Jutta about it when you give her a call."

Zoe sighed. Trey's belief in reincarnation was fading again, as it had off and on all week. It seemed to her that Trey was beginning to side with his father's views again.

"Okay, I'll call her now," she said. "With all the books we've just read, I know enough now to at least ask halfway intelligent questions."

Jutta answered Zoe's call on the first ring. When Zoe commented on the fact, Jutta said, "I'm psychic, I knew the phone was going to ring." Then Jutta laughed and said, "I'm just kidding! I happened to have hung up the phone two seconds before your call came through. What can I do for you, Zoe? Karem . . . er, I mean Dr. Azzam, told me you might be contacting me, and I'm so glad you have."

"Well, I apologize for calling you at home," Zoe said.

"No apology necessary. I'm divorced and have lived alone for several years, so I've gotten into the habit of doing most of my work out of my home. My clients are able to relax and regress easier in this environment, as opposed to the more formal atmosphere of my office," Jutta explained. "How are things going with your daughter?"

"So Dr. Azzam discussed the situation with you?" Zoe asked.

"Yes," Jutta said. "And it definitely sounds to me as if Skylar is having spontaneous memories of a former lifetime. It's not as uncommon as you might think. It just tends to be a taboo subject. People are afraid of looking like they're crazy, off-the-wall, so they don't talk about it too much."

Zoe understood completely. She spoke with Jutta for several minutes before posing Trey's question. Jutta assured her it was a common question among non-believers. "Why should one believe there is a limited number of souls, or a limit to life within the universe?" Jutta asked. "It's quite conceivable that earth is one of many other inhabitable planets in this vast universe. Perhaps the populations on various other planets are decreasing as this planet's population increases. Or perhaps souls are spending less time in spiritual form between lifetimes than they did centuries ago. There are many theories and I don't profess to know all the answers."

Zoe was not convinced that Trey would be satisfied with that explanation, but she was enjoying the conversation with Jutta. "So, if we have previously lived as different people in different places, why can't we remember those lives?"

"Ah, well, that's another interesting question that evokes many different theories."

"What's your opinion?" Zoe asked, laughing softly. She knew she was presenting a challenging question to Jutta.

Jutta chuckled and said, "You are talking to someone who can't remember what happened last week. I certainly can't recall anything that occurred in my life before the age of four or five. Can you? So how can we expect to remember anything from many decades ago, or even centuries ago?"

"That makes sense," Zoe agreed.

"Many children, more than you'd imagine, have memories of former lives, but they don't often vocalize them as Skye has been doing recently. And if one does, it's often seen as the rambling of a child with an active imagination. As these children become older, the memories of past lives begin to fade, as do their current life memories of being an infant and toddler," Jutta explained. "But have you ever experienced a feeling of déjà vu, as if you have been somewhere before but can't recall when?"

"Yeah, I guess I have," Zoe admitted. She fiddled with the

coiled telephone cord with her left hand, as she listened and jotted down occasional notes with her right. She knew she wouldn't remember everything Jutta said that she wanted to pass on to Trey. Perhaps Jutta was right; Zoe wasn't sure she could remember by tomorrow what she ate for lunch today.

Jutta coughed raggedly several times and then continued. "Yet under hypnosis, children, as well as adults, can often recite incredible details about a time, a place, a language, a culture, or even a religion they've never been exposed to in their current lives. These details are validated in many instances. In most cases these regressed individuals do not recall a former incarnation as Joan of Arc, or Napoleon. Instead they recall lives as normal, everyday people from all walks of life, who often have lived very mundane lives."

"That would make it more believable. We can't all have been Napoleon or someone of his caliber," Zoe said, drawing small circles with her pencil on a corner of her notepad.

"I also think that if we knew we could return to physical form again and again, we wouldn't give much effort to working our way through hard times and adversity in any one lifetime," Jutta continued. "We'd throw in the towel, slash our wrists, and hope the next life will be easier. So it would defeat the purpose of incarnating into physical form to learn new lessons. For what lessons would have been learned? In other words, all this may just be a way to protect us from ourselves."

Before breaking the connection with Zoe, Jutta recommended a book written by Dr. Brian L. Weiss, a psychiatrist and graduate of Columbia University and Yale Medical School. She told Zoe the book was titled *Many Lives, Many Masters* and was based on the experiences of a patient named Catherine whom Dr. Weiss had regressed back to childhood. To his surprise, Jutta explained, Catherine regressed farther back in time to a previous lifetime, and since this first unique experience, Dr. Weiss had now become one of the most renowned past-life psychotherapists in the world. Zoe decided to purchase the book to read on the plane trip to Bombay.

That same week she spent a lot of time encouraging Skye to talk about her memories as Radha. She noticed that sometimes Skye was receptive, and sometimes she wasn't. Zoe used a notebook to record details of the memories Skye was able to recall and speak about. She was born in 1951, she remembered a younger brother named Mohandas, and a grandmother who had died when Radha was just an infant. Skye talked about a fishing trip she had taken on the Arabian Sea with her father. They caught big fish from a small rowboat. She also mentioned the Bal Anand Community Center again. This prompted Zoe to return to the library and check out a reference book on Bombay.

After verifying the existence of Malabar Hill and Chowpatty Beach, Zoe found a short article about the community center that Skye had mentioned. Bal Anand was a small center for the urban poor and was located at the base of Malabar Hill. Nandini Mechta had created the center in 1954 in the garden of a colonial home. Its purpose was to be a place for less privileged children of the community, where they could come to play, sing, and learn to paint. Originally the center was sustained with the help of volunteer workers, and Zoe assumed Radha's mother, Asha, must have been one of the volunteers. In 1968, enrollment had increased to the point Bal Anand had to move to the garage of a high-rise building on Dongersi Road, where it was still located.

Verifying this information all but eliminated any doubt Zoe had on the authenticity of Skye's recollections. She was relieved to see Trey was becoming less skeptical, more convinced Skye really was remembering a past life she'd experienced as a young Indian girl.

"Pretty overwhelming evidence, isn't it?" Trey said, shaking his head in bewilderment. "I had rather hoped this entire thing had been a figment of Skye's imagination, kind of like Freddy, the Talking Frog."

Zoe smiled as she thought about the invisible frog Skye used to conjure up for her amusement during moments of boredom. Skye would talk a mile a minute to the frog as she walked it around the yard on an invisible leash, stopping on occasion to listen to responses only she could hear. "That was so funny," Zoe said.

"Not to me," Trey responded. "I thought it was just further proof Skye needed real friends to play with."

"Yes, I imagine you would." Zoe didn't want to rehash the old argument, so she closed the book, set it down on the table, and left the room before Trey could reply.

"What's going on?" Zoe asked, popping straight up in bed like a bagel in the toaster. She and Trey had just gone to bed when they heard a loud noise down the hall.

"I think it is Skye hollering," Trey said. "Sounds like she is having another nightmare. I told you not to press her about what happened to Radha when she was fifteen. It upsets her too much," he chided. "Why can't you listen to me once in a while? There's no sense stirring up these traumatic memories Skye appears to be having."

Trey followed Zoe down the hall to Skye's room, to find their daughter thrashing about in her twin canopy bed.

There was a look of sheer terror on Skye's face. Her small body was bathed in sweat. Zoe gently touched Skye's forehead and woke her, but could not persuade her to discuss her nightmare. It took a long time to calm Skye. Zoe held her in her arms and stroked her back with soft, tender strokes, until Skye fell asleep again.

Earlier in the evening, Zoe had broached the subject of what had occurred in Skye's life as Radha to cause her to leave her family, and as before in Dr. Azzam's office, Skye's discomfort was apparent. *I suppose I should've listened to Trey and not pressed her,* Zoe thought. *The memory must just be too painful for her to deal with.*

Even without that important piece of information, Zoe felt she was gathering enough useful details to be helpful when they arrived in India. And if nothing else came of it, at least Trey was showing more interest in his family than he had in a long time, she thought. Maybe she was loosening up a bit, too. As much as she disliked admitting it, she knew she also had been too uptight in recent months. Losing her father to cancer earlier that year hadn't helped any. An only child like Trey, Zoe had lost her mother in a car accident caused by a drunk driver many years before. It was important to Zoe to keep her family together, if at all possible. Skye was a talkative but often melancholy child; she needed both her parents involved in her life. Zoe couldn't bear the thought of a potential dissolution of her marriage. *I'm going to work harder at recapturing the love Trey and I once shared,* she vowed, *for Skye's sake, as well as my own.*

Six

Kansas, 2001

Pulling weeds from the flowerbed behind the house, Zoe paused and glanced up when she heard the distinctive rattle of Trey's old pickup coming down the long, gravel driveway.

"I picked up some boards at Capital Lumber," Trey said, gesturing at the small stack of two-by-sixes in the truck bed.

Zoe's eyes darted toward the barn and back. She lifted a questioning eyebrow.

Trey scowled in disgust. "No, not for the barn. You know I can't start a major project like that when we're leaving for India in a few days. I'll get to the barn when I have more time. These boards are to replace the steps leading up to the front porch. The old ones are beginning to rot, and I'm afraid one of them will give out."

"Oh," was Zoe's short response.

"Where's Skye?"

"Taking a nap. She stayed up pretty late last night."

Trey nodded and said, "Oh, yeah, I forgot. She had to see how *Lion King* ended. She's only watched that movie fifty times before."

"She loves that movie," Zoe said with a look of mild surprise. She was reminded again of the change in Trey's recent attitude. He usually wasn't so easily agitated over insignificant things like Skye's staying up an hour or two past her bedtime. Until lately he'd encouraged Zoe to be more lenient and flexible about the exact things for which he now showed no tolerance.

"She knows every line of it by heart. She doesn't need to stay up late to see how it ends," he said irritably.

"She doesn't stay up late all that often, Trey. What's it hurt to let her do it once in awhile?" Zoe asked, her hands placed firmly on her hips.

"What's it help?" Trey countered. As Zoe turned to walk away, he said, "Oh, and by the way, I ran into Sam at the lumberyard, and he invited us over for supper. It's up to you, I guess. Anyway, I told him I'd have you call Ellie this afternoon."

Zoe turned back around, "Let's go, Trey," she said, happy to have an invitation to go into the city for at least a few hours. "We haven't gone anywhere in weeks. It would be nice to get out for a change. I can ask Victoria to watch Skye. I know Skye would be tickled. It's been a while since she's seen Victoria."

Victoria was a promising young barrel racer whose family owned the horse stables up the road from the farm. She was a reliable and trustworthy babysitter, and Skye adored her.

Luckily, Victoria was available on such short notice and agreed to watch Skye that evening. Zoe showered, then put on her faded denim skirt with a new western blouse that had just arrived the day before from a mail-order company. She was ready shortly after five o'clock, anxious to visit the Boyers. Although they were initially Trey's friends, Zoe had become very fond of Sam and Ellen over the years since she'd first met them on a double date.

Zoe recalled that Sam and his wife Ellen had been friends with Trey since junior high school. Samuel Boyer had gone to work for the local water department shortly after graduation and had worked his way up to assistant manager of the local office. Ellen now worked as a waitress at the Main Street Diner, one of the best restaurants in town, and Sam often joked that they hired her as a waitress instead of a cook because they couldn't afford the malpractice insurance. Zoe smiled. It was no secret Ellen was better at serving food than she was at preparing it. It would be fun to spend the evening with them and catch up on the local gossip. Working at the diner, Ellen heard about everything going on in town.

The Boyers lived in an older, well-established neighborhood in town. When Trey pulled Zoe's mini-van up to their house at about ten minutes before six, Sam flung open the door and exclaimed exuberantly, "Welcome to the *Sam 'n Ella Café!*"

This play on words was an old joke they all still found amusing. Several years prior, Trey had stopped by to borrow a ripsaw from the Boyers and was invited to stay for lunch. The next day, Trey spent most of his time in the bathroom, leaning over the toilet. Ellen had been concerned Trey's illness was the result of something she had fed him the previous day, and Trey had been a bit suspicious of her beef stroganoff, which hadn't tasted quite right. But Zoe and Skye had succumbed to the same illness a couple days later, and since food poisoning wasn't contagious, Ellen was let off the hook.

Zoe and Trey laughed as Sam led them into the house. Sam told Zoe that Ellen was in the kitchen doing fowl things to a chicken. Zoe walked into the kitchen, and Ellen looked up from a dog-eared cookbook and asked, "Do you know what braise means? I'm trying to make Cordon Bleu and am about ready to give up on the recipe and just wing it."

Zoe flinched as she imagined the results. "Here, let me help, Ellen, even though I'm no Betty Crocker myself!"

"Do you think we should tell Sam and Ellen about this situation with Skye and our trip to Bombay?" Zoe had asked earlier on the drive over to the Boyers.

"Well, I'd like to see what they think, but I'm not wild about looking like a couple of pistons not firing on all cylinders, if you know what I mean," Trey replied.

"Yeah, I know what you mean," Zoe said with a sigh, not real fond of his analogy. "I have no idea what their views on reincarnation are, but I'm anxious to discuss Skye's situation with someone. Aren't you?"

"No, not really. I'm in no hurry to have my best friend think I've lost touch with reality. Let's just play it by ear," Trey said. "If it comes up in conversation, that's okay."

Zoe and Trey found themselves relating Skye's entire story to the Boyers while they choked down an overspiced, undercooked chicken, washed down with three bottles of Spumante. Sam and Ellen were fascinated with their tale, and Zoe was relieved to find their friends were supportive of their plans to travel to India and do further research into Skye's recollections of a former lifetime as Radha.

"Do you remember me talking about a sister named Joyce who lives in Kentucky?" Ellen asked. At Zoe's nod, Ellen continued. "I think something similar is happening with her seven-year-old son, my nephew, Nick. He was watching some media coverage on the conflict in Kosovo the other night when he suddenly hung his head in his hands and said, 'I hope I never have to go to war again. I haven't lived through one yet.' Isn't it odd? It was almost as if watching the frightening events on television triggered an old memory of a history of his having died in battle. It gives me chills just thinking about it."

"Yeah, me too," Zoe agreed. "Yesterday I was on the Internet and went onto a Web site called *childpastlives.org.* I was reading through message board topics on the site, and it seems like that kind of TV coverage triggers past-life memories in a lot of people, especially in children."

"Makes sense," Ellen said. "A gal who cooks part time at the diner told me once she was baking cookies one day when her three-year-old son asked her if she remembered when he used to bake cookies for her when she was his son. She was a real skeptic when it comes to reincarnation, but that question sure made her stop and reconsider. She's not quite as close-minded now."

"In all of this literature Trey and I've been reading, it says friends and family members often reincarnate in groups, and often in different relationships to each other."

"I've read that too. Just think, Zoe, I could've been your grandfather in a previous lifetime."

Sam laughed and broke into the conversation. "That's a scary thought. But, all joking aside, it is an odd phenomenon. Ellie and I'll be anxious to see how your trip pans out. Y'all fly out in what, three days?"

"Yes, Saturday morning," Trey answered.

"Would you like me to drive you to the airport so you don't have to leave your van in long-term parking? I have no plans for Saturday," Sam offered.

"That would be great," Trey said, accepting his friend's offer, to Zoe's relief. She'd feel better knowing her van was in the garage and not the airport parking lot.

Since they didn't know how long they'd be gone, the parking fees could mount up in a hurry. The return date of their round-trip tickets was open-ended. It would be an expensive trip, Zoe knew, but she believed it was the perfect thing on which to spend part of the inheritance she'd received from her father. Trey didn't agree, but he didn't agree with her on much of anything anymore, so his attitude didn't bother Zoe as much as it would have in the past.

It will be money well spent, if for no other reason than it'll force Trey to spend more time with his family, Zoe thought. *I can't wait to just get away from the farm for a few days—for any reason whatsoever!*

SEVEN

Indian Ocean, 1936

"Ahoy there, matey!" Rafael greeted his older brother, entering their cramped cabin in the hull of the cargo ship. Eduardo groaned and smiled sheepishly at him. It was the first time Rafael had seen Eduardo sitting upright on the cot in days, and it was a welcome sight. The almost constant pitching and rolling of the vessel hadn't bothered Rafael at all, whereas Eduardo had been seasick from almost the moment he had stepped onboard.

Eduardo had always been the stronger of the two brothers, protecting and watching over Rafael. Now their roles were reversed. Rafael was proud to be caring for his brother, bringing him food and water, holding his head while he retched into a bucket, and trying to keep Eduardo's spirits lifted despite his discomfort. Having always been the weaker brother, it now felt good to Rafael to be the stronger one.

Day after day, Eduardo had lain sprawled across the room's only cot, trying in vain to keep down anything he ate. But each heave of the ship's belly seemed to result in a similar heave in Eduardo's. Rafael felt almost relieved when Eduardo occasionally lapsed into semi-consciousness; at least in this state, Eduardo was unaware of his suffering. Each night, Rafael and his father, Juan, curled up under thin blankets on the musty floor, often without Eduardo even knowing they were there. It was only for his brother's sake that Rafael prayed for a speedy arrival in India.

While sailing aboard the cargo ship, Rafael found himself happier than he could ever remember. He loved the salty taste of the air and the feeling of the ship's motion beneath his feet as he moved about the vessel. He was curious about the activity of the crew and quickly became a favorite among them. They answered his many questions with patience and amusement, taught him how to tie a sailor's knot, and explained how they charted a course using marine maps and coordinates. Rafael was enjoying every minute of the voyage, and he felt stronger and more at home on the sea than he'd ever felt on the ailing cattle ranch in landlocked Wyoming. He dreamed at night of one day becoming a sailor himself. Working in a cotton factory didn't sound half as alluring as sailing the high seas. In fact, working in any kind of factory just sounded like work! *But I will do whatever I have to do to help Papa fulfill his dream of rebuilding the cattle ranch,* Rafael thought. Rafael was not certain this was the way to go about it but felt surely Papa knew best.

Eduardo had been skeptical about the recent upheaval and reluctant to leave the ranch, but Rafael had embraced the opportunity to see more of the world. He had a wanderlust nature Eduardo lacked, and although he had no qualms about returning to the ranch some day, he looked forward to new and exciting experiences in the meantime—even if it meant working long, hard hours in a cotton factory.

Rafael was young, but observant, and old enough to see how unhappy his father had become. Juan hadn't been the same since the day Rafael's mother, Maria, had walked out the door, leaving her husband and sons behind on the ranch. Her defection had upset Rafael and Eduardo, but not to the extent it had devastated their father. Juan and Maria had often become embroiled in bitter arguments, flinging true and imagined slights and accusations at each other. Theirs wasn't the most solid of marriages to begin with, Rafael realized, but having his mother there had given his father a purpose to keep struggling. It was obvious to Rafael that Juan now felt like a failure, with no self-esteem and little incentive to continue striving to keep the ranch afloat.

In recent weeks on the ranch, Rafael had rarely seen his father. Juan had been spending most of his time in the chicken coop, drinking to excess, which only seemed to make him more irritable and depressed. It seemed to Rafael his father had given up trying to solve his problems, and chose to hide from them behind a bottle of Scotch. It was the old "head buried in the sand" technique. If Juan couldn't see the problem through his drunken fog, then as long as the alcohol lasted, the problem ceased to exist. This reasoning didn't make sense to Rafael, but it seemed to work for his father. Sober, Juan was a kind and pleasant man. But pour a little alcohol down his father's gullet, and a cold and testy Juan emerged. He became as ornery as a bull in a pasture with one heifer in heat, and a dozen other bulls wanting to oblige her.

Rafael often prayed for his mother to return, not because he missed her all that much, but because he longed to see his father in a better disposition. His mother had never shown any obvious attachment to him, and not much to his healthier brother, Eduardo. For all the love and concern she showed his father, Rafael could not fathom why Juan was so upset that she'd left them. It had to be pride, simple as that!

At first, Rafael had held himself responsible for his mother's abandonment. As a sickly toddler, he knew he'd been a burden to her, a responsibility she didn't welcome; he was a child not even his own mother could love. Rafael felt his father must have blamed him as well, but Rafael didn't know how to even begin to make it up to him. When he could no longer stand the guilt he'd shrouded around himself, he asked his brother about it.

"It's not your fault, Rafael," Eduardo assured him. "It's not the fault of any of us. Mama just needed a more exciting life than she could have here on the ranch. She needed to go places and see things, have a life that didn't involve trying to keep a few skinny cows alive. Papa doesn't blame you for her leaving us, so please don't blame yourself. She isn't worth beating yourself up over."

Now traveling across the Indian Ocean on the cargo ship, Rafael began to understand the way his mother had felt. Getting out in the world gave him an almost euphoric feeling, even though he felt badly because it'd been such an unpleasant trip for his brother so far. His father was rarely sober enough to have any feeling at all, Rafael thought despairingly. He felt a moment of hopelessness each time he spied his father sneaking tankards of ale out of the ship's galley. Rafael was well aware that the crewmembers were not oblivious to Juan's pillaging either. Rafael imagined the theft was overlooked as a means to keep Juan out of their way. His father had made little attempt to converse with the crew and was most likely tolerated for Rafael's sake.

Rafael, Eduardo, and Juan were provided with water and coffee, but were responsible for feeding themselves. They'd dragged an old steamer trunk down from the rafters above the chicken coop, cleaned it up, reinforced the weathered wood, and replaced the rusty hasp. Two changes of clothes for each of them, almost all they owned, were placed in the trunk along with their bedrolls. The remaining space in the trunk had been crammed with hard tack, beef jerky, and other nonperishable provisions.

Many of the crewmates, including the captain, were suffering from beriberi and scurvy. Rafael hoped the three of them would be lucky enough not to acquire one of the vitamin deficiency diseases on their lengthy voyage. It was the last thing his brother or father needed at this point.

The cargo ship on which the Torres family had booked passage was no luxury liner, but it was cheap, and it was slowly taking them to their destination, Bombay, India, where Rafael was certain a new, exciting way of life awaited them.

EIGHT

New York, 2001

"I'm hungry," Skye whined, looking up at Zoe as they sat in the JFK terminal on Saturday evening. "What's taking Daddy so long? He's been gone, well, like forever."

Zoe dug around until she found a hard peppermint candy in her fanny pack. She removed the wrapper and handed it to Skye. It was the best she could do at the moment.

"I know, punkin, but he should be back soon. This is a busy airport. He's probably in a long line at the deli. Here, suck on this until Daddy comes back with our food."

Zoe was hungry too. They'd been served tiny packs, containing about nine peanuts each, on both their flights that day. The energy obtained from eighteen nuts didn't last all that long. Zoe knew they'd burned off more calories than that just making their connection at O'Hare Airport in Chicago, because it had been a hectic one.

When they disembarked the commuter jet on the tarmac outside the gate, there were only a few minutes to catch their next flight at a gate at the opposite end of the terminal. They made the next flight only because the takeoff had been delayed for a short time while the technicians worked on a problem with the plane's engine. It was a good news/bad news situation, Zoe thought. The bad news was the plane they were about to take off on was not mechanically sound. And the good news was, because it wasn't mechanically sound, they were granted an extra few minutes to catch the perilous flight. Zoe wasn't the calmest passenger to begin with. But the flight was a smooth one and, much to her relief, it had landed in New York without incident.

And now, nearly a half hour later in the waiting room area, Trey returned from the nearby bar and grill with three hamburgers. Zoe thought they cost just a wee bit less than her entire wardrobe. She had agreed the burgers were enough to tide them over when she discovered the price of a full meal for the three of them would've been somewhere around the GNP of a small third-world country. Zoe wondered why airport food was so overpriced. Wasn't sticking it to their customers on the airfare enough? Shouldn't they be embarrassed to charge more for a teeny hamburger than a full prime rib dinner would cost in most restaurants?

Zoe ate her burger slowly, nibbling at the stale, dry bun that overlapped the wafer-thin hamburger patty. They had a lot of time to fill, and she wanted to savor the bland but greasy sandwich as much as possible. Trey had his burger wolfed down before Zoe had gotten her pickles arranged just the way she wanted them, and even Skye was halfway finished with hers before Zoe took her first bite. It was probably neurotic behavior, Zoe realized, but it was the way she'd always been. Playing with her food kept her hands busy and helped make the time seem to pass more quickly. Idle time didn't begin until the last morsel was swallowed.

It would be another two hours before their Cathay Pacific flight was due to depart for Hong Kong, the next stop on their journey to Bombay. Once the hamburger was, at long last, ingested, Zoe spent much of the remaining time listening to Skye recite the alphabet, while Trey read through the latest edition of the *New York Times*.

Zoe applauded each time Skye made it all the way through the alphabet without a mistake. She was amused when Skye flashed her slightly off-kilter smile, looking like a jack-o-lantern, with several of her front teeth missing. With undisguised pride, Skye asked her, "Now do you want to hear me count to one hundred?"

Zoe noticed Trey was getting tired and cranky. She was thankful when they were allowed to board the jumbo jet at 10:30 P.M. The 747-400 was the largest commercial jetliner ever built according to the airline's onboard magazine. They were on the main deck of the double-decker, in row eleven, the first row in business class seating. Up against the wall, they were directly in front of the large television screen in the middle section. Zoe was pleased that there were not passengers reclining their seats in front of them for the duration of the twenty-hour flight. On the other hand, when the movie *Gladiator* was being shown on the oversized television screen, she felt as if she could crawl into one of Russell Crowe's nostrils and still have room to stretch out. It was difficult to enjoy a good free-for-all when you were two feet from the screen. It wasn't Zoe's type of movie anyway, so she read through the Brian Weiss novel she'd brought along, while Trey watched the movie and Skye drew in her coloring book. Zoe occasionally read passages of the book to Trey, until she realized he was becoming annoyed at the interruptions while he was trying to concentrate on the movie. *Jeez*, Zoe thought, *he's not near as much fun as he used to be. It sure would be nice to have the old Trey back again.*

By the time they landed in Hong Kong, Zoe was past ready to get off the plane and stretch her legs. She'd spent most of the last twenty hours napping, reading, and then napping some more. She'd lost all track of time, not sure if it was morning or evening. She was beginning to understand how taxing jet lag could be.

Trey had complained that watching *Gladiator* at such close range had given him a headache, so Zoe had dug a Tylenol P.M. out of her purse for him, and he'd rested fitfully for the remainder of the flight. It was almost a relief to Zoe not to have to work at making pleasant conversation with Trey.

As a break from the monotony, Zoe had appreciated the meals served on the flight. They were either better than she'd anticipated, or she was just pleased to be served food that didn't come in a miniscule foil bag. And Zoe could make a full meal last throughout an entire in-flight movie if she took itty-bitty bites and paced herself just right.

The layover in Hong Kong was a lengthy one. The three of them browsed through every gift store in the airport, while Zoe purchased a few souvenirs along the way. She bought an Oriental silk scarf for Trey's mother, a stuffed panda bear with *Hong Kong* imprinted across its chest for Skye, and a jade sitting Buddha figurine for herself. As she lifted the small statue off the shelf, Trey grumbled, "We'll be broke before we even reach India. Don't forget, Zoe, we have limited space in our suitcases for extra items."

As she was in the habit of doing recently, Zoe ignored his remarks and headed toward the checkout counter. She picked out several postcards on the way. After buying stamps and filling out the cards, they searched for a mailbox to post them. After an hour of searching in vain, Trey suggested they return to the shop where the postcards had been purchased. Zoe asked the clerk if she could post them for her. The clerk looked at Zoe as if she'd been asked to scale Mount Everest in her mini-skirt and high heels, so Zoe wasn't really expecting the cards to find their way back to her friends in America. But by then she no longer cared.

Their last flight soon left Hong Kong, bound for Sahar International Airport. Eight hours after takeoff, they landed in Bombay, and Zoe was well rested, well read, and sick and tired of flying the friendly skies.

Zoe was relieved to find their luggage had arrived in India on the same flight as they, even though all of their essentials had been packed into their carry-on bags. Going through customs proved to be a nuisance, but before long they were on a public transit bus heading for the hotel. Their accommodations had been reserved at the Taj Hotel in the southern region of Bombay.

The first thing Zoe noticed about Bombay was the poor air quality. The smog was so dense she could feel its gritty texture clinging to her lungs. Her eyes burned and her nose stung. It was not a pleasant-smelling city. Trey scrunched up his nose, but made no comment. Skye's wild, excited eyes were so busy looking around, she didn't seem to notice the offensive smell at all, or it was not unfamiliar to her.

Zoe was shocked to see the overwhelming mass of people, mostly on foot. People seemed to fill every inch of the streets and sidewalks. It was obvious overcrowding and poverty were serious problems in Bombay. A vast number of inhabitants appeared to be beggars. As the bus inched along, they passed a couple of children standing in the median, looking as thin as the stick people Skye often drew on her sketchpad. They were begging for change from passing motorists. It was a heart-rending scene to Zoe.

Every time the bus halted, women in long colorful saris would converge on it. One arm was invariably clutching a pitiful-looking child, while the other was extended up to the bus windows requesting handouts from the passengers.

The children the women carried were often malformed and almost always malnourished with distended bellies. Zoe passed out coins to every one of the beggars and street urchins as more and more of them gravitated to her window.

A fellow female passenger with a strong British accent tapped Zoe on the shoulder. "You have to harden your heart when you're here and tell yourself you can't save the world. You couldn't carry enough money in your suitcase to give to all of them."

The older woman pointed out a woman toting what looked to be a dead infant, and continued, "Chances are it's not even her child. When a dead baby's available, the women take turns carrying it around. And worse, on occasion, babies are even maimed because it makes the begging more profitable."

Zoe flinched at the woman's words and looked around at the swarms of pedestrians. She'd never seen such a mob of people in all her life. "Where do all of these people live?" she asked.

The other woman's male companion said, "In cheap housing developments in the outlying neighborhoods primarily, and many in flimsy shanties without proper sanitation. Thousands of them just live on the streets. The homeless rate here is unbelievable."

A few blocks later he said, "Look over there, under the little mango tree. You'll see that all over this city."

Under the tree a man lay sound asleep in a threadbare, faded sleeping bag. On a bench a few feet away, another man lay sleeping with no covering at all. Zoe began to realize how much she took for granted in her own life.

The driver stopped abruptly to let a mob of people cross in front of the bus. Skye spoke out for the first time since stepping onto the bus, "Mickey D's!"

Zoe and Trey both turned in surprise to look at the McDonald's restaurant Skye was pointing at.

"They're everywhere," the British man said. "McDonald's and Coca-Cola are pretty much worldwide symbols."

Zoe nodded and attached a zoom lens to the camera she had removed from her carry-on bag. She aimed it out the window and focused on the fast-food restaurant. There were no golden arches, she noticed.

"Daddy, can I get a Happy Meal?" Skye asked.

Her father laughed and replied, "I can't promise you a Happy Meal, but we'll get something to eat as soon as we get settled. We're all hungry."

The other man smiled at Skye and said, "In India, the cow's a sacred icon. I'm not sure you'd like what they're apt to put into a Happy Meal here, sweetie."

With a puzzled look on her face, Skye looked up at the stranger and stated, "Why not? I've always liked chicken, and we used to eat lamb burgers when I lived here many years ago."

The British gentleman looked at Skye in amazement while Trey looked at Zoe in the same way. Not another word was spoken until the bus pulled up into the circular drive of the Taj Hotel.

Soon, the threesome enjoyed an early dinner in the hotel restaurant. By any standard, the Taj was an impressive structure. The beautiful five-star hotel boasted several fine restaurants and an appealing bookstore. Zoe was pleased to discover their room was in the new wing, offering a lovely ocean view from their windows.

It was late in the afternoon when they finished supper, but there were still several hours of daylight left, so they strolled across the street to get a closer look at one of India's most famous landmarks, the Gateway of India. The monument was made of yellow basalt and modeled after the Arc de Triomphe in Paris, which Zoe and Trey had seen during their honeymoon in 1995. The enormous arch was built in 1927 to commemorate the visit of King George V and Queen Mary in 1911, when India was still under British rule.

A young man with a Polaroid camera snapped a photo of them in front of the arch and offered it to Trey for 250 Indian rupees, the equivalent of approximately five American dollars. Trey indicated he wasn't interested. Zoe, being much more sentimental than her husband, talked Trey into purchasing the photo to put in the scrapbook of mementos she planned to assemble once they returned to Kansas. While Trey paid for the photo, Zoe bought a pack of postcards from another vendor for 100 rupees.

After walking around the area for a time, Trey asked, "Anybody want ice cream? There's a stand just ahead with some tasty-looking sundae cones."

"I do, Daddy, I do!" Skye answered with enthusiasm. Zoe was also ready for something cool. Though it was early evening in Bombay, it was still warm and sticky.

Sitting on the curb to eat their ice cream, they watched two young native girls about Skye's age feeding breadcrumbs to a flock of pigeons. Zoe took several snapshots of the endearing children with her Minolta, turning back around just as Trey tossed his ice cream wrapper on the pavement.

"Joseph Jackson!" Zoe said in teasing admonishment.

"Every litter bit helps," he quipped with a sheepish smirk on his face. He laughed as he bent over to retrieve the paper, and then he shoved it into his back pocket. It was a brief reminder of the lightheartedness that had attracted Zoe to him at the beginning of their relationship, a trait she had sorely missed the last couple of years.

In no hurry, they strolled back to the elegant Taj Hotel. Worn out from traveling, they retired early, anxious to begin their search for Skye's previous family the following day.

After a quick breakfast the next morning, they made their way over to Malabar Hill in a rental car. As they followed the map in a tour guide, they drove alongside Chowpatty Beach. They watched a lot of people strolling, sitting, or lying on the sand. Not one person was actually in the water. Zoe wondered why they all seemed to be avoiding the water and commented to Trey about it.

"Take a closer look at the water, Zoe," Trey said. "It looks too hazardous and much too unsanitary to swim in."

At closer inspection, Zoe saw the water was dark brown, and the surf had chunks of miscellaneous debris floating on it.

Trey pointed out a number of men hand-washing clothes in the surf and asked, "How would you like to wear clothing washed in that, Zoe?"

"No thanks! In fact, I think I'll kiss my Whirlpool washer and dryer when I get home, just to let them know how much I appreciate them."

"Let me know when you are going to do that so I can take a photograph. Which reminds me, according to the tour book there's a huge outdoor laundry called Dhobhi Ghat in the middle of town I'd like to see."

"Okay," Zoe agreed. "I'd also like to go to Mani Bhavan if we get the chance."

"What's that?"

"It's a home where Mahatma Gandhi once lived and worked, but it's a museum now."

Skye leaned over the front seat and in a soft, thoughtful tone said, "Gandhi was killed, you know, just a few years before I was born. He was a great leader. Everyone called him the 'Father of India.' "

Trey drew in a long sigh as Zoe turned to look at her

daughter. The look in Skye's eyes was pure excitement, but her facial expression was unrecognizable to Zoe. *It was like looking at a stranger,* Zoe thought.

Zoe turned back around and told Trey the guidebook had stated Mahatma Gandhi had been assassinated in 1948, and had indeed been known as the "Father of India." Trey nodded without responding. Zoe noted he was becoming accustomed to Skye's remarkable observations.

Here in Bombay, Skye seemed to be flooded with memories of her former life, and of Bombay in general. She stared out the back window, noting familiar places and commenting on things that had changed in recent years. Zoe felt as if she and Trey had their own personal tour guide in the back seat. Skye's intelligence was more pronounced here in this land, which was once her home. It was hard for Zoe to believe that her daughter was not even six years old yet and could speak with such maturity.

"See up there?" Skye asked as she pointed to the top of a nearby hill. "That's called the Tower of Silence. It's where the Parsis place their dead relatives to be eaten by vultures."

Oh, nice, Zoe thought. *Anyone for lunch?*

Reading out loud from the tourist guide, Zoe told Trey that Bombay was home to the largest community of Parsis in the world, along with Muslims, Jains, Buddhists, Christians, and Hindus. Hindus made up over two-thirds of the population, with Marathi being the predominant language. "There are over nine hundred million people in India, with over fifteen million in Bombay alone," Zoe recited to Trey. "The population of India is expected to top a billion this year because of the lack of birth control practices. Wow! Where will they put more people when there isn't enough room for all the people they have here already?"

Trey stared straight ahead, saying nothing in response, as if Zoe had not even spoken. She stopped reading out loud.

Several minutes later Skye said, "There used to be a beautiful temple right over there."

Skye was pointing toward a corner lot occupied now by a small, open-faced building. Papers, cigarettes, candy, film, and postcards were displayed on the front of the ramshackle hut. It was Bombay's version of a Quik Trip, Zoe decided.

Trey pulled up in front of the little shop, hoping to buy an English edition of the morning newspaper. The shop owner, like most of the natives they'd met, spoke to him in unfaltering English. Trey complimented him on his competency with the language, and the man replied, "We're taught English in school as a secondary language. It's the international language of business and finance. You will find most people here can speak at least some fundamental English, enough to communicate with you, anyway. There are those rare exceptions, of course."

"I'm impressed," Trey said as the man dropped a few rupees of change into his palm. "You will find very few Americans who can speak even one word of your language, and I imagine that we should be ashamed."

"No, not really. I doubt you find many occasions where you'd need to know any of the languages spoken here."

"Well, I guess that's true enough," Trey agreed.

"Actually, the literacy rate here's only about fifty-two percent. Our government doesn't generally encourage education."

"Why wouldn't they encourage education?" Trey asked, surprise registering on his face.

"They prefer the common people not be too informed. It helps the politicians get re-elected to their positions every four years," the shop owner explained. "On the other end of the scale, however, is the Indian Institute of Technology. ITT graduates are some of the brightest and most highly recruited engineers and scientists in the world. What's more, the Indian government subsidizes eighty percent of the cost to educate them. And where do most of them end up after they graduate? Well, in America, of course. My son studies there and will end up in your country, too," the shop owner stated with obvious pride. "The competition to be accepted at ITT is fierce."

"I can well imagine. Congratulations. You must be very proud of your son," Trey said with sincerity. The shop owner nodded and smiled at the compliment.

"By the way, sir," Trey continued. "Was there a temple located at this site at one time?"

"Yes, a Buddhist Temple, but it burned down in 1981."

Zoe was not surprised, and neither was Trey, to hear Skye's observation confirmed.

Trey received directions to Little Gibbs Road before they all climbed back into the rental car and headed east. "Little Gibbs should be the next street," Trey said.

"It is, Daddy," Skye assured him, "just past the alley."

The surrounding neighborhood was quite posh, and it was obvious to Zoe some of the city's elite lived in the Malabar Hill area. It was not where a person would expect to find a cotton-picker and his volunteer wife, Zoe decided.

"Stop here!" Skye exclaimed. "This is it!" Skye led her parents up to an apartment on the third floor.

Trey knocked on the door of the apartment Skye indicated once belonged to her family.

Footsteps were heard shuffling inside, before the door cracked open just enough for an eyeball to peer out at them.

"Is there an Asha or a Nirav living here?" Trey asked.

A thought suddenly occurred to Zoe. Skye had never mentioned the family's last name in any of her past-life recollections. Why hadn't Zoe thought to ask her?

When the eyeball looking out at them didn't respond to Trey's question, he repeated it, louder and slower this time.

The door opened wider revealing a plump, older woman.

"*Hain,*" the woman said at last, shaking her head. The woman wore a long red sari wrapped around her ample body, and had a matching red tika in the middle of her wrinkled forehead. She held a heavily bundled infant in the crook of her right arm. The baby sucked on its thumb and stared at Trey with wide-open, dark brown eyes.

"Do you know where they could be found?" Trey asked.

The woman responded in Hindi as she shifted the infant to her left arm, and used her right hand to grasp the doorknob.

Again Trey repeated his question in hopes she'd answer in English, but it was clear she was one of the rare exceptions the shop owner had spoken about.

After a short pause, Skye stepped around in front of her father and said, "Joshi. Asha and Nirav Joshi."

"*Hain, namaste,*" the old woman said, shaking her head and shutting the door.

"*Namaste,*" Skye said in response just before the door closed, her head bowed in obvious disappointment.

Zoe and Trey were in a quandary about what to do next, but Zoe refused to give up hope. "We have every reason to believe Skye led us to the right apartment, but there's still a remote possibility she didn't," Zoe said to Trey. "Should we find the office of this complex or look around for someone else to ask?"

"Nah, not yet anyway," Trey said, shaking his head. "It's more likely they moved from here a long time ago, if any of them are still alive."

"Well, then, we might as well spend the day touring the city," Zoe suggested, "while we work on a plan."

"Yeah, there's a lot of interesting things to see here until one of us comes up with a brilliant idea."

Not far from Malabar Hill was a temple with lavish decorations. On either side of the entrance were large, heavily bejeweled elephant statues. Tied to a post in front of the temple was a cow, standing in a resigned, sedate fashion on the sidewalk. This was a common sight in Bombay; they'd seen cows in front of other temples around the city.

"We used to worship at this Jain temple," Skye said.

"Really?" Zoe inquired. "It is so interesting on the outside. I'd like to see the inside, too. Do you know if tourists are allowed in the temple?"

"I think so," Skye answered, "but you have to take your shoes off and leave them outside."

They approached the temple and placed their shoes on a long, sturdy table. Near the table, piled high with shoes of all descriptions, stood a bald, elderly man wrapped in a large sheet of plain white cotton. He appeared to be the attendant in charge of footwear being deposited on the table. Behind him was a sign requesting cooperation from visitors in observing a number of rules and restrictions. Included on the list was a rule prohibiting ladies "on monthly period" from entering the temple, and another one instructing people taking photographs to not turn their backs on the idols. Zoe took a quick photo of the sign and shoe attendant, and then another of the gaudy elephant statues, before following Trey and Skye into the temple.

Around the perimeter inside the Jain Temple were many statues of Buddha and other gods and goddesses. Incense was burning everywhere and the odor was almost overpowering. They remained silent, watching an Indian woman rub a powdery substance on the belly of one of the statues.

Skye pulled Zoe down to whisper into her ear. "My family used to pray to Shiva at this temple too." At Zoe's puzzled expression, Skye continued. "Shiva is the Hindu God of Destruction, and I prayed to him to provide me with a good husband." Skye giggled at the recollection. "My mama and papa poured milk on rock sculptures of lingam to help them have lots of children, though they only had me and Mohandas."

Zoe felt again as if someone much older was speaking to her, which was typical when Skye spoke from the perception of Radha. Skye used words that would seem mature even coming from a teenage girl. "What is lingam?" Zoe whispered back.

"It would be Shiva's phallus."

"What'd you say?" Zoe wasn't sure she'd heard correctly. She had, she soon discovered, when Skye repeated her response.

"Uh, okay," Zoe blushed and nodded, thinking, *Oh my, what have we gotten ourselves into?*

After collecting their shoes, they were surrounded by beggars while they walked back to their car. A man crossed in front of them, balancing a basket of bananas on his head, while another hawked oranges from his position propped up against the outer wall of the temple. A young girl offered to sell Zoe a fan constructed out of peacock feathers. Zoe snapped a photo of the girl before handing her the asking price for the fan, afraid of offending her by offering her less. Before she could place her wallet back into her fanny pack a half-dozen street vendors, peddling everything from gaudy necklaces to avocados, encompassed her. None of them were selling film, however, the one thing she needed.

Next they paid a visit to the Hanging Gardens, a park full of beautiful flowerbeds and topiary art, with tall hedges cut to resemble things like a two-humped camel and a man behind a team of water buffalo. Outside the gardens a young male snake charmer puffed on a wooden flute as a hooded cobra, protruding from a wicker basket, swayed back and forth before him. After Zoe took a photo of him, he laid down the flute as the snake recoiled back down into the basket. The boy put a lid on the basket and walked over to Zoe, with his hand palm up in the international gesture for "Pay up!" She dropped an

American dollar into his hand.

Later in the day they visited Dhobhi Ghat. The outdoor laundry was enormous and nestled right in the middle of town. The skyline surrounding it resembled any large American city, which made the laundry seem even more out of place. Zoe stopped at a small souvenir stand to buy more film before joining Trey and Skye, who were looking down at the laundry, which was located at a level lower than the bustling street.

They watched hundreds of men, in their own separate cubicles, beating and scrubbing the clothes in pools of dark brown water. They listened as a nearby guide addressed a group of American tourists. The guide said the water was changed just once a day, and each man paid the Indian government an equivalency of five American dollars per month to rent their space. The men picked up and delivered the laundry to the locals. The fabrics didn't hold up long with this kind of treatment, so most people had cotton garments laundered here, but not their finer clothing. Only men were allowed to work at the laundry, the guide informed the group. Zoe took several photos and loaded a fresh roll of film.

"Now don't you feel even more privileged to have your very own washer and dryer?" Trey joked.

"Yes," Zoe laughed. "It is just one of many things I haven't appreciated as much as I should have."

"DOSA, VADA, and FRITTERS" read the sign above the concession stand. Small stands such as this occupied almost every street corner, Zoe noted as they wandered around an outdoor bazaar in downtown Bombay.

"What's your pleasure?" Trey asked his wife and daughter.

For all Zoe knew, dosa and vada could be pig snouts and kumquats. She chose a fritter, as did Trey.

Skye requested a dosa. "It's my favorite," she said. "I like the crispy shell."

Her father didn't bat an eye. "Two fritters and one dosa, please."

Trey paid the vendor for the pastries and pocketed the change. He was whistling an unrecognizable tune as he handed Zoe her snack. Zoe felt happy to see him in such a good mood.

Skye offered each of them a taste of her dosa, and Zoe agreed it was much tastier than her fritter. She liked the crispy shell also. The dosa looked like a pancake made out of rice and lentil, folded in half with a potato filling, and deep-fried.

They spent the rest of the afternoon visiting the Gandhi Museum and the Prince of Wales Museum. It had been a full day of sightseeing, and they had only scratched the surface. Driving back alongside the harbor, Zoe yawned and asked, "So what's on tap for tomorrow?"

Her question was soon answered when Skye pointed out the window and exclaimed, "Hey, there's our old cotton shop!"

Nirav was obviously no run-of-the-mill cotton-picker. Across the front of the huge building a sign read *Deshpande Cotton Factory—Worldwide Shipping*.

"I thought you said your last name used to be Joshi," Trey said to Skye.

"It was, Daddy. Deshpande was the name of my grandparents, and my mama's before she married Papa."

NINE

Bombay, India, 1941

From where Asha Deshpande stood, outside the Cotton Exchange building, which was a beehive of activity, she could see the acrid smoke belching out the chimneys of the factory mills along the harbor. Her father, Ajay, stood beside her. It was one of the rare occasions when he'd permitted her to leave the confines of the home they shared. Asha didn't enjoy his company, but she cherished any opportunity to get out of the house and see for herself what was going on in the city. At her father's insistence, Asha led a very sheltered life, and she was an inquisitive person at heart. She watched with interest now as activity ran rampant around her father's cotton factory. The commotion resembled an army of soldiers scurrying to serve the queen bee. Asha could well imagine her father wallowing in that self-appointed role.

It was 1941, and with World War II in full swing, the need for cotton had accelerated. The mills were operating twenty-four hours a day, and more employees were being added to the payroll daily. Even then, they couldn't produce cotton fast enough to keep up with the demands of the war efforts abroad.

As Asha and Ajay passed the Sassoon Dock they heard a loud whistle signaling a shift change, and Asha saw her father's stern expression transform into a pompous smile. Being prosperous at a time when so many others were struggling obviously gave him a great deal of satisfaction.

They passed by a crew of construction workers, busily erecting more chawls adjacent to the factory. These low-income family dwellings were five stories tall, cheaply constructed, and contained up to ten people crowded into each room. With the addition of many new employees on the payroll, Ajay had found it necessary to build more chawls to house them. He didn't build them out of compassion or generosity, Asha knew, but more as a way to keep employees working for nominal pay at his mill. Her father had a compelling need to amass wealth and power. He should feel guilty and ashamed, Asha thought, but guilt and shame had never been a part of his character; only greed and gluttony.

The time and effort Ajay had expended to ensure the success of his business had kept him far too busy to lead much of a social life. He'd never remarried after Asha's mother, Laxmi, had died giving birth to Asha in 1926. Asha, now fifteen, took care of his house, prepared and served his meals, and kept his clothes laundered. She felt like an indentured servant and knew Ajay had no regard for her happiness. As long as she kept his life orderly and waited on him as if he were royalty, he was content. It was evident to Asha he had no desire or intention to ever form any kind of emotional bond with her, his only child. The feeling was mutual; she felt nothing for him but contempt.

Had Asha been the son he had so coveted at the time of her birth, she knew things would have been much different. He'd never had any respect, and little use, for the female gender. *What did my mother ever see in this overbearing tyrant?* she wondered. *He is self-absorbed and belligerent.*

As the blazing sun beat down on her, Asha adjusted her cotton dress, which was wrapped around her waist and draped over her shoulder. She did this to cover her head and protect the perfect complexion of her face. She had a dainty figure, small-boned and graceful. Her skin was very fair, from both a lack of exposure to the sun and the light-skinned genes she'd inherited from her mother. Asha bore no resemblance to her father, who was dark-skinned and had a husky build that seemed to border on becoming soft and flabby.

"Ajay," she addressed him because she'd never been able to bring herself to call him Father or Papa to his face, "why won't you allow me to work in the office of your factory? I promise to be a hardworking, devoted, and efficient employee."

"Never," he retorted. "You will work in my home as you always have. I want to hear no more about this silly desire to work at the factory. You hear? No more about it! You're not smart enough to work at the factory. Cooking and cleaning are all you know or will ever need to know."

Asha ignored his remark, having expected a rebuff. Asha had become so accustomed to his insults and belittling comments, she was no longer emotionally affected by them. She refused to let Ajay's verbal abuse damage her self-image, but with every day that passed, she despised her father a little more.

Ajay had made it clear to her his brother's son, Manoj, would eventually inherit the business, as well as the bulk of his estate. Asha would inherit nothing more than a monthly allowance, doled out by her younger cousin, Manoj. It would be a meager pittance that would be barely enough to feed and clothe her. Asha was surprised that Ajay appeared to be reading her mind when he stated, "Manoj is thirteen now, old enough to begin learning the ropes of the cotton industry. By the time I'm ready to retire, he should be well prepared to take over the reins at the factory."

Asha sighed as she kneaded the bread dough on the kitchen counter. Before heading home from their stroll down to the harbor, Ajay had informed her he was bringing a guest home for supper that evening. "My newly promoted second-shift fore-man will be dining with me, and as always, I expect the repast to be served precisely at eight."

Ajay also mentioned the new foreman was young, but a hard worker and a quick study. It was an unusual comment, not only because Ajay rarely spoke to her about anything concerning business, but also because he seldom had a complimentary thing to say about anybody other than himself. "I want to discuss the job requirements of a foreman with him, so you're to serve the meal and then remove yourself from the dining room so we may converse in private," he had told her.

This was agreeable with Asha, who had no desire to be around her father any more than she had to be. She'd borrowed a book about modern finance and wanted to study it that evening. She could only do this when she wasn't in her father's presence. In his opinion, she didn't need an education. Asha felt differently. *It's my only hope to escape and have a life of my own,* she thought. *I can't tolerate this enforced confinement much longer.* Asha was determined that the entirety of her life would not be spent as a servant in her father's grand home, a home that had become little more than a prison to her.

Asha always waited until she knew Ajay wouldn't be return-ing from work until late to sneak out and run the dozen or so blocks to the regional library. Covered from head to toe in a dark cotton wrap she'd stitched for herself from remnants found lying about in Ajay's study, she would borrow books about a multitude of subjects. Over a number of years she had taught herself reading, writing and arithmetic, and after mastering the "three R's," she'd advanced to more intricate subjects like chemistry, business management, and foreign languages. At Ajay's insistence, only English was spoken in the household, and she had no trouble learning all the intricacies of the complicated language.

The more she learned, the more confident she felt. She was careful not to display any of her self-taught knowledge in front of her father. *One day,* she vowed, *I will walk away from this prison and never look back.*

As Asha placed platters of skewered lamb and potatoes on the table for Ajay and his handsome, Spanish-looking guest, her hands trembled slightly. Against her will, she was drawn to the endearing smile of the broad-shouldered young man who sat across from her father. He appeared to be about her age, but had a maturity that suggested an older man. He was very gracious as he stood up when she entered the room.

"Good evening, miss," he greeted her, extending a hand in welcome. He smiled again with a charming grin that revealed white, perfectly shaped teeth.

As she grasped his warm hand in a solemn shake he introduced himself, "My name is Eduardo Torres, the new second-shift foreman at your father's mill. I've had the pleasure of working for him for over five years now."

Asha felt her hands become clammy and beads of sweat break out along the back of her neck, but despite her better judgment, she couldn't take her eyes away from his. "It's nice to meet you, Mr. Torres. I am Asha."

"Eduardo, please," he answered pleasantly. "When I hear the name Mr. Torres, I look around for my father."

"Eduardo, then," she repeated, trying to emulate the way he had rolled the R-sound in his name.

"Perfect!" he said, grinning. He was charmed and amused at her attempt to pronounce his name with a Spanish accent.

She smiled back at him, aware she was flirting for the first time in her life. As she averted her eyes and blushed, she glanced at Ajay and knew he realized as well that she was flirting, and was not at all pleased about it.

Ajay flashed her a look of scornful impatience as he said, "You may go now, Asha."

"Yes, sir," she responded, turning to leave the room.

Eduardo rose to his feet once more. "Thank you for the meal, Asha. It looks and smells delicious," he stated sincerely as she closed the dining room door behind her.

On the other side of the door, Asha nearly collapsed. She clung to the doorknob as she attempted to pull herself together. Leaning against the door she heard Eduardo's voice, "You have a very beautiful daughter, Mr. Deshpande."

Asha's heart leapt to her throat, and then she nearly choked on it when she heard her father's reply. "Yes, well, don't get any ideas, boy. She's off-limits to any of my employees. That goes for my foremen, as well."

It was a steamy day in 1943, and Rafael was sweating profusely in nothing but a pair of thin cotton shorts as he leaned over a large spool of unbleached cotton fabric. The unfiltered air in the factory made it difficult for him to breathe. The heat and humidity threatened to drop him to his knees, but somehow he managed to remain standing and continue his labors. *I can't afford to lose this job,* he thought. *We need my paycheck even more than ever now that Papa can no longer work at the mill.* Liver damage had weakened his father, Juan, to the point he could barely get out of bed. Yet he still insisted on his daily intake of alcohol.

Since arriving in Bombay seven years ago, his father's drinking had escalated. Scotch was no longer his drink of choice. He now saturated his liver in bevda, a potent brew made from an assortment of rotten fruits and a coarse brown sugar called jaggery. Rafael couldn't tolerate the smell of the vile stuff. He had long ago given up hope Juan would stop trying to drown his sorrows in alcohol.

Juan, Eduardo, and Rafael occupied one of the flimsy chawls

furnished by the factory. Rafael rarely saw his older brother. Eduardo had been working as the second-shift foreman the last two years, while Rafael still reported for the first twelve-hour shift. They only seemed to meet each other coming and going, and despite the fact he missed spending time with Eduardo, the schedule allowed them to take turns administering to their father's needs.

Juan was totally dependent on his two sons now. It was only a matter of time before Juan met his maker, Rafael was certain. His father had relinquished the dream of ever seeing his homeland again. Rafael made a promise to himself that one day he would return to the ranch and make it bigger and better than ever, but as far as his father was concerned, the Torres cattle ranch was all but forgotten.

"Asha? Is that you?" Asha heard someone whisper, leaning over her back as she sat at the library desk. She gasped in alarm. She'd removed her scarf and cloak, and had been so absorbed in reading the back cover of a history book she hadn't heard him approach.

"Yes?" she whispered back, uneasily.

"I apologize for frightening you. You looked engrossed in your reading. I hate to bother you, but I had to see if it was really you."

"Eduardo? Is that you?" she asked, looking up into the face that had haunted her dreams for over two years. He was even more handsome than she'd remembered.

He nodded, and she continued, "What are you doing here?"

"Looking for a medical journal. My father is very ill with cirrhosis, and I am hoping to find some information on how to help alleviate his pain," he whispered. "Do you come here often?"

Asha hesitated before responding, "Yes, as often as I can, but please promise me you won't mention seeing me here to Ajay. He would be very angry with me if he knew."

"I promise. He would be angry with me, too, if he found out I spoke with you. May I sit down?" he asked, motioning toward the chair across from her.

"Yes, of course."

"Thank you. How have you been, Asha? You are looking well. You're even prettier than you were the first time I met you, if that is possible."

Asha blushed at Eduardo's compliment, which was given with such sincerity that it did not seem like mere flattery. She chatted with him for a while longer, until she realized she must return home soon if she were to have supper on the table on time. Ajay became very indignant when supper wasn't served exactly at eight, and she had no wish to raise his ire. He was unbearable enough without encouragement.

As Asha gathered her books and prepared to leave, Eduardo clasped her hands in his and asked, "Will you make me a promise also?"

She nodded. "If I can."

"Promise me you won't tell your father, but I'd very much like to become better acquainted with his charming daughter." He gave an exaggerated bow as he leaned over to place a light kiss on the top of her hand.

Asha giggled and looked away. She felt her face become flushed. Eduardo released her hands and went on to request she meet him at that very table the following week.

"I can't promise, Eduardo, but I'll try. If it's at all possible, I'll be here."

The dawn of 1944 brought little change to Asha's life, other than the fact she was desperately in love with her father's trusted foreman. She and Eduardo were both eighteen, and anxious to be married and raise a family.

The only obstacle standing in their way was her father. Asha knew Eduardo couldn't marry her and keep his job, because Ajay would never allow it. But Eduardo couldn't afford to give up his position at the factory. He and his younger brother, Rafael, whom he spoke of often, could barely make ends meet as it was, and Eduardo had his own father to consider. According to Eduardo, his father was hanging on to life by a thin thread.

Asha couldn't endure the thought of continuing to see Eduardo for only a few minutes at the library each week, but for them to make a public acknowledgment of their love for one another would bring about an adverse chain of events, she was certain. Asha prayed frequently for a solution to their dilemma.

In mid-March, Asha's prayers were answered. Eduardo had been offered a job in the motion picture industry, which was becoming more prominent every year. Bombay was well on its way to producing more movies than any other country on earth. The largest number of feature films in any one language was coming out of the Hindi studios of Bombay. Hollywood could not even match the sheer number of films being produced in Bombay.

The films were fairly unprofessional, flawed, and predictable. The heroes nearly always conquered the villains against whom they were pitted. Happy, if unlikely, endings were the norm. But the movies were profitable; the vast Indian population had no other real form of entertainment to compete with the movie industry.

Fortunately, a friend of Eduardo's knew a producer looking for a costume director for his studio. Eduardo, with his natural charisma and knowledge of fabrics, was able to land the position, which included a salary over twice that of a cotton mill foreman.

The producer also had access to an apartment for Eduardo and his family, which was essential because they'd no longer be able to reside in one of the factory's chawls, Asha was quite sure. The rent was higher, but within their budget with Eduardo's higher income factored in.

Eduardo, who was well aware of the deplorable treatment Asha suffered at the hands of her father, asked Asha to elope with him and move into the apartment with his family. Asha accepted without reservation, thrilled to soon leave her father and her current lifestyle behind.

She knew she could be an asset to Eduardo in his new role as costume director. She'd perfected the ability to stitch clothing from years of fashioning her own wardrobe from fabric samples she'd found scattered about her father's home. She could assist Eduardo in designing and creating costumes for the production studio.

"Our marriage will be an equal partnership," he told her one day after they exited the library. "You'll not be expected to cater to my every whim. I want you to feel free to pursue your own dreams."

"Thank you, Eduardo. I'm so grateful you came into my life," Asha said. "I didn't really have a life until I met you. Just an existence."

"Me either. I didn't live. I just survived," Eduardo said as he guided her along the sidewalk. "I hope you'll not be too disappointed in the apartment. It's a bit sparse compared to what you're accustomed to."

"A fancy prison is still a prison, Eduardo," she responded. "It's not what you have in life, but who you share it with."

Eduardo was slated to begin his new job on the fifth of April. When his shift at the factory ended on the fourth, he'd go directly to the Deshpande home, where Asha would be waiting.

She'd have all her personal belongings, basically clothes and a few toiletries, packed and ready to go. She'd already written a note to leave for her father. The note stated, *By the time you read this I will already be Mrs. Eduardo Torres. Effective immediately, Eduardo resigns his position as your second-shift foreman, and I resign my position as your personal servant. Do not expect to see either of us again, nor any of the offspring our union may produce in the future. I'm afraid our children will be off-limits to you. Sincerely, Your daughter, Asha.*

Asha knew she could have softened the blow by writing a more tactful message but couldn't bring herself to do so. As hard as it was to admit, Asha knew the loss of his dependable foreman would be a harsher blow to Ajay Deshpande than the loss of his only daughter. He could more easily hire a new servant than replace a trained foreman.

Asha and Eduardo would proceed to exchange vows soon after Eduardo picked her up on the evening of April fourth. They'd spend the night alone in the new apartment to consummate their marriage in privacy. The idea of that didn't frighten Asha in the least. She looked forward to sharing her passion with Eduardo. It'd be the first time she would ever receive any affection in her life. Asha couldn't recall her father ever kissing or hugging her in all her eighteen years. And, of course, a couple couldn't display much affection in a public library either, so she and Eduardo had been limited to holding hands and exchanging a few quick pecks on the cheek.

The day after she and Eduardo exchanged vows, Rafael, who'd been sworn to secrecy, would assist Eduardo in moving Juan and their few possessions to the new apartment. Rafael would continue working at the factory, unless Ajay let him go in retribution. Due to the difficulty of keeping enough trained employees on the payroll, Asha thought this was not apt to happen.

If it did happen, she thought, it was a situation they could deal with later. Rafael was a reliable, trained employee who could find employment at any cotton factory in the region. There wasn't a mill around that wasn't desperate for help. Asha thought it might even be in Rafael's best interests to find a position elsewhere, lest he become the brunt of her father's anger.

Asha told Eduardo she was anxiously anticipating her new life with him and his family. "I will be thankful to see the last of my father," she said earnestly.

TEN

"Could the last two weeks have passed any more slowly?" Eduardo asked Rafael in jest. Rafael was aware Eduardo and Asha had agreed to forego their weekly meeting at the library, unwilling to push their luck with the marriage date fast approaching. It'd been a trying time for his brother, who professed to miss his fiancée a great deal. Eduardo told him, "Asha is the most delightful woman I've ever met. She's a woman of integrity, Rafael, and I know you'll come to love her as I have. She'd be almost impossible to dislike."

"I'm sure I'll adore her, Eduardo, considering how hard you've fallen for her. Do you promise that she's not at all like her father?"

"I promise. I'm thankful I can truthfully say her personality is not at all like Ajay's." Eduardo grimaced at the mere thought. He loathed the man who was to be his father-in-law, a man he'd been forced to tolerate in order to keep his job. "It's hard to believe they're even related."

"That is a bit hard to fathom!" Rafael agreed, punching his brother's shoulder playfully.

Eduardo winked and walked out the door. Rafael thought it was just as well his brother hadn't spent time at the library with Asha the last couple of weeks, since he and Eduardo had been taking turns standing vigil at their father's bedside. Juan's condition had deteriorated further; he was drifting in and out of consciousness and refusing all food and drink. Rafael sadly realized Juan's days on earth were nearing an end.

But it was now April 4, 1944, a day his brother had greatly anticipated. Rafael hugged his brother as he prepared to leave the chawl and report for his final day of duty at the Deshpande Cotton Factory. Eduardo would be a married man when next he saw him, something Rafael could hardly imagine. He smiled at the thought.

Rafael waited until Eduardo had headed off to the mill and his father had fallen into a deep slumber before he went to purchase food at the market. *There's no sense preparing a meal Papa will only decline,* he thought. *And Eduardo won't be coming home for dinner. He'll be spending the evening in the new apartment with his bride.*

Rafael whistled as he walked toward the center of town, feeling happy and thankful for his brother's good fortune. Suddenly, the ground beneath him shook as the force of a mighty blast knocked him to the ground. Looking back over his shoulder in the direction of the thunderous roar, he saw large comets of flame shooting upward toward the sky above the harbor. Rafael swallowed hard, his mouth had turned dry, and his hands had turned clammy. He could feel his heart pounding in his chest. Filled with an impending sense of doom, he realized the explosion was centered in the area of the cotton mills and the chawls that housed the mills' employees.

Rafael jumped to his feet and raced toward the shoreline. As he approached, the thick smoke gagged him and burned his eyes but he ran blindly into the smoke.

"A ship has exploded in the harbor!" Terrified voices cried out. Rafael knew, due to the war, there were ships loaded with ammunition anchored in the harbor, and ammunition dumps located near the docks. He fought his way through the smoke and floating ash and debris, while rubbing his eyes and breathing into the cuff of his work shirt. The raw cotton raining from the sky reminded him of a Wyoming blizzard.

The entire harbor area had been decimated. The building his family lived in was flattened. Rafael knew, buried beneath the rubble, lay the battered body of his father. Juan could not have known what hit him. Knowing his father was most likely now at peace was almost a relief to Rafael. He couldn't dwell on that thought now, however. His first priority was to locate his brother, Eduardo.

Rafael ran on toward the location of the cotton factory. Through the cloud of smoke and dust, he saw only a small section remained standing. The majority of the building had been blown to bits. Rafael faltered and almost fell over a large spool of charred cotton fabric as he crossed the street to what remained of the Deshpande Cotton Factory.

Running through pools of blood, broken glass, and twisted steel, Rafael searched in desperation for his brother. Dead bodies, many he recognized, and miscellaneous body parts littered the ground. By the time he found Eduardo, shameless tears were streaming down Rafael's face, and he was coughing uncontrollably.

Eduardo lay in a twisted heap, his torso trapped beneath a steel beam. Rafael was further horrified to see Eduardo's right leg was mangled, almost severed, with the femur bone ripped clear of the pelvic socket and protruding through his hip. Blood was pouring out of the gruesome-looking wound at an alarming rate. It was obvious Eduardo could not survive his injuries. Rafael blanched at the realization his beloved brother was dying.

Eduardo grasped Rafael's hand weakly and whispered in a hoarse voice, "*Adios, hermano.* Take care of Papa, he will need you."

Not anymore, Rafael thought. But he nodded his head, not

wanting to further distress Eduardo. They will meet each other on the other side soon enough. Time was but a blink of an eye in heaven, he had heard.

"Please find Asha and tell her I will always love her, and I will wait for her in heaven. She may need you, Rafael, and I trust you to make sure that she's all right."

Rafael held tight to his brother's hand and promised to fulfill Eduardo's last requests. "I love you, *hermano,*" he said in a voice choked with emotion. He leaned down to hear Eduardo's next words. His brother's voice weakened as he struggled to draw in a breath and speak.

"I know you do. I love you, too. I am proud of the man you've become, Rafael. Please don't be afraid. I promise we'll be together again someday. Take care of yourself and Papa, and remember you have a home in Wyoming to return to when the time's right. I must go now," Eduardo said, before taking a ragged and final breath.

Rafael cradled his brother's head in his lap and sobbed, unaware the bottom of his shoes had melted and hot cinders were burning his feet.

That day, Ajay Deshpande and his nephew, Manoj, also perished in the explosion caused by the ammunition ship. The explosion had leveled three hundred acres of docks and warehouses. Many lives were lost in what would come to be known as one of the worst catastrophes in Bombay's history.

Three weeks later, Asha had hardly eaten or slept since the explosion that had taken the lives of her fiancé, his father, her father, and her cousin, Manoj. She rose from her bed, filled with new resolve and determination. She was light-headed and shaking like a leaf in the breeze. She had to force herself to leave the confines of her father's home, now as quiet as a monastery.

She knew Eduardo would want her to go on living, and no matter how hard it'd be for her, she'd have to do just that. *I can't lie in bed and wallow in self-pity indefinitely,* she told herself. She must force herself to pull together and concentrate on what needed to be done to rebuild the mill, because there were individuals in even more desperate situations than her, whose livelihoods depended on the future of the factory. *And it will be successful,* Asha vowed to herself. *Bigger and better than ever.*

Asha was now Ajay's only living heir. She had never had his love or respect, but she now had the one thing that had meant the most to him—the Deshpande Cotton Factory.

Eleven

Bombay, India, 2001

"Do you remember where Nirav's office was located?" Zoe asked Skye as they walked into the cotton factory a few blocks from the Taj Hotel.

"Yes, follow me."

Skye led Zoe and Trey to a dimly lit corridor winding to the back of the massive building. Skye was skipping as she rounded a corner and continued down a long, unadorned hallway. She paused before a door bearing a placard inscribed "Mr. Joshi—Plant Manager."

Trey knocked as Zoe stood back, twisting her hair between restless fingers. A petite, middle-aged woman opened the door. She introduced herself as "Mrs. Joshi," and then asked if she could help them. Skye's puzzled expression indicated to Zoe that she didn't recognize the woman. Zoe stared at her daughter as Skye stared at the stranger.

"Is Mr. Joshi available?" Trey asked.

"Yes," Mrs. Joshi replied. "He's in his private office. Who would like to see him?"

"I'm Trey Robbins, and this is my wife and daughter. We would like to speak to him about a personal matter."

"One moment," she said. She exited the small office through a door behind her desk.

Skye tugged hard on the hem of her mother's shirt. There

97

were slight furrows in her brow as she looked up.

"That's not my mama," Skye said, pouting. "I mean, the mama I had when I was Radha." She corrected herself, looking up at Zoe. "I don't know that lady."

There was no time for Zoe to consider Skye's statement before she observed a medium-framed man, possibly in his mid-forties, enter the room through the same door Mrs. Joshi had used. His salt and pepper hair was slicked back, and his wire-rimmed glasses seemed to balance precariously on the very tip of his nose. His complexion was smooth and swarthy.

"I am Mr. Joshi. May I help you?" he asked.

Skye squinted her eyes, staring at the man for a moment before asking, "Mohandas?"

"Yes, that's correct," he answered, obviously confused. He looked down at Skye and asked, "Do I know you?"

"Well—er, yes, sort of . . ." Skye whispered.

"That's what we'd like to speak to you about," Trey broke in. "It's kind of an unusual situation. Do you have a few minutes to spare?"

Mohandas nodded, held open the door behind the desk, and said, "Let's go back to my office. My wife can take my calls while we talk."

His wife! Of course, Zoe thought. It suddenly occurred to her that Skye wouldn't recognize Mohandas's wife. Mohandas was Radha's younger brother, and he would've been much too young to be married when Radha was fifteen.

The three of them followed Mohandas to a bright, airy office with floor-to-ceiling windows. He motioned for them to choose between the half dozen chairs haphazardly placed about the room.

Trey completed the introductions of himself, Zoe, and Skye, before shaking hands with Mohandas. Pulling their chairs close to Mohandas's desk, they sat before him.

"This is going to be a hard story for you to believe, I'm afraid," Trey began. Settling back in her chair, Zoe felt relieved that Trey had opted to be the spokesperson.

"At the risk of sounding crazy, let me explain what's been going on the last few weeks," Trey continued.

Mohandas listened intently, saying nothing, but glancing across the desk at Skye numerous times. His deep brown eyes blinked only occasionally, with long intervals separating the flutters as he concentrated on Trey's dialogue.

When Trey completed the story, Mohandas folded his hands together and finally spoke. "First of all, I don't think you're crazy. Our religion is based strongly on the beliefs of reincarnation, and also karma. We believe a person's life is determined by their previous deeds. In Hinduism, these deeds are called karma.

"Souls who do good karma will be rewarded with a better life in the next incarnation. Souls who do bad karma will be punished for their sins, if not in this incarnation, then in the next, and will continue to be born in this world again and again. The good souls will be liberated from the circle of rebirth and receive redemption, which is called Moksha, meaning freedom. Hindus cremate their dead so the souls will go to heaven."

Zoe listened intently, fascinated by Mohandas's explanation of the Hindu view on reincarnation. She leaned slightly forward as he continued. "I truly want to believe your daughter, Skylar, is the reincarnated soul of my sister, Radha. Skylar did recall many accurate details and directed you to the apartment we occupied when Radha disappeared. And there's something in Skye's smile that reminds me of my sister. But it will take me some time to assimilate this information and accept it. It comes as a shock to me, as I'm sure you can understand. After all, we don't even know for certain if Radha is deceased. It's been suspected, but never verified."

Mohandas lifted his lightweight glasses off his face and placed them on his desk. He rubbed his eyes in a circular motion with the fingers of both hands, seeming suddenly weary and fatigued.

Zoe waited for Mohandas to put his glasses back on and asked, "What happened to Radha?" She wasn't sure she wanted to hear the details.

Skye squirmed uncomfortably in her chair as Mohandas answered Zoe's question. "We don't really know what happened to her. Radha was working at the front reception desk one day in 1966. She was fifteen," he said. Zoe knew Mohandas was aware of the significance of Radha's age in relation to the events Trey had just explained.

Mohandas drank from a water glass on his desk. His pronounced Adam's apple bobbed as he swallowed, and then he spoke again. "Another employee went to relieve her for her lunch break, but she wasn't at her desk. Although it was unlike Radha to leave her post unannounced, it was possible she'd gone to use the water closet, or restroom, as you'd call it. It was assumed she'd return in a matter of minutes, but she never did. We never saw her again."

"Where did she go? Does anyone know?" Trey asked.

"No, but we do know someone abducted her. My father received a ransom note the following day. The abductor was demanding two million rupees in exchange for the safe return of my sister. My father scraped up enough cash to meet the demands and arranged to make the transfer. He left a suitcase filled with bills exactly where the note had instructed. A week later the suitcase was still there, still jammed with the two million rupees."

Mohandas paused, allowing Zoe and Trey to absorb his information. "My parents were distraught, naturally. We all were, but my father was particularly inconsolable. He was extremely fond of Radha and felt responsible for her disappearance. He was convinced her abduction revolved around a disgruntled employee. With many employees at the factory, there were always disputes and disagreements within a handful of workers at any given time. My father died from a virus just a few months later. The case regarding Radha's abduction was never solved. To this day, I occasionally wake up in the middle of the night, bathed in sweat, full of remorse I couldn't do more to help locate my sister."

"I'm sure you did all you could. After all, you were still a young boy at the time," Trey said. "So Nirav is gone? Well, I am so sorry to hear that, Mohandas. And your mother, Asha? Is she still living?"

Skye now sat still, her hands gripping the sides of the chair. Zoe knew her daughter was anticipating and dreading Mohandas's response. Skye's head hung down. Her chin almost touched her chest.

"Yes, my mother lives with my wife, Sitha, and me. She was never quite the same after Radha disappeared."

Skye perked up. A look of relief spread across her face as Mohandas responded to her father's question.

Mohandas went on, "I guess none of us were. Mother now suffers from Alzheimer's. She's also blind, a complication from diabetes. She was diagnosed with the disease about fifteen years ago."

Mohandas sighed deeply and drummed his fingers absent-mindedly on his desk. His fingers stilled as he looked up at Zoe. He then looked down at his fingers as though they were foreign objects he'd never seen before. He frowned and placed his hands on his lap.

He continued to speak. "Mother did well enough with oral medications until just a few months ago, when we had to start giving her insulin injections three times a day. But she gets by okay, all things considered. Sitha, bless her, watches mother's diet and takes good care of her. I administer the insulin injections only because Sitha grows faint at the sight of needles.

"Knowing my mother," Mohandas said as he smiled for the first time, "if she could see to fill the syringe with the correct dosage, she'd insist on giving the injections to herself. She's always been a strong, independent woman. Right now she is sleeping—she sleeps a lot these days, but I'll have to wake her soon for an injection. Would you folks like to meet her when I deliver her lunch? I can take you up with me then, and Sitha can watch the office while we visit Mother."

"That would be wonderful," Zoe replied enthusiastically, "if you're sure it wouldn't be too much of an imposition. We'd all be grateful for the opportunity to meet her." Zoe looked over at Skye and saw her daughter was now grinning from ear to ear, as she squirmed about in her chair.

"It would be no imposition at all. Why don't you meet me here at that time? We live above the factory now. About five years ago, we moved from the apartment on Malabar Hill, so Sitha and I can take care of my mother and run the business at the same time. It has worked out well for all three of us. We're able to check on Mother often."

Mohandas glanced at Skye with a rueful expression. "Sitha and I have recently begun to regret our decision not to adopt children after we learned a childhood disease had left her unable to bear children," he said. "We are both forty-six now, and feel we're too old to reconsider the decision. You two are lucky to have one another, and such a beautiful child. You should feel very blessed."

He's right, Zoe told herself, *and it's a shame it takes an offhand remark from someone I've just met to make me realize I haven't fully appreciated how fortunate I am.*

When they walked out the door of the cotton factory, Trey put an arm around Zoe, and another around Skye. He pulled them both toward himself in a tight embrace. "We are lucky, aren't we? We have a lot to be thankful for, so let's try hard not to lose sight of that fact."

Tears glistened in Zoe's eyes as she heard Trey's tender words. Her lip quivered as she leaned into her husband's loving embrace.

"Mother? Wake up. It's time for your insulin shot," Mohandas said to seventy-five-year-old Asha as he gently shook her shoulder. He filled the syringe, swabbed the injection site, and plunged the needle swiftly into the loose flesh of her upper arm. Asha showed no reaction, unaware her son had even administered the shot.

"I will be returning in thirty minutes or so with your lunch. Okay?" Not expecting or waiting for a response, he continued. "I will be bringing some people up with me who are anxious to meet you. Can you stay awake if I turn the radio on for you?"

"Of course I can," Asha said, nodding. "I need to get up and put a chicken in the oven to roast soon, anyway. Can you let the dogs out before you leave?"

"Yes, Mother," Mohandas replied. It was easier, he thought, to just agree with her than to try and explain that she could not get up from the recliner without assistance, hadn't cooked for ten years, and the dogs had been gone for over fifteen.

While he gathered up the syringe, alcohol wipe, and insulin bottle, Asha began drifting off to sleep again. Mohandas sighed and shook his head in exasperation. He turned the radio on and fiddled with the knobs to eliminate the static. Before leaving the room, he cranked the volume up another notch or two.

Now he wasn't sure about having the Robbins family come up to meet his mother. It might not have been such a good idea. But he knew it was very important to them to do so, and he didn't know what to think about the possibility of Skye having his long-lost sister's reincarnated soul. He certainly had no idea how to propose the possibility to his mother, who didn't recognize him much of the time.

"We've got two hours to fill until we return to the factory, Zoe. Any ideas?" Trey asked.

"Let's visit Churchgate, and then wander around the Crawford Market until it's time to go back to the factory."

"Sounds like a plan to me."

They toured through Churchgate, the historic train station, and then retraced their steps to the market, as Zoe had suggested. Individual stalls at the market offered everything from fruits and vegetables to shoes and clothing. Small pharmacies were also abundant. People were milling about everywhere; peddlers were very vocal in hawking their wares. There was a lively atmosphere.

Zoe noticed Trey made no snide comments this time as she went from stand to stand collecting souvenirs, including cotton t-shirts for the three of them, a hand-carved mahogany elephant statue for Joe Junior, and an onyx Buddha figurine for herself. She was fascinated with the Buddha statues, which seem to be made out of every imaginable type of material. Zoe had decided to begin a small collection of figurines. She'd give them to Skye when she was older.

The next stall sold reasonably priced jade and amethyst jewelry. Trey pointed at a concession stand and said, "I'll get us a snack to tide us over till lunch, since we skipped breakfast. You two can select some jewelry for yourselves and then wait for me here. Okay?"

Zoe nodded as he continued, "And I'd like you to pick out a watchband for me too. Something that's not too gaudy or elaborate—in silver and jade—to go with the watch you gave me for my birthday."

"I thought you didn't like that watch."

"Why would you think that?" Trey asked.

"I haven't seen you wear it."

"I love the watch, Zoe, but the band it came with is too tight and it pinches the hair on my wrist. One of these bands will be ideal for it and a nice souvenir of our trip."

Zoe smiled as her husband left her side. She was pleased to discover that he hadn't disliked her gift. She would buy his mother a necklace while she was selecting jewelry to purchase.

Trey returned with three dosas a few minutes later. As they sat on a bench and ate their pastries, Zoe and Trey discussed their visit with Mohandas. Zoe thought Mohandas's skepticism was apparent, but he'd appeared hopeful that Skye was the soul reincarnate of his sister, Radha.

"I'm sure there's doubt in his mind. How could there not be at this point? He got blindsided by all this, after all, and he probably doesn't know what to think," she said.

Trey nodded, then motioned for Zoe to look at Skye, who sat quietly taking small bites of her snack. She had a contented, happy look on her face.

"There's no doubt in her mind though, is there?" he asked.

Carrying a small bowl of sambar, a form of curried vegetable stew, from the mill's small cafeteria, Mohandas pushed open the door to his mother's room. The Robbins family followed behind him. For a few moments no one spoke. Mohandas was uncertain about how to introduce the Robbins family to his mother. He'd given it a lot of thought the last two hours, but still found himself tongue-tied.

Then to his surprise, Skye moved quickly across the room to the old woman who was half dozing in her recliner. She knelt down next to the chair. She then picked up Asha's frail right hand, stroked it lovingly several times with her own, and whispered breathlessly, "Mama?"

Asha sat up straight, instantly alert, and reached out to enfold Skye into her arms. Crushing the little girl to her chest, she said, "Radha? *To mera jaanu.* Oh, my baby, my dear sweet baby. I always knew you'd come back to me. What took you so long to come home?"

Mohandas's eyes darted from the touching scene to Trey and Zoe and then back again. His mother couldn't see the little girl, but had recognized Radha's spirit instinctively. *It's true,* he realized, *my sister's soul has been reborn into the body of this little blond-haired girl named Skylar Robbins.* It was a bittersweet realization for him; he now had to accept the fact that Radha, as he'd known her, was never coming home.

Mohandas walked across the room. At the recliner, he wrapped his arms around both Skye and his mother. "Welcome home, my dear sister," he said softly, as a lone tear escaped his eye and moved slowly down his cheek. It was a tear of mixed emotions. It was one of pure joy for finding his sister's soul still existing in the body of Skylar Robbins, and a tear of disappointment for the verification of his sister's death many years ago.

TWELVE

Bombay, India, 1944

Rebuilding the cotton factory and chawls was a tougher challenge than Asha could have imagined. To her dismay, there was nothing left of the original building that could be salvaged. The entire area had to be cleared off and hauled away before she could begin the reconstruction. She'd have to start from scratch, and it was a massive undertaking.

Ajay Deshpande had never been one to leave anything to chance when it came to his own welfare. He'd always covered all the bases, and Asha was relieved to discover he hadn't gambled on the fate of the factory either. A substantial insurance policy had been maintained on the cotton mill, and on the chawls her father had furnished for his employees. His prudence was a bright spot in a dark and dire situation. But it wasn't the only one, Asha thought, as she mulled over how much her life had changed since the tragic explosion. She was enjoying a freedom she'd never been allowed to experience when her father was alive. She was now at liberty to socialize with anyone. She could come and go as she wished. More importantly, she had the opportunity to accomplish something worthwhile, a chance to help needy people.

And there was a tremendous amount to accomplish, Asha soon realized. But at least deciding where to begin had been easy for her. Most of the employees and their families had been killed on that fateful day in April. But there were still a few dozen people, including Eduardo's younger brother, Rafael, who hadn't been at work or at home in the chawls when the explosion occurred. These individuals now found themselves on the streets with no home, no food, and no paycheck. This was Asha's primary concern.

She quickly organized crews to begin erecting new chawls, more substantial and roomier than the original ones. Proper sanitation was also a priority in the new structures. *No one should be forced to live in filth and squalor,* Asha thought.

With the clamor of saws and hammers in the background, Asha combed the streets for what she'd come to think of as her extended family. She also searched for rooms she could rent to house as many of these displaced individuals as she was able to find. She dipped even further into her father's reserves to supply them with an emergency relief allowance to meet their needs until the factory was up and running again.

Her actions were almost unheard of, her compassion overwhelming. She was determined to do what she felt was right for the people who'd been loyal to her father's business, a business over which she now had complete control. *Never again,* she vowed, *will the Deshpande factory employees be treated as a commodity, something to be used as a means to an end. They'll be treated as family, as worthy human beings with hearts and souls that need to be protected and cherished.* Like Asha, they were all suffering from the loss of loved ones, and she'd do everything in her power to help them rebuild from the terrible catastrophe. Helping others recover was helping her recover, serving as a balm for her own wounded heart. Only very late at night did Asha have time to sit back and think about Eduardo, and reflect on what might've been. She tried to avoid the temptation of reflection, for it only brought on more tears and sorrow.

Not feeling comfortable occupying her father's palatial home,

Asha put it up for sale. To her relief, within a few weeks she was presented with a contract to sell the property to a successful movie producer for twice what she would have thought it could bring. The extra money would be welcome to help provide for the surviving factory employees.

Asha secured a smaller, more modest flat on Little Gibbs Road in the Malabar Hill district. It was within convenient walking distance to the harbor and had everything she needed. She loved the feeling of independence as she decorated the new third-floor apartment with the barest of necessities. The remaining contents from her father's home were sold off. The proceeds went to the relief fund she had established for her new family.

As Asha scoured the area for the suddenly homeless survivors, she frequently asked if anyone knew where to find Rafael Torres. Several mentioned seeing him, but no one could tell her where to locate him. She'd never met Eduardo's younger brother, but felt a personal responsibility for his welfare.

One afternoon while strolling along the harbor that now resembled a war zone, she spotted an attractive young foreign-looking lad, several years her junior. Despite his wiry frame, he had a strong muscular build, the kind obtained from years of hard, manual labor. Other than his wild, tousled hairstyle and lankier frame, he bore a striking resemblance to Eduardo.

As Asha approached, she saw he was sitting on a pile of charred debris and staring out to sea. There was an angry look on his face as he absentmindedly picked up bits and pieces of debris and tossed them into the surf. He did not appear to notice her.

"Rafael?" she asked softly, not wanting to startle him.

He turned his head quickly, and after studying her for a moment, replied, "Yes, I'm Rafael. Rafael Torres. Are you Asha?"

"Yes, I'm Asha Deshpande. I was to be your brother's wife," she answered, tears welling up in her eyes.

Rafael ran his fingers through his disheveled hair before rising and then wrapping his arms around her in an awkward embrace. "I'm so happy to finally meet you, Asha. You're as beautiful as Eduardo said."

"Thank you, Rafael," Asha murmured. "It's wonderful to meet you, too. I'm sorry it has taken me so long to find you."

"I wanted to find you also. I am ashamed to admit I've been too busy feeling sorry for myself to look for you. But I would've made a concentrated effort to find you in the near future. I need to give you a message from Eduardo. It was the last request he made before he died."

Asha attempted to reply, but the image she was visualizing from Rafael's words impeded her ability to speak. She nodded instead, as she looked into Rafael's eyes and waited to hear the message from her late fiancé.

"He told me to tell you he would always love you," Rafael said softly. He looked at the sand around his feet. Asha concealed a slight smile as she realized Rafael was embarrassed to be repeating his brother's words of endearment to her. "He said he will meet you in heaven one day," Rafael continued. He made circles in the sand with his bare toe.

"You meant the world to him, Asha," he said, lifting his eyes to gaze at her. "I had never seen him as happy as he was the last few months. He loved you with all his heart, and always will."

Asha placed her hand on Rafael's forearm, her smile fading and her eyes pooling with tears. "Thank you for the message, Rafael. I will always love Eduardo. He was the first and only person in my life who truly cared about me, and I'll always cherish his memory.

"But there's nothing we can do that can change the events of that painful day, Rafael," she said stoically. "You and I must go on and live our lives in a way that would have made Eduardo proud. I may meet another man someday to share my life with, but your brother will always own a very special piece of my heart. Being with Eduardo made me whole. He had a way of making me want to be a better person, to want to live up to his expectations of me."

Rafael understood and nodded in agreement. He had felt the same way. "I must get on with my life, too," he said. "It's been hard for me to get motivated these last few weeks. But I can't continue to just sit here along the shore of the Arabian Sea, wishing I was aboard one of the many ships I've watched sailing in and out of the harbor. Perhaps it's time to pursue my dream of becoming a sailor. There's nothing left for me here." Rafael stared out to the distant horizon.

"Oh, but I think there might be, Rafael," Asha said. "Where are you living, now that the chawls have been destroyed?"

"You're pretty much looking at it," he replied, spreading his arms out and gazing at the devastation. "I've been living here on the beach. I've had nowhere else to go, and nobody I could ask for help. I was fortunate to have had a little money in my pocket when the ship exploded, so at least I've not gone hungry."

Asha thought for a moment. "I've just moved into a small flat," she said. "It's not fancy, but it's comfortable and it has a spare bedroom. I'd like for you to stay with me, make use of the extra room for the time being."

"Thanks for the kind offer, Asha, but I couldn't possibly accept. Your reputation would be at stake, and I wouldn't want to see it tarnished for my sake. People would talk," he said, a blush spreading across his cheeks at the implication.

"Oh, pooh! At a time like this, the last thing I'm concerned about is my so-called reputation," Asha assured him. "We were to be family, Rafael. We were to have lived in the same home had this tragedy not occurred. I don't care what other people have to say about it. I don't have to justify my actions to anyone, and frankly, Rafael, I could use your assistance and your company. I need help in getting the factory rebuilt and the business back up and running."

Rafael raised his eyebrows in surprise. Eduardo had been right; Asha was a spirited young lady even to consider taking on the responsibility of rebuilding the mill. "How can I help you? What can I do?" he asked.

"You worked for my father long enough to know what the new factory needs to make it a better workplace, and you can help me deal with contractors. You see, I'm not just offering to help you. I'm also asking you to help me."

"Well, put that way, Asha, how can I refuse?" Rafael said, grinning. "If it's what you truly want, I'd be honored to occupy your spare room and assist you in any way possible. Eduardo would have wanted me to."

Asha smiled broadly and put out her hand. Rafael grasped it in a friendly shake. "Partners?" she asked.

"Partners," he agreed. Following their handshake, they turned and strolled back toward the construction site.

As they ambled at a relaxed pace, Asha noticed Rafael was hobbling along in an awkward gait. "Why are you limping?" she asked. "Have you injured a leg?"

"My feet were burnt on the day of the explosion," he explained. "There are some blisters still a bit sore and tender, but they'll eventually heal. Nothing to worry about, Asha."

"Have you seen a doctor, Rafael?"

"Well, no, but . . ."

"No 'buts' about it, Rafael. I'll take you in to have them checked out at the clinic tomorrow. Those blisters could be infected. I need you healthy to be of help to me."

Rafael was touched by her concern. "Okay, you're the boss," he said contritely.

"No, I'm not your boss, Rafael. I'm your partner," Asha corrected.

Over the next several months, Rafael and Asha worked together to accelerate the reconstruction project as much as possible. They spent long, arduous days studying blueprints and collaborating with the contractors. They were on the construction site by dawn and rarely left until after sunset. They ate late suppers and talked well into the night over hot tea. A strong bond was formed between the two. They made a young, but formidable, pair as they supervised the rebirth of the Deshpande Cotton Factory.

As the first row of chawls was completed, they were quickly filled by those survivors spread around town in rooms that had been rented by Asha. She made sure everything the new occupants needed was available in order to set up their households. It became increasingly difficult for anyone to imagine she could have been the offspring of a man as dispassionate as Ajay Deshpande.

Meanwhile, construction crews had broken ground on the new factory. There would be many additions to the factory to make it safer. Cotton factories had been notoriously dangerous places to work; many people were killed in accidents. To Asha, this was unacceptable.

"Rafael, I want you to tell me all the changes you think should be implemented. I don't want employees being killed or maimed in senseless accidents, nor do I want them miserable and suffering throughout their work days."

"I've given it much thought, Asha, and I've come up with a list of suggestions," Rafael said. "I think we can create a safe, comfortable working environment, without sacrificing the financial success of the business. I've also thought of a few ways the mill can operate with more efficiency."

Together they went through Rafael's list, checking off each idea as they drafted in modifications to the blueprints. They learned all about load-bearing walls, electrical configurations, plumbing fixtures, and duct work in the process. Asha and Rafael worked together in perfect harmony.

Clean, sanitary water closets for the employees' use were added to each end of the main floor. Large fans to circulate air throughout the building were also drawn into the plans. A comfortable break room would be located beside a small canteen in the center of the factory. When work resumed, employees would be granted scheduled breaks from their labors; in the cafeteria, low-cost tiffens, or lunches, would be available to them.

After studying the meticulous ledgers and records her father had kept, and then had the foresight to store in his home office, Asha and Rafael determined they could establish three eight-hour shifts, as opposed to the previous twelve-hour shifts. This would provide more job opportunities while increasing the productivity of the mill. Asha was certain a worn-out worker couldn't be as productive as one who was fresh and well rested. Rafael agreed, thinking back to the days when after ten or eleven hours of intense labor, he had devoted most of his energy to trying to keep from fainting on the floor. At times, just staying on his feet was all he could manage to accomplish in the last hour or two of his work shift.

They could also increase the workers' hourly pay and still allow the factory to remain solvent. Unlike her father, Asha's goal was to make the factory efficient and self-supporting, while providing the employees with a fair income and a safe, pleasant place to work. No longer would it be just a vehicle for fattening the owner's wallet. Asha had no need or desire to live a lavish lifestyle.

★ ★ ★ ★ ★

While sitting alone, eating lunch one day, Rafael thought about how his life had changed since he'd met Asha. Working and living together, an easy, comfortable relationship had formed between them. She was the first female figure of any importance in his life. He scarcely remembered his mother, Maria, who had abandoned him when he was four. He knew he was three years younger than Asha, and it would require a small miracle to take Eduardo's place in her heart.

But he also knew he was becoming more than a little in love with her. If there were any way possible to replace Eduardo in Asha's heart, he would try hard to do it. Eduardo was gone, and no matter how much it grieved him, Rafael could not bring his brother back to life. He and Asha had to go on living. *Would it be such a bad thing if we were to go on living together? Would it be wrong for us to have an intimate relationship, or to one day be married?* Rafael wondered. *I wouldn't want to show any disrespect to Eduardo's memory, but I've grown to love Asha as he assured me I would.* He had been correct in that she was impossible to dislike.

Asha was beginning to be an almost regular feature in his dreams at night and in his fantasies during the day. He longed to hold her in his arms and kiss her passionately. Asha Deshpande was the woman he yearned to spend his life with, but could he approach her with his feelings?

Asha treated him as a friend and companion, but certainly had never given him any indication she had romantic feelings toward him. *She treats me,* he thought rather dejectedly, *as if I were her brother. I don't think I'm ready to risk making a fool of myself. Better wait until she gives me some kind of sign she feels the same way about me as I feel about her. Then I will take a bold, romantic stand for her.*

In 1946, with war no longer raging in Europe, the demand for cotton had settled down to a less hectic pace. The Deshpande Cotton Factory was back in full operation, and Rafael was proud of the part he'd played in its impressive rebound. The turnover rate was minimal; the workforce was contented with their new living quarters, their safer, more employee-friendly working environment, their healthier paychecks, and their compassionate new bosses, Asha and Rafael.

Along with the new gregarious atmosphere came an eighteen-percent increase in production. Rafael encouraged Asha to introduce a new profit-sharing program for employees, and production rose another twenty percent. Financial incentive was a powerful tool in Rafael's view.

Possibly he was the youngest plant manager in the city, yet he was pleased his subordinates treated him with respect, although most of them were older than Rafael. Once he feared they wouldn't take his leadership seriously, and now he was relieved to realize his concerns were groundless.

Rafael continued to reside with Asha on Little Gibbs Road. He could now afford to rent his own apartment, or at the very least occupy one of the modernized chawls, but he had no desire to put distance between himself and Asha. She seemed in no hurry for him to move out, either, so he didn't force the issue. Asha still had not given him the sign he prayed for, but he was willing to wait if she was the reward for his patience.

Wading through water almost up to his knees, Rafael made his way across the street to the factory. It was late August 1947, nearing the end of the monsoon season, and Bombay was experiencing torrents of rain. Building the new factory on a higher foundation had been a wise decision. Less raw cotton was now lost to the frequent flooding conditions when the yearly rains came. He felt a great sense of pride and accomplishment that his idea to raise the factory above flood level had been adopted.

On August fifteenth of that year, India had achieved dominion status. independence from British rule, and the country had been partitioned into India, a Hindu majority, and Pakistan, a Muslim majority. Things were changing at a rapid pace in the country.

Rafael awoke one morning just after his eighteenth birthday, full of purpose and hope. He knew this was the day that would set the course for the next stage of his life. His patience had run out, and he'd decided it was time to declare his love for Asha. He felt comfortable enough with her now to ask her if she felt they had a future together. Maybe Asha was waiting for him to make the first move toward a more intimate relationship. He dressed hurriedly, anxious for the day to begin.

"There's a Mr. Joshi here to see you," Asha's receptionist announced through the open door of Asha's office.

"Send him in," Asha said, neatly stacking a pile of papers she'd been working on and moving the pile to the edge of her desk.

Nirav Joshi, formerly a laborer on a plantation in Gujaret, India, where cotton was grown in the fertile, black soil, was now in charge of soliciting factories to buy the raw fiber for production of cotton fabric. He was cordial and courteous as he elaborated on the high quality of the plantation's product and the terms of the deal he was offering. Asha was impressed with the offer and took little time agreeing to contract the plantation to provide raw material for her factory. She was also highly impressed with the professional manner of the salesman, Mr. Joshi.

Nirav was trim-figured, handsome, and impeccable in his

tailored three-piece suit. He didn't try to hide the fact he was impressed with Asha also. "Would you do me the honor of dining with me this evening?" he asked as he gathered up his belongings and prepared to leave.

Asha agreed without hesitation. *I'm twenty-one, and this will be the first real date of my life,* she thought. After all, a thirty-minute rendezvous with Eduardo at the local library once a week could not really be classified as a date.

Asha and Nirav enjoyed a Gujarti meal at one of the finest restaurants in Bombay. When he escorted her home to her Malabar Hill apartment, she invited him in for tea. They consumed many cups of the hot, aromatic beverage while talking late into the night.

His own plans dashed for the evening, a somber Rafael sat in his room and fretted when he heard Asha and her companion talking and laughing in the kitchen. Rafael had been giddy with anticipation all day, determined to profess his love to Asha that evening. Instead, he now sat forlorn in his room, hating the stranger in the kitchen more and more with each outburst of Asha's joyous laughter.

Over the next few months, Asha was often in the company of Nirav. He took her out to eat, to movies at the theatre, and on romantic picnics to Chowpatty Beach. She enjoyed spending time with him. He made her laugh when he referred to himself as a "cotton-picking fool." And she cried when he told her about losing his father in a cotton gin accident the previous year.

"I live with my sister, her family, and my mother, who suffers from a heart condition," he told Asha. "My brother-in-law is a laborer in the cotton fields, as I used to be, and we're all housed in a small bungalow on the plantation. My mother's parents both died young of the bubonic plague in 1896, and my father's parents have both died within the last ten years."

Unlike Asha, Nirav grew up in a happy, loving environment. She enjoyed hearing him tell stories of his happy childhood. She told him very little about her own early years. She didn't want his pity, but she wasn't a liar, and she couldn't make her childhood sound enviable no matter how much she embellished the truth.

Asha also found Nirav to be very physically attractive. His appearance was always immaculate, which caused her to want to appear more attractive in his eyes as well. She began taking greater pains with her wardrobe, and displaying colorful tikas, which were decorative red Hindu marks on her forehead. Tikas were more of a fashion statement than a religious one, and Asha had never been particularly fashion conscious.

These changes in Asha did not go unnoticed by Rafael. He became more sullen and withdrawn with each passing day. There was no love lost between himself and Nirav. When introduced, they'd become instant adversaries. Rafael was jealous of Nirav's prominence in Asha's life, and was convinced Nirav felt the same toward him. By mutual consent, all three of them determined it was time for Rafael to seek alternate living arrangements. He moved out of Asha's flat in early December. Aside from burying his brother, it was the hardest thing Rafael had ever done.

Later that month, Rafael heard through the factory grapevine that Nirav had asked Asha to marry him, and Asha had accepted the offer.

The news hit Rafael like a wrecking ball to the chest. He hadn't allowed himself to consider the possibility that Asha would not tire of Nirav once the newness wore off their relationship.

Rafael felt like a bug that had been ground into the dirt

beneath Nirav's shiny, black heels. What he wouldn't give to be able to pound Nirav's perfectly proportioned face into a bloody pulp!

But Rafael knew any act of revenge toward Nirav would not change the way Asha felt about either of them. It wouldn't change anything, other than make Asha want nothing at all to do with him.

Rafael couldn't even bring himself to congratulate Asha on her engagement. He found it hard to admit he'd been preempted by his foe, the supercilious salesman from Gujaret. Rafael was even more crestfallen to realize his love for Asha had never been reciprocated.

When Rafael could no longer face seeing Asha and Nirav together, he applied for a position as a deckhand on a ship that transported cotton to China and other ports around the world. His love for the sea had never abated. Only his love for Asha had prevented him from following his dream and becoming a sailor after the death of his father and brother.

Rafael left the cotton factory without uttering a single word to Asha about his intentions.

Asha learned of Rafael's resignation from her receptionist. She felt his defection very deeply, having been quite fond of her former fiancé's younger brother. She could not fathom what had happened to their relationship to cause him to desert her in this way. She had noticed his change in demeanor and his gradual distancing of himself from her in recent months, but she'd been too preoccupied with her burgeoning relationship with Nirav to dwell on it. *I thought we were partners,* she said to herself. *I feel as though I've lost my best friend.*

Asha and Nirav were married two weeks later, in January 1948, just two days before a young Hindu fanatic gunned down Mahatma Gandhi, the preeminent leader of Indian nationalism.

With the country in such turmoil, she and Nirav decided it would be best to cancel their honeymoon plans and get right back to work. Asha knew Nirav was anxious to begin learning about the business of producing cotton fabric. He had much to learn if he were to fill Rafael's shoes.

Nirav replaced Rafael as the plant manager, and as the man of the house in Asha's flat on Little Gibbs Road. Although he could never hope to possess Asha's heart to the extent Eduardo had, he was kind, faithful, and reliable. Eduardo had been her soul mate, a kindred spirit, and no man, not even Nirav, could ever replace him as the love of her life. But Asha knew Nirav would be a considerate husband and a good father to their children in the future. She was satisfied they would work well as a team at raising a family and managing the cotton factory.

By 1951, Nirav was competent enough to manage the business without Asha's daily presence at the mill. She was heavy with child, and Nirav suggested it was time for her to stay home and prepare to raise their family. Radha was born in November. Asha and Nirav couldn't have been more thrilled or delighted with their tiny, beloved daughter.

Their family expanded in 1955 with the birth of their son, Mohandas, who now slept in the wooden crib Nirav had built for Radha four years before. Radha had graduated to the room Rafael had once occupied. Asha often thought about Rafael and wondered what had ever become of the young man whom she had grown to love like a brother.

THIRTEEN

Bombay, India, 2001

"Help! Let me out of here!"

As Skye's scream filled the room, Trey jumped up from the large bed. He rushed to the rollaway cot the hotel had provided for Skye, as Zoe tumbled out of bed just one step behind him. They found Skye flopping and writhing in her sleep, her pajamas saturated in sweat. The damp sheets were twisted around her like a pretzel. When Trey woke her, she was gasping for air, almost hyperventilating. As before, Skye refused to discuss the nightmare she had experienced.

Sitting beside Skye on the cot, Trey pulled her to his lap and gently rocked her while he stroked her back. He kissed her forehead and assured her he was there and she was safe.

After Skye had fallen asleep again, Trey motioned for Zoe to follow him to the far corner of the room. "We've got to do something, Zoe. Skye needs relief from these frightening memories of her past-life trauma."

"That's what I've been saying all along." Zoe's hands trembled as she pushed the hair back that had fallen across her eyes.

"I know you have, and you've been right. What can we do? Mohandas and Asha need closure too." Trey knew Mohandas was still haunted by the disappearance of his sister, Radha, a case that had never been solved. Mohandas had told him Asha still spoke of Radha as if she were there in the house. She often told Mohandas to let his sister know Sitha had supper ready to serve, and then was disappointed when her daughter did not show up at the dinner table. Being in the latter stages of Alzheimer's made comprehension elusive for Asha. The disease had robbed her of crucial facets of her memory.

"We've got to do more research, Zoe. There had to have been some media coverage when the abduction occurred."

The next day Trey and Zoe poured through newspaper clippings that had been saved in an old cardboard box Mohandas had pulled out from his office storage closet. Trey was discouraged when they learned little more than Mohandas had already told them. "How can we tap Skye's memory for more information without causing her emotional havoc?" he asked Zoe.

"I don't know. Do you think Jutta Meyer might be able to give us some suggestions?"

"Possibly. I'll call her if you can dig up her number for me."

"I have it right here in my fanny pack." Zoe searched unsuccessfully through the pack for a while and then dumped the entire contents on a nearby desk. She picked out a scrap of paper with Jutta's phone number written on it and handed it to Trey.

Trey calculated the time difference, and rented an international phone to contact Jutta. He brought her up to date on the situation that had unfolded in Bombay. "How can we obtain more details of her past life without upsetting her too much?" he asked. "It's harder for her to deal with here in Mumbai."

"I'm not surprised. Did you purchase the Brian Weiss novel I recommended?" Jutta asked.

"Yes, Zoe did. She brought it to India with her."

"Good. At the end of the book is a written dialogue of the hypnosis meditation that Dr. Weiss uses to regress patients. Practice reciting it in a soft, soothing voice. By following Dr.

Weiss's instructions, you should be able to take Skye back to that previous lifetime as an observer, rather than as an actual participant. But if the memories seem to be affecting her physically or emotionally, you can bring her out of it by telling her to open her eyes. Okay?"

"Okay," Trey said, with obvious doubt in his voice.

"Don't worry. Once she can see for herself that what happened to Radha has nothing to do with her life now, her nightmares might stop. Hopefully she can recall enough information to help you in your search for the truth."

"Okay, Jutta, I'll give it a try. Thanks."

"Keep me posted, and please don't hesitate to call if I can be of any further help. That's what I'm here for."

"Want to play a game with us?" Trey asked Skye the following day.

"Sure, Daddy. What kind of game?" she asked with a grin on her face.

"Well, it's a meditation game," was his vague response.

"Uh, okay . . ." Skye had no idea what meditation meant, but knew the word "game" was a good thing.

Zoe helped Skye become comfortable, sitting in an upright position on the king-sized bed. Zoe propped Skye's back and head up with several thick pillows. Trey explained the game to Skye, "Now as I read from this book, I want you to concentrate on what I'm saying and follow my instructions. Okay?"

"Uh-huh."

"If anything happens that scares you or makes you uncomfortable, just open your eyes. Okay?"

"Uh-huh."

Trey began reciting his own version of Dr. Weiss's meditation from *Many Lives, Many Masters* in a very soft voice, almost a whisper. "Close your eyes and take a deep relaxing breath."

As Skye took a deep breath, so did Zoe in an attempt to calm her nerves. She twisted the ends of her hair in a nervous reaction to the possible effect this attempt at regression might have on their daughter. She listened as Trey continued.

"Imagine that all the stress from your body is completely gone and your arms and legs are beginning to become limp. Take long deep breaths and feel yourself get even more relaxed and limp with each breath. If you get scared or uncomfortable, rise above your body and watch the scene unfold as if you were an entirely different person than the one you are seeing in the scene in front of you. If you are still too scared to relax, come back to full consciousness."

Zoe watched Skye tense up temporarily, as if she were just realizing what kind of game it was she had agreed to play. Almost immediately, Skye began to relax again. As Skye was drifting off into a hypnotic state, Zoe was becoming more anxious and nervous. She was still not convinced that putting Skye through this regression was the right thing to do. Just then Skye's head pitched forward as if her neck was made of Jell-O, and her arms went completely limp.

Trey continued talking in almost a whisper. He was speaking slow and dreamily in a low, barely audible tone. "Imagine an alluring tunnel in front of you. This is a tunnel that leads to your past lives with you in a spiritual state of being. You want desperately to walk through that tunnel to see what is on the other side. You know going through the tunnel will benefit you greatly in your current life. The more you look at the tunnel, the stronger is the urge to pass through it. As you slowly approach the opening of the tunnel you see a bright light on the other side, which beckons you to approach it. Go ahead and approach it, give in to your urges, and go through the tunnel into the light. I want you to become a participant in the scene taking place in front of you."

As Trey spoke out loud in a low soothing voice, Skye appeared to be settling into a deep trance. Her head was listing rhythmically from one side to the other. Trey then told Skye to visualize a pretty country lane, which led past an entrancing, rippling stream. "I want you to go back to a time before you were Skylar, back to when you were fifteen. Imagine yourself as this fifteen-year-old girl as you stroll down the country lane. Now imagine yourself walking beside the relaxing stream. There is a small cove off the stream where the water is still. It is so calm and clear you can see your reflection on the surface of the water. Look into the reflection and tell me what you see," Trey instructed his daughter.

"I see a young woman," Skye said after a short pause. Trey looked up at Zoe over the top of his reading glasses. Zoe knew he was as astonished as she that he had succeeded in regressing their daughter.

"Are you that young woman you see?" Trey asked Skye.

"Yes."

"What do you look like?"

"I have short dark hair and dark eyes. I'm wearing several layers of clothing," Skye said, describing her vision in an almost monotone voice. "The clothes are light and comfortable and swish around my legs. I'm barefoot."

"Where are you?"

"I'm in the kitchen, frying eggs and a rasher of bacon on a wood stove."

"Can you go outside and tell me what you see there?"

"Yes." She paused a few moments and continued, "I'm going out the front door, stepping over an orange tabby on the doorstep. He is my cat. I call him Zeus."

"Are you outside now? What does the area look like?"

Zoe reached over and grabbed a notebook beside her to record anything Skye said they might need to remember later.

She felt as though Trey had the situation under perfect control but was still apprehensive, knowing it was the first time he'd ever attempted a past-life regression in his life. She couldn't help being drawn in by her curiosity to know what had happened in Skye's past life, but was afraid of doing further harm to her psyche. But she sat still and silent as she listened to Skye describe the area she was visualizing.

"The house is fairly large and made out of big square rocks. There's a cobblestone path leading up to the thick wooden door. The houses on either side of it look a lot like this one. So do the ones on the tier above and the tier below. Looking down the hill I can see Mandraki Harbour, and a number of boats out on the water."

"Where is this Mandraki Harbour located?" Trey asked.

"Rhodes."

"Roads? What roads?"

"Rhodes," Skye repeated. "The Greek island. Through the gap where the Palace of the Grand Masters used to be, I can see the walls of the Fortress."

"Why are you on the island of Rhodes?"

"Nikos brought me here."

"Nikos?"

"Yes, Nikos Colotto."

"What does Nikos do?" Trey asked. Zoe could see he was getting more and more excited as the regression proceeded. She was getting more and more fearful.

"He works with fabric."

"Look forward in time now. How long do you stay in Rhodes?"

"Until I die."

Zoe gasped and covered her eyes with her hands. She considered covering her ears instead, not sure she wanted to hear any more of the details.

"How did you die, do you know? What happens to you?" Trey asked as he leaned forward in anticipation of Skye's next response.

Shrugging her shoulders with indifference, Skye said, "I just leave my body, like all the times before."

"Why did you stay in Rhodes?"

"I had to. I couldn't leave, I had to take . . ."

Just then a loud bang startled all three of them as a door slammed across the hallway from their room. Skye opened her eyes, blinking rapidly. "Daddy?" she asked, as if she weren't quite sure she recognized Trey.

"Yes, honey, it's Daddy. Are you okay?"

"I'm okay. But I don't want to play this game anymore today."

Zoe didn't either. Trey met her eyes and said, "We won't play it anymore then. Would you like to go with Mommy and get some ice cream instead?"

Skye nodded. Trey spoke quietly to Zoe. He told her that he wanted to go speak to Mohandas without Skye present. Zoe agreed and she and Skye left to walk across the street from the hotel to the same vendor's stand they had patronized before.

While Zoe and Skye were gone, Trey drove to the cotton factory. Mohandas told him he'd never heard the name Nikos Colotto. "Many of the ships that transport cotton are registered out of Greece, and of course have a lot of Greek crew members," he said. "Radha looked a lot like our mother, pretty and petite. She caught a lot of men's eyes. She could have been abducted randomly by a sailor in port off one of those ships, I suppose," Mohandas continued without any real conviction. "I can't remember any particular conflict my parents had with any of the transport contractors, Greek or otherwise. I was eleven at the time, though. They wouldn't have discussed that sort of thing around me anyway."

Like Mohandas, Trey wasn't too sure they were on the right path either. He was wary of putting too much stress on Skye and wasn't sure she would be very receptive at being hypnotized again. When he returned to the hotel, Skye was taking a nap, so he and Zoe sat out on the balcony and discussed their next move.

"Sitha volunteered to reserve us three seats on a flight to Athens, and from there we could catch a smaller jet to the island of Rhodes," Trey said. "No visas are necessary to enter Greece, so we could fly out tomorrow, which is Tuesday, and back to Bombay on Thursday. Do you honestly think it's something we should do?"

"Yes, I think it's something we need to do," Zoe said.

"Okay, I'll give her a call soon and tell her to book the flights for us." Trey mulled over what they needed to try to find out, once they reached Rhodes, should they be fortunate enough to track down this Nikos Colotto. "Skye said Nikos worked with fabric. There is a cotton connection here, I'm sure. But in what way is Colotto connected to the Deshpande Cotton Factory? Did he snatch Radha and take her to his home on Rhodes and force her to stay there in captivity? How did she die? Did she die at Nikos's hands? Did he torture her and kill her in his home? She said she couldn't leave there, and she died there."

Zoe had been silent as she listened to Trey thinking out loud, then she asked, "Why would he not have collected the suitcase full of money before taking Radha back to Rhodes? Why kidnap her and send a ransom note demanding money, and then not collect it?"

"Good question, Zoe. I don't know. It doesn't make much sense, does it? Skye mentioned cooking bacon and eggs."

"Can you believe she used the word 'rasher'?" Zoe asked.

"Yeah, that surprised me too. And I don't surprise easily these days."

"I hope we can find out who Nikos Colotto was and how he was connected to Radha."

"Me too," Trey said. "Did this Nikos Colotto force Radha to cook for him? Did he force himself on her sexually? Maybe keep her as a sexual slave until she died? Could he have killed her in a fit of rage?"

Zoe flinched. "Do you think Colotto is still living?" she asked. "He would be pretty old by now."

Trey paced back and forth as he considered Zoe's remarks. "Yes, I thought about that aspect. I guess there's no way to know unless we go to Rhodes and search for him, or at least search for information about him in public records there. Are you absolutely certain going to Rhodes is what you want to do, Zoe? Can you accept and live with what we might discover there?"

"Yes, I'll have to accept whatever we find out about Radha's life and death. I need to know the truth about what happened to Skye when she was Radha. I also hope the truth will not be too much for Skye to handle, but Jutta said the truth should relieve her of her nightmares. And even if the truth is difficult to swallow, it would still provide closure for the Joshis, something they've long been denied."

"You know, Skye didn't seem upset or emotional at all when she was talking about her abductor," Trey said. "But then, I guess, it could be because the meditation dialogue instructs the regressed subject to view visions from a distance. She may have felt an emotional and physical detachment from the scene. She didn't really seem to have witnessed anything traumatic, no violence or anything of that nature. Maybe the door slammed before she got to the traumatic portion of the memories." He stopped pacing, sat down, and dropped his head into his hands.

"Trey, do you think it's possible Radha had been previously involved with Nikos? Possibly even eloped with him? Maybe

Radha was a runaway and not a victim of kidnapping."

"Well, maybe, but then why the ransom note?" Trey asked as he lowered his hands and looked at Zoe.

"Maybe to steer the authorities off on the wrong track in their investigation?" Zoe asked.

"I guess anything's possible, but Radha was from a close, loving family. It's hard to imagine she would knowingly put them through that kind of pain and agony."

Zoe nodded. "Too bad the regression session ended so abruptly before we could find out more."

Trey suddenly felt like they were on a wild goose chase. Even if they caught the wild goose, what would they do with it? If they should happen to track Nikos Colotto down, they could hardly ask him point-blank if he abducted and/or killed a young woman named Radha thirty-five years ago. Trey wasn't sure whether he even wanted to approach the man. He was even less sure if he wanted Zoe or Skye involved. *Maybe if we find him, we should contact the local police and let them handle it from there. But what can I even tell the police that wouldn't make them more apt to lock me up instead? I'd look like some kind of lunatic!*

Trey was totally unsure about how to handle the possibility of finding Nikos Colotto on Rhodes. The next few days would be interesting. That was about the only thing Trey felt sure about.

FOURTEEN

Rhodes, Greece, 2001

Zoe was greatly relieved when the small commuter jet touched down at the Diagoras International Airport on the Greek island of Rhodes. She didn't like flying to begin with, much less flying on small planes that made every slight bit of turbulence seem life-threatening. The airport was sixteen kilometers from Rhodestown, and Mandraki Harbour. They took a taxi to Eleftherios Square and were dropped off in front of the new market near the harbor.

Zoe was captivated by the city's charm, with its rock walls and pebble stone streets. There were huge rock balls lying about. They were told they'd been catapulted into the city centuries ago. It was if they'd been left as conversation pieces. Near the entrance of the harbor was the Fortress of St. Nicholas that had been built to protect Rhodes from invaders approaching from the sea.

It seemed to Zoe as if they'd stepped back in time to medieval days. She expected to see a knight in full armor come riding up on a horse at any second, or the town crier walking by, bellowing out the news of the day.

Zoe noticed that on either side of the harbor's entrance there were statues of a male and female deer, marking the site where the enormous bronze statue of the Sun God, Helios, once straddled the harbor, towering more than a hundred feet over it.

She'd read about the Colossus of Rhodes, one of the seven ancient wonders of the world, and how an earthquake had toppled it around 225 B.C.

There were three large old windmills lining the long pier along the harbor. Zoe snapped photos of them from several angles. After taking a dozen more snapshots of the harbor, fortress, and rock walls, Zoe placed her camera back in its case. She slung the case's strap over her shoulder and turned to her husband.

"Should we go on into the city?" she asked.

"Are you sure you don't want to take another three or four dozen pictures first?" Trey asked.

"Hey! There's a lot to photograph here and . . ."

"Chill out, Zoe," Trey cut in. "I was just kidding."

"Oh, sorry." It had been so long since Trey had joked with her that Zoe no longer knew when he was serious or not.

Trey held her hand as they walked through the Eleftheric gate, or Gate of Freedom, into the city of Rhodestown, past the Inn of the Tongue, and on toward Argyrokastro Square.

The city was teeming with stray cats, hundreds, maybe thousands of them. Many of them didn't look too healthy to Zoe. Most were thin and mangy. When a pitiful-looking orange tabby crossed the path in front of them, Skye said, "He looks just like Zeus, the cat I used to have when I lived here. Except Zeus was a lot fatter than this one. He got all the leftover scraps from dinner."

Zoe looked over at Trey with wide eyes. Skye was beginning to recall memories of the time spent here in her past life. Zoe thought that it was odd that a man who was vicious enough to kidnap a young woman would let the woman keep a pet and let her feed it dinner scraps.

"Do you remember this place, Skye? Do you recall how to get to your home when you lived here on Rhodes?" Trey asked.

Skye looked around thoughtfully, her brow wrinkled in intense concentration.

"I think so. This all looks very familiar. I don't think much has changed. Follow me, and I will try to lead you to my old neighborhood," Skye instructed.

They followed Skye through a maze of alleys and back streets until they reached an ancient residential area with several tiers of old rock homes.

"Up there," Skye said, pointing about halfway up the hill to a cluster of closely spaced homes. "I think it's the one over on the second row with the big tree in front, but I'm not really sure. It didn't used to have a tree in the yard. Least not that I remember."

"Well, we'll trust your instincts, Skye," Zoe said and turned to Trey. "Now what do we do?" she asked. "Just walk up and knock?"

"I reckon so. Maybe we can find out who lives there without actually saying why we want to know."

"And if no one named Colotto lives there now?"

"Then we can ask if the current tenants have any idea where Nikos Colotto lives or what might have happened to him. I know it's a long shot, but I don't have any better idea, do you? I just hope whoever lives there can speak English. My Greek is a little rusty," Trey said jokingly. "In fact, *gyro* and *baklava* are pretty much the extent of my Greek vocabulary."

"I used to make good baklava," Skye said. "Nikos and all the children loved it." Zoe noticed Skye's faraway look, just before she saw the look of pure shock on Trey's face. Skye had slipped into the mindset of a long-ago incarnation. She seemed to be straddling both worlds as she spoke—with a young girl's voice, and a woman's maturity.

"All the children?" Zoe and Trey asked in unison.

"Yes, we had nine of them altogether, six boys and three

girls, but we lost twin boys at birth," Skye explained. "I was only fourteen at the time. The twins were our first children, and they were born too early to survive."

"Fourteen? You were fourteen?" Trey asked, an incredulous lilt to his voice. "How could that be? You didn't even come to Rhodes until you were fifteen. Isn't that right, Honey?"

"No, actually I was younger than that, because Nikos brought me to Rhodes, from Alexandria, to marry him when I was thirteen. He owned a tailor shop here and made me beautiful flowing gowns to wear. Nikos was a good father to our children, and a good provider for the family. I lived here with him for the rest of my life, until I died of a heart attack at sixty-four, that is."

Comprehension seemed to set in, as Trey asked, "You couldn't leave Rhodes because you had to take care of your family, right?"

"Of course. But I never wanted to leave. I lived a very happy life here."

Trey gave a hard thump to the side of his head. He laughed as he turned to his wife, and said, "Jeez, Zoe, do you realize what we've done?"

"Chased the wrong incarnation halfway around the world?"

"Exactly. What a pair of master sleuths we'd make." Turning back to Skye, he asked, "Do you remember what year you died here, when you were Mrs. Colotto?"

"Yes, I believe it was in November 1907."

Zoe began to laugh, and Trey joined in as she said, "We forgot the high probability Skye had lived many other lifetimes other than just the one she had experienced in India. She was speaking to us from the perception of a Greek woman, not Radha."

"Yes, the lifetime she visited during my past-life regression with her was one that was many years prior to her lifetime as Radha," Trey said.

"Just as Dr. Azzam did in his office, we tapped into a past-life personality. The memory of that personality was probably triggered by suddenly seeing the place she knew as home for many years in her previous life as Mrs. Colotto," Zoe said, and shook her head in astonishment. "Jeez, I just can't picture her as an old Greek woman. Can you?"

"No, and I can't get used to hearing her talk like she was a full-grown woman instead of a little girl," Trey whispered to Zoe, as Skye picked little wildflowers that were growing in a clump along the side of the road. "It kind of weirds me out, to tell you the truth."

Trey shuddered in a comical display of revulsion, and then he and Zoe began to laugh.

"What's so funny?" Skye asked her parents.

"Nothing, punkin," Zoe told her. "Let's go back to town. This really is an interesting place and we should go explore it." Turning to Trey, she added, "Okay with you, Sherlock?"

As they ambled down the Street of the Knights, they reached the Palace of the Grand Masters, an imposing structure with huge turrets. Zoe thought back and remembered Skye saying this palace no longer existed.

Trey must have been thinking along the same lines because he turned to Skye and said, "You said when you lived here before you could see the walls of the fortress through the gap where this palace *used to be*. What did you mean by that? Do you remember?"

Skye just looked at him blankly and shrugged dramatically. Her memories of Rhodes seemed to be fading fast, almost as if she had lost interest in the long ago lifetime.

Zoe approached an engraved, historical stone marker outside the entrance of the palace. It mentioned that the palace had been demolished in 1856 by an explosion of gunpowder the

Turks had stored in its basement. It had been rebuilt in strict accordance with the original plans and finished in 1940. In that lifetime, Skye would have been thirteen the year the explosion occurred, Zoe figured out in her head, the same year Nikos brought her to Rhodes to become his wife.

"If we had done a little research on the Grand Masters Palace, we would have known the past life Skye visited during her regression wasn't the one she lived as Radha," Zoe said to Trey.

"If I had asked Skye her name in that lifetime or instructed her to go back to her life as Radha Joshi, and not just back to a time when she was fifteen."

"If the door across the hall hadn't been closed so loudly and brought her out of the hypnosis before we found out more of the details of the life she was recalling." Zoe added.

"If-if-if," Trey said quietly to Zoe. "We can't beat ourselves up about what happened. It is all hindsight now, anyway. Besides, getting a glimpse into another of Skye's former lives was worth the trip."

"I agree. It tempts me to see if Jutta will perform a regression on me someday. I'd love to discover some of the secrets of my soul's journey, wouldn't you?" Zoe asked.

"Yeah, that would be an incredible experience. I can't believe how close-minded I once was, discounting the possibility of reincarnation without even knowing a thing about it. But, hey, speaking of incredible, we're here until Thursday, so we might as well enjoy the sights."

"This is a fascinating place," Zoe agreed. "I'm glad we came. Let's grab some lunch and then go exploring. You know, despite the reason we made this trip, we are on a vacation of sorts."

Zoe purchased a tourist booklet at a small shop along the Street of the Knights before they stopped at a little tavern for lunch. Trey and Skye ordered bifteki, Greek hamburgers, and

Zoe opted for an eggplant dish called mousakka. They all had baklava for dessert. "This is not nearly as good as I used to make it," Skye bragged to Zoe.

As they ate their lunch, Trey flipped through the information pamphlet. "There are small excursion boats leaving Mandraki Harbour daily on cruises to Lindos and Kallithea. Both are towns down the east coast of the island. This guidebook says Lindos has perfectly preserved medieval character and beautiful beaches. There's a Byzantine Church there with eighteenth-century frescoes and an acropolis with the ancient Doric Temple of Athena. Doesn't that sound like a neat place to visit?" Trey asked. "It might be fun to take a boat there."

"No! No! Please don't make me go!" Skye pleaded with a look of sheer terror on her face. "I can't go on the boat. I just can't, Daddy. Please don't make me go on the boat!"

"Okay, baby. It's okay," Trey said, putting his arm around her shaking shoulders. "Relax, honey. We won't go on the boat. You've never even been on a boat. Why are you so afraid of it?"

There was no response as Skye shrugged and looked away. *I wonder if she even knows why the idea of being on a boat terrifies her,* Zoe thought. If she did, maybe she just couldn't bear to talk about it. Maybe it was time to get Jutta more involved in the situation.

Back at the hotel that evening, another international call was made to Jutta Meyer. This time Zoe made the call. Jutta told Zoe she was becoming more and more intrigued by the situation with Skye. Zoe was thrilled when Jutta volunteered to fly to Bombay at her own expense if someone could pick her up at the airport. Jutta said, "I can perform a past-life regression on Skye inside the cotton factory where her memories seem to be the strongest. I'm a professional, and you can rest assured I won't do anything that could potentially harm your daughter. She needs relief from these memories, or they could haunt her

138

indefinitely."

"But won't this interfere with your schedule, Jutta?" Zoe asked. "Or your personal life?"

"No, this is perfect timing actually. I've been divorced for several years, and my ex and I had no children, so there's really no problem there. And I've taken a month-long hiatus from my work with no particular plans for my vacation. I would be grateful for the opportunity to fly to Bombay and see if I can help in any way."

After the connection was broken, Zoe worked on a crossword puzzle to pass the time while she waited for Jutta to call back. It was about an hour later when Jutta telephoned with her itinerary. She told Zoe she would be arriving at Sahar International Airport in three days.

Jutta, a tall, large-boned German, arrived in Bombay three days later as promised. Zoe was surprised to find the dark-haired woman was many years older than she had sounded on the phone, late fifties or better.

Jutta was attractive in an almost masculine way with a short haircut and broad shoulders. She had a low, gravelly sounding voice, like that of a woman who had smoked for forty-odd years and was approaching a chronic problem. Zoe was reminded of a rottweiler her family had owned when she was young. It was not just the deep growl of Jutta's voice, but the tenaciousness in her demeanor. It was her "never say die" attitude.

Jutta was very assertive, with an outspoken, aggressive personality. But she had a good sense of humor and seemed friendly and concerned. Zoe felt relieved to turn the situation over to an expert.

Jutta decided to perform the past-life regression the very evening of her arrival. *She's not the kind who is prone to procrastination,* Zoe thought.

Zoe helped Skye get comfortable on a small sofa in the Joshis' apartment. Skye was reluctant to be hypnotized again, and Zoe was apprehensive about it too. But Zoe trusted Jutta to know what to do, and to handle the situation in the best interests of her daughter.

Jutta began her meditation, very similar to Dr. Weiss's, and Zoe could feel her heart racing as she watched Skye drift deeper and deeper into a meditative trance. Zoe held her breath as Jutta instructed Skye, "I want you to visit your past life as Radha Joshi. Go back in time to 1966 when you were fifteen and living in Bombay, India." Jutta waited a few moments before asking in a soothing voice, "Do you see yourself as Radha?"

"Yes."

"How old are you? Are you fifteen?" Jutta asked, as if steering her toward that period in her life as Radha.

"Yes, I am fifteen."

Zoe looked up at Trey as she, Trey, and Mohandas sat in absolute silence, observing the exchange. Asha was in her recliner; her eyes aimed sightlessly at the wall. She seemed not quite aware of what was occurring in the room.

"What do you see yourself doing right now?" Jutta asked Skye.

"I am walking to the market with my brother."

"Mohandas?"

"Yes."

Zoe glanced over at Mohandas and saw his dark brown eyes were wide and unblinking. There was a trace of sweat across his forehead. To her, he looked as if he had just spotted a ghost. As it was accustomed to doing, his Adam's apple bobbed as he swallowed deeply.

Jutta continued with her questioning, "Where are your parents? Where are Asha and Nirav?"

Zoe saw Asha sit up straighter in her recliner and become

more alert at the sound of her name. Zoe's attention turned back to Skye as her daughter answered. "They're at work, at the cotton factory."

"Can you go to the cotton factory now, too?"

"Yes," Skye said. After a short pause she added, "I am at the factory now. I'm in my father's office. Alone."

"Go to the desk where you work in the front office."

"Okay."

"Are you there now?"

"Yes, I'm there now," Skye said, nodding her head.

"Go forward in time now to the last day you remember ever being in the front office of the cotton factory," Jutta instructed.

"Okay."

"Tell me what you see, what you're feeling. Tell me what is happening to Radha."

Zoe was twisting her hair so hard, her head was beginning to hurt. She forced herself to stop and to clasp her hands in her lap. She watched in nervous apprehension as Skye sat still for several long moments. Zoe was startled when Skye began to squirm on the sofa, thrashing her arms against the cushions. There was pure terror visible on her face.

"I am being dragged out the door by a man who calls himself Rafael," Skye said at last. "This man is very unfamiliar to me. I'm sure we have never met before. I don't know what he plans to do with me, and I'm terrified. I am trying to scream, but he has his hand over my mouth. I can't talk. I can barely breathe. I am so very scared."

Zoe had stopped breathing herself. The room remained in absolute silence until Skye said in a louder, more agitated voice, "Help me! Somebody please help me!"

Jutta glanced over at Zoe, and Zoe shook her head, dragging her hand across her throat to indicate she wanted the regression halted. Jutta nodded at her in agreement and turned back to

Skye, "Back away from the scene you're witnessing, Skye. Remove yourself from the scene and open your eyes for me. You are Skye again. The scene you just witnessed was from a lifetime a long time ago. It has nothing to do with your present life as Skylar Robbins. Release the memory and open your eyes," Jutta said.

Skye stopped squirming and slowly opened her eyes. She looked around the room and said, "Mommy?"

"Yes, punkin, I'm here. It's okay now. Daddy and I are here with you," Zoe said as she crossed the room to comfort her daughter. She wiped the sweat off Skye's forehead and kissed her tenderly on the cheek.

Zoe cradled Skye in her lap as Jutta turned to Mohandas and asked, "Rafael? Do you recognize that name, Mohandas?"

Before Mohandas could reply, Asha leaned forward in her recliner, speaking in a slow and articulate manner, "I do. Before I met Nirav I was engaged to Rafael's older brother. The two brothers came from America with their father. They left their family's cattle ranch in the Great Divide Basin of Wyoming and all went to work for my father in the cotton factory."

Along with everyone else in the room, Zoe sat in stunned silence. This was the most lucid she'd ever seen Asha, and the most she'd ever heard her speak. She listened as Asha continued, "My fiancé was killed in the same explosion in 1944 that killed my father. Rafael Torres stayed in my spare room for several years. He left without saying goodbye, right before I married Nirav."

Asha leaned back and began to pick at loose threads on the armrest of her recliner, and resumed staring blankly at the wall through unseeing eyes.

Mohandas appeared shocked by his mother's detailed recollection. Zoe knew he'd seldom seen his mother that cognizant in recent years. "I vaguely remember hearing the name Torres a few times during my childhood," he said to no one in particular, "but I don't recall any of the details."

Mohandas then turned toward Asha, and asked at length, "Mother, do you remember why Rafael left, or where he went?"

"Who?"

"Rafael, your former fiancé's younger brother. The man you were just speaking about, Rafael Torres," Mohandas answered impatiently.

"Who's that?" Asha asked her son with a vacant expression on her face. Zoe sighed, as all evidence of Asha's lucidity vanished. There would obviously be no more pertinent information coming from Asha at that point. *Alzheimer's is a horrific thing,* Zoe thought, *a fate I would not wish on anyone.*

Asha looked around the room in confusion, pointed a gnarled, bony finger at Mohandas, and asked, "Just who the hell are you? And what are all you people doing in my house?"

FIFTEEN

Bombay, India, 1964

"Radha! Wake up! It's time to get up and get ready for school."
Radha felt her mother, Asha, stroking her long, dark hair. It was
an early Tuesday morning in 1964, and as always, Radha was
eager to get up and go to school. She sat up, stretched, and
leaned in to her mother's embrace. It was her favorite way to
start the day.

"Good morning, Mama," she said. "I need to wash, and then
I'll get dressed and be in the kitchen for breakfast in just a few
minutes."

Radha loved school. She knew her mother had been determined that both she and her younger brother, Mohandas,
receive an extensive education. Her mother had insisted that
they attend a private school where English was the primary
language, and the curriculum had a more western flair than the
public schools. Mohandas was four years younger than Radha
and a little less enthusiastic about school, but he still managed
to earn superior grades at a school that maintained high
standards and avid academic competition among its students.

Radha, on the other hand, was happy to work hard to stay at
the top of her class to enhance her chances of receiving a
scholarship. *I will attend Bombay University in the future. After
that, medical school,* she thought. She dreamed of becoming a
doctor. Radha's grandmother on her father's side of the family

had died of a massive coronary just days after Radha had celebrated her first birthday. In honor of the grandmother she never really knew, Radha wanted to become a cardiologist. Nothing and nobody would stop her, Radha vowed to herself.

At thirteen, Radha was frequently told she was an exact image of her mother. She couldn't have been more flattered, except to be told that her personality resembles her mother's too.

Radha was petite and light-skinned like her mother. And, like her mother, she had a small-framed, perfectly proportioned body, a long mane of thick dark brown hair, straight pearly-white teeth, with the exception of one somewhat tilted bicuspid, and deep-set brown eyes that seemed to sparkle like diamond chips. *But mother is blessed with a sparkling personality to match,* Radha thought. She herself was much too reserved and introverted. She should try harder to be more outgoing. She wasn't shy, but she was less boisterous than her mother, and much more introspective. She took after her father in that respect.

Radha was devoted to her mother and wanted to be just like her when she grew up. She had a lot of respect for her mother's values and integrity.

Still, it was her father, Nirav, whom she idolized. She was Daddy's little girl and she reveled in his attention. He had taught her to fish when Mohandas had shown little interest in the sport, and Radha's most cherished days were those spent with him, fishing for tuna and shark on the Arabian Sea. Her father had a friend who lived near the marina. He kept a little rowboat in the friend's shed for those rare occasions when he could take time away from work to spend the day fishing with her. Daddy seemed to enjoy her company as much as he enjoyed the fishing, Radha thought. That's why he made her feel so loved and special.

Radha washed, dressed, and finished her grooming in a flash

and entered the kitchen to have breakfast with her brother and mother. Her father had left the apartment to go to work at the cotton factory. He was usually up and about long before dawn, not returning to the apartment until just before suppertime.

"Have you got a big day at school today, honey?" her mother asked her as she sat down at the table.

"No, not really. I have an oral report to give in economics, and probably a surprise test in my history class, but that's about all," Radha replied.

"Is the oral report the one you were practicing last night? Something to do with investments and interest rates?"

"Uh-huh," Radha replied around a mouthful of oatmeal.

Radha finished breakfast and gathered her books for school. As she was walking out the front door, her mother asked, "Are you still planning to meet me at the center after school?"

"Yes, I should be there around four o'clock. I'll see you then," she said, kissing her mother on the cheek before exiting the apartment. She turned and waved at Mohandas before she closed the door.

Radha looked forward to the afternoons she spent helping her mother at the Bal Anand Community Center, where Asha worked as a volunteer, supervising the less fortunate children who attended the center. Radha enjoyed playing with the children and teaching them new games and songs she had learned at school.

As she walked to school, she thought about her mother's role at the small community center. Asha had begun working there as a volunteer about four years ago, in 1960. Her mother had become restless and bored and needed something to fill her days, she had told Radha. "I need to feel useful and contribute to society in some way," Asha had said. "Sitting around doing nothing is just not for me."

Underprivileged children from the area were taught to sing

and paint at the community center, which was now in its tenth year of operation. Although her mother wasn't particularly artistic or musical, Radha knew she was terrific with the children. Asha's main responsibility was to supervise them as they played in the garden of the colonial home where the center was located.

Whenever she could, Radha met her mother at Bal Anand after school. She enjoyed interacting with the children and teaching them the importance of good sportsmanship and showing respect for others. She'd been told many times that she, like her mother, was a natural in dealing with children. *I'm going to have a large family of my own someday,* she told herself. *It will be filled with happy, laughing kids.*

In the latter part of 1964, Radha decided she also needed more to do and convinced her father to begin training her to help out at the factory. She was taught the fundamentals of working in the front office, everything from answering the phone to filling out contracts. The work added to her self-confidence, and she anxiously awaited the opportunity to work the reception desk by herself.

At thirteen, her life was full and rewarding. She was preparing herself for an even more rewarding future; she knew her life was going someplace. But she could never have imagined where that place would be in just two more years.

SIXTEEN

Rawlins, Wyoming, 2001

"That crazy old fool in fourteen is throwing food again," Mark told Oscar at the nurse's station of the Wallingford Institute in Rawlins, Wyoming. As Mark walked closer to the desk, he saw Oscar was absentmindedly fiddling with his palmtop computer while watching Jerry Springer on an old black and white portable television.

Oscar turned and looked up at Mark. "Where does Springer find all these nuts that appear on his shows?" he asked. "They should all be residents here, you know. So what's Rafael's problem now, Mark?"

"Don't know. He's just in one of his moods, I guess. Yelled at me to get out of his room, and then beaned me in the back of the head with a bagel as I was leaving."

"Well, Mark, look on the bright side, at least bagels don't pack much of a punch when they bounce off your head."

"I didn't say it hurt, Oscar, but now I got cream cheese in my hair." Mark ran his fingers through his bushy red hair for the tenth time, certain he'd somehow missed a glob of the gooey stuff.

"He's a case, ain't he? You know, sometimes I just wish he'd die and get it over with," Oscar said. "People who won't talk to me make me nervous."

"Aw, come on, Oscar, he's not that bad. He'll even talk to

you a little once you get to know him." Mark had never had any major problems with Rafael. He felt sorry for the old guy.

"How could you ever get to know him? I've been here almost as long as he has, and you know, I still don't know him. And what's the point of lingering when you have no quality of life? He lies in bed and stares out the window most of the time," Oscar pointed out. "You gotta admit, he ain't got much to live for."

"Well, that's true. But," Mark said jokingly, "for an old guy in his condition, he's sure got good aim."

"Yeah, I know," Oscar laughed. "I took a pork chop to the shoulder the other day."

"Do you remember the cottage cheese incident, Oscar?"

"Yeah," Oscar said, slapping his knee as he chuckled at the memory. "Now that was a classic! Oh, and by the way, I forgot to tell you that Rafael woke everyone up again last night, yelling out in his sleep."

Rafael had not had one of those episodes for several weeks, and Mark had hoped the reoccurring nightmares had ceased. "Anything new?" he asked wearily.

"No, same old stuff. You know, 'Thunder, whoa!' and things like that. I say we play horror flicks on his TV all day, 'cause he needs some new material for his nightmares. That new medicine Dr. Wheeler prescribed for him sure ain't doing much."

Mark couldn't help but think Oscar was getting a bit too callous and sadistic. "You've been working here far too long, pal," he said. "And I'll agree he's an odd one—but who around here ain't? Has Rafael got any family at all?"

"Not that I know of. Been here thirty-three or -four years and, other than homicide detectives, he hasn't logged in a visitor yet."

"That's really sad." Mark could not imagine a person lying in bed for thirty-some years and not have one single person in the world care enough to come and visit him in all that time. *It wouldn't hurt me to start spending a little more time with Rafael,* Mark thought, *I can make small talk at least, even if he doesn't often respond to it.*

"Yeah, it is sad," Oscar agreed in mock sorrow. Then he smirked and said, "Know what's even sadder? The old broad in room eleven just crapped in her bed again, and it's your turn to clean it up!"

SEVENTEEN

Kansas, 2001

"Skye!" Zoe yelled out the back door of the farmhouse. "Get over here away from the barn! Come play on the porch where I can keep an eye on you. I've told you a dozen times that it's not safe for you to play around the barn."

Zoe was glad to be back home in Kansas, but very disappointed they'd come to a dead end in Bombay. She had been somewhat surprised to discover she'd actually missed the farm and the old house after being away for just over a week. Maybe country living was growing on her after all. She was also surprised Skye hadn't mentioned anything about her past life as Radha, or anything to do with her life spent in India, since they'd arrived back home. Instead, she'd been jabbering nonstop about her sixth birthday party scheduled for the upcoming weekend.

Zoe had been busy planning the party for the last couple of days. She'd invited Jutta, Trey's parents, Skye's barrel-racing babysitter, Victoria, and Trey's old school chums, the Boyers. *Maybe Trey has been right,* she thought a little guiltily, *Skye had no friends her own age to eat cake and help her celebrate her birthday.*

Trey had been busy too. Since taking Zoe out to eat at the Main Street Diner for their anniversary, he'd spent most of his time out in the fields surveying his crops. He had told Zoe he was relieved to find both the wheat and the milo crops were doing well. Joe Junior had been irrigating the entire section while the three of them had been abroad. Zoe had also noticed Trey's dad had tacked up a few boards as reinforcement along the back wall of the barn. Apparently, he was concerned about the barn's imminent collapse, too.

But Zoe had resolved never to mention the barn to Trey again. It just wasn't worth fighting over, particularly when they'd been getting along so well since going to Mumbai.

"Happy Birthday, my dear," Grandma Robbins said, stooping down to kiss Skye on the head as Zoe led her and Joe Junior into the house. It was Skye's sixth birthday, on a cool, damp Saturday, and the sky was overcast with off and on light showers forecast for the entire day. Due to the dreary weather, Zoe decided to hold Skye's party on the screened-in back porch. She'd placed a double-layered chocolate cake in the center of the picnic table and surrounded it with gaily wrapped packages of various sizes and shapes. She even had silly-looking hats for the guests to wear when they sang "Happy Birthday" to Skye.

The guest of honor, dressed in a frilly yellow jumper with white lace trim, was showing off a new tooth that was just beginning to erupt from her lower jaw. The baby tooth it was replacing had been knocked out in a tumble from her bicycle earlier in the summer. Even with the training wheels on Skye's bike, Zoe knew the gravel driveway could be treacherous at times. She tried to encourage Skye to limit her riding to the paved portion. It extended out fifty feet from the garage, but occasionally Skye ventured out farther onto the loose rock, and usually with disastrous results.

After "Happy Birthday" was sung and the cake and ice cream was served, Skye opened her presents. She and Trey had bought Skye a new computer. It was loaded with games and educational software, and would be an excellent and necessary learning tool once Skye started school. Zoe hoped it would encourage Skye to put more of an effort into learning to read and write.

"Thanks, Mommy and Daddy," Skye said with sincerity.

Sam and Ellen Boyer had brought Skye an Ariel the Mermaid lunchbox and a matching pink backpack. Jutta Meyer had arrived with a set of picture books and a box of alphabet flash cards. Grandma Robbins had made Skye a new doll, along with several outfits that matched the outfits she had stitched for Skye. "We'll be twins!" Skye exclaimed. She turned to look at Zoe, and asked, "Can I change my clothes after I open my presents, so I'll match my new doll?" Zoe nodded with a smile, knowing Skye was not at all comfortable in the yellow dress. Like Zoe, Skye preferred the comfort of denim jeans and cotton shirts.

Victoria arrived a few minutes late. With her she brought what became Skye's favorite gift of all, a porcelain statue of a black stallion. The stallion had white markings on its front legs and was depicted reared up on its hind legs with its front legs pawing the air.

"Wow! Thanks, Victoria! He looks just like Thunder!" Skye said, beaming with pleasure and delight.

Zoe laughed and said, "Yes, you're right, Skye. He does look a lot like the horse in front of Wal-Mart, doesn't he?"

"Not that one, Mommy. That horse is just a toy. I'm talking about the real Thunder, the horse I used to ride in Wyoming."

For a few seconds the room was filled with total silence. Zoe was sure everyone could hear her heart beating in double-time. Too stunned to speak, she glanced over at her husband in bewilderment. He shrugged his shoulders at her and looked over at Jutta for guidance.

Finally, Jutta turned to Skye and asked, "When were you in Wyoming, Skye? Was it when you were called Radha?"

"Yes, it was when I was fifteen. Rafael took me there. He

trapped two wild horses and gave one of them to me. I named him Thunder. I really loved that horse. I felt so free when I rode him," Skye said thoughtfully.

"Why did he take you to Wyoming? Did Rafael hold you captive there?" Trey asked. Zoe sat silently praying Skye would respond to his questions and not clam up as she was prone to do.

Staring down at the porcelain statue with a wistful expression on her face, Skye shrugged awkwardly. But to Zoe's dismay, Skye didn't reply to her father's questions.

"Do you remember where in Wyoming he took you?" Trey asked, his voice taut with impatience. "Or anything about the place at all?"

"No, I don't know where it was, or anything about it."

"What do you remember about the time you spent in Wyoming or about this man you call Rafael?" Trey asked, pressing for more information, any little clue that might be useful.

"Nothing," was Skye's clipped response. "I don't remember nothing except how much I loved riding Thunder."

Although Skye didn't appear agitated or upset, it was obvious to Zoe she was reluctant to discuss the details of her memories in Wyoming. She knew her daughter well enough to know she remembered a lot more than she was telling them, Zoe realized. *Skye obviously doesn't want to be badgered about her memories of Rafael and Wyoming. Maybe the memories are just too painful for her. Well, other than the memories of Thunder.* Zoe thought that subconsciously Skye wants to keep those memories to herself and not share her thoughts and feelings with anybody else. And they couldn't force them out of Skye, as much as they'd like to.

Skye broke into her thoughts when she said, "Mommy, Victoria said she'd help me set up my new computer. Can we go inside and do that now?"

"Of course, punkin, you two go right ahead. Have Victoria set it up on the desk in your bedroom."

After the two younger girls had gone inside, Trey asked the assembled group on the porch, "Do you think Rafael Torres could have taken Radha back to his family's cattle ranch in the Great Divide Basin? He might even still own the property, I reckon."

"Possibly," Jutta answered. "I wonder how we could find out where the property is located and who owns it now."

"I bet I could find out," Sam Boyer stated, scribbling a few notes down on his napkin. "I can log on the Internet at work and do some research. I can access public records and databases, maybe locate his whereabouts if he's still in Wyoming."

"That would be great, Sam. I'd sure like to find out what happened to Radha if there's any way possible," Trey told him. Sometimes Trey wished he wasn't so computer-challenged. He could barely manage to log on to the Internet. He was one of the few people he knew that didn't even have an e-mail address. "I can't imagine why Rafael would take her back to Wyoming though, or how he could take her there without alerting the authorities."

"Don't know, but it sounds like it's exactly what he did. If he captured a wild horse and gave it to her, it doesn't sound like he was too abusive to her," Sam concluded. "Of course, there could be much more to this story than any of us realizes."

"That's certainly true," Trey agreed. "We don't know what his motives were, or what the real story behind all this entails. I'm really anxious to see what you can come up with about this man. Odd as it sounds, I hope he's still alive so I can track him down and drag the truth out of him. Apparently he's escaped justice for over thirty years as it is."

"Well, what do you say we run over to my office right now? Ellie can drive our car home, and you can drop me off at my house afterward," Sam suggested.

"It sounds good to me. Let's go!"

Zoe had been quietly listening to the exchange between Trey and his friend, and was having mixed emotions about the idea they could be back on track in their quest to discover what had happened to Skye in her former life as Radha. She was intrigued by the possibility of finding out the truth behind Radha's disappearance, but apprehensive and concerned about what they might discover.

Zoe looked over at Trey's father as he rolled his eyes and shook his head. She knew he still thought they were a bunch of fools. In a nervous response, Zoe jumped to her feet and asked, "Anybody for more cake?"

There was a comfortable silence in the cab of Trey's truck as he and Sam drove to Sam's office in town. Trey was filled with a new sense of determination. Trey was on a mission and wouldn't rest until the truth had been revealed. *We've gone too far to give up now,* he thought. *I want to find this man, if he's still alive, so I can demand answers from him. I want him to face up to his past; I want him punished for his crimes no matter how long ago they were committed.*

At Sam's office, Trey and his friend searched through public records, land plats, online phone directories, and utility databases for several hours before locating a 1,280-acre tract twenty miles northeast of Wamsutter, Wyoming, deeded to a Juan Torres. By Wyoming standards, this was a small ranch, even though to Trey it sounded large compared to his 320-acre spread.

"Sam, something tells me this is the place we're looking for. It's in the Great Divide Basin," Trey said as he studied the Rand McNally atlas on the desk in front of him. He removed his reading glasses and looked over at his friend, who was still moving his mouse around on the mouse pad and staring intently at his computer monitor.

Sam nodded. "I think so too," he said. "I'll make some calls on Monday morning, Trey. Maybe I can get some information out of the Sweetwater County Treasurer's office, or even the post office there."

"Thanks Sam." Trey knew Sam enjoyed a challenge of this nature. If anyone could dig up the information regarding Rafael's whereabouts, it was his friend Sam Boyer.

"Trey, it's Sam here," Trey heard as he lifted the phone to his ear on Monday afternoon. "I think I've pinpointed your man, Rafael Torres."

"Really?" Trey asked, unable to conceal the excitement in his voice. "What did you find out?"

"That tract of land was apparently owned by Rafael's father, Juan, and his father's father, José before that. It's been handed down for generations. But since 1945, the real estate taxes on the property have been paid for out of a trust account in the name of R. J. Torres. The land has been listed as vacant since the late thirties."

"But, if the property's vacant—" Trey began.

"Hold on," Sam interrupted, "there's more to it. They gave me the address that's been on file as the current owner's since 1967. This address is in Rawlins, Wyoming. I ran a crosscheck on the address and it's listed as the Wallingford Institute."

"I don't get it."

"I didn't either, so I called the Institute and found out that it's a home for the mentally insane, an asylum of sorts. And, yes, there's been a patient there for over thirty years by the name of Rafael Torres."

"Oh, my God, Sam! I can't believe it!" Trey exclaimed as he paced frantically around the living room with the cordless phone at his ear. "This is incredible!"

"So, I guess he's still alive—and apparently insane," he heard his friend's voice say over the handset.

"Somehow that doesn't surprise me. How insane, I wonder," Trey replied. "Do you think it would be worth our while to go out there and try to talk to him?"

"It might be. I don't think it could hurt, but don't be too disappointed if you don't get much out of him. According to Mark, who's the nurse assigned to him, Rafael's not very communicative."

"Well, I think it's worth a shot. I know Zoe will be game to go, because she wants to see this mystery solved as much as I do. Skye doesn't start school for ten days, and we could drive out there in less than a day. I wonder what Skye's reaction will be if she meets this man."

"I'm not altogether sure she should be allowed to meet him. If she does, and she shows an obvious aversion to him, I'd get her away from him as quickly as possible. You don't want to make a basket case out of her," Sam advised Trey. "We already know that the memories of him are upsetting to her."

"Yes, and that's something to take into consideration. Those memories seem to put her into instant emotional turmoil every time," Trey said, pausing to reflect on the situation. "Still, I have a gut feeling it's important for her to face him—to free herself of the hold the memories of him seem to have over her. I may be dead wrong, but I hope not. Should I call the Wallingford Institute and ask them if it can be arranged for us to come out and visit with Rafael?"

"Yes, probably. I anticipated the possibility, so I registered your names as potential visitors."

"Good, thanks!" Trey replied. He wasn't surprised that Sam had instinctively known his friend would not be able to let it rest until the situation had resolved itself. They had been closer than brothers for years.

"No problem, buddy," Sam said. "And I must say, Mark, the nurse I spoke with seemed totally shocked by the idea Rafael might be having visitors."

Eighteen

Rawlins, Wyoming, 2001

"The results of Rafael's biopsy came back this morning, and it's not good news, Mark," Dr. Wheeler reported, as he flipped through pages in his notepad. "The oncologist has found malignant cells, I'm afraid."

Mark sighed. He wasn't surprised Rafael's biopsy had come back positive, but it wasn't what he'd wanted to hear. He knew Rafael had been having to get up numerous times every night to urinate, and his PSA level had been higher than normal at his last physical. "I had expected as much, Doc. Is the cancer localized to the prostate?" he asked Rafael's physician.

"No, unfortunately it has metastasized to the surrounding tissue, lymph nodes, lungs, and possibly even to the bone."

"Terminal?"

Dr. Wheeler nodded and said, "I'm afraid so. The cancer has spread enough by now that neither chemo or radiation seed therapy would be effective. It's a moot point anyway. He's refusing any kind of treatment. He almost seems to be relieved to know his life is nearing its end."

"I'm not surprised. I would be too if I were him, I suppose. What about pain medication? Can you prescribe something for me to give him to control the pain?"

"Well, yes, but we'll have to be clever about it because he's refusing that too, told me he deserves to suffer. Repentance or something, I guess. Is he still having those nightmares, Mark?"

"Yeah, same one over and over, I'm sure. Yells out the same things every time he has one," Mark responded.

"I'll order some morphine patches for him. See if you can sneak them onto his back. The morphine may exacerbate the nightmare problem, but he'll need something for the pain whether he wants it or not. As far as I'm concerned, no one deserves to suffer that much."

"Okay, Doc. By the way, he might be having some visitors this week, a family from Kansas. Ironic, you know. Now that he's dying, he may have some visitors for the first time in thirty-four years. Probably some long-lost kin who want to see if he's got any money left they can cabbage on to." Mark was still bothered by the idea no one had ever come to the Institute to see Rafael, and he'd always had a tendency to feel very protective of the patients in his care.

Dr. Wheeler patted him on the back and said, "Get a grip, Mark. We've only known about the cancer for a few hours. It usually takes at least a week for the so-called grieving relatives to start coming out of the woodwork. You had any vacation time recently, Mark?"

"Nah. It's been a long time."

"Maybe you should think about taking a vacation." Dr. Wheeler winked at Mark, but Mark knew that he was only half joking. He was a compassionate man and concerned about Mark's frame of mind.

Doc's probably right, Mark thought. He did need to schedule some time off. He was getting too emotionally involved with his patients, and it was starting to show. Maybe he should take a couple of weeks off to go visit some Mayan ruins, and do some snorkeling off the coast of Cancun and Cozumel. He could relax on the beach, drink a few tequila sunrises, and forget about his mentally unstable patients for a while. It would be good for him to unwind and rejuvenate his spirits.

Dr. Wheeler broke into his meandering thoughts. "Who are these visitors anyway?"

"Don't know. The guy on the phone just said he had some friends who were trying to locate Rafael. He didn't explain why, though."

"Guess it's hard to say why anyone would want to visit Rafael after all these years. There's no statute of limitation on murder charges, you know, so it could even relate back to that case in the sixties."

"I hope not," Mark answered. "There's nothing to be gained by dredging that whole thing up again."

"Well, until we find out more about these visitors, I wouldn't tell them about the cancer. Unless they ask, of course."

"Rafael, are you done with your lunch?" Mark inquired from the slightly ajar door of room fourteen at the Wallingford Institute.

"Yeah, don't want any of it," Rafael answered gruffly.

Mark went on into the room and noticed Rafael hadn't touched anything on his tray. "You're going to have to start eating, *mi amigo,* or I'll have to start forcing it into you through little tubes. You're wasting away to nothing."

"Just try it!" Rafael spat out.

Mark ignored Rafael's retort. "I'm going to move this tray over to the side here, just in case you decide to eat some of this later."

"It's a pile of garbage. Take it away."

"Later," Mark said. "Right now there's a very nice family out in the lobby who'd like to visit with you."

"Don't want any visitors. Tell them to leave."

"I can't do that, Rafael," Mark responded. "These folks came all the way from Kansas just to see you."

"Don't know anyone from Kansas. Tell them to go away and leave me alone," Rafael ordered.

"You've been left alone for far too long as it is, pal. I think having company will be good for you. I'll give you a couple of minutes, and then I'll be bringing them in to see you," Mark insisted. He was a little apprehensive about how Rafael would react to having visitors. Visiting with folks was certainly not something he was accustomed to.

He straightened the bedding around Rafael and patted the seventy-two-year-old man on the shoulder. "Now you be nice to these people, you hear?"

As he walked out of the room, Mark felt an overripe orange careen off the small of his back. He rolled his eyes, shook his head, and shut the door.

Trey stood up and wiped his sweating palms on his jeans as Rafael's nurse approached them in the lobby. "I want to warn you folks Mr. Torres can have a pretty volatile temper," Mark told them. "He suffers from an anxiety disorder, which makes him a little unpredictable at times. I'll be sitting in the corner of the room, just in case he gets out of hand, but y'all can just pretend I'm not even there. Okay? Visiting hour's over at two." Mark then marched them up the corridor to room fourteen.

"Okay, fine," Trey replied. Trey was actually relieved someone familiar with Rafael would be in the room with him and his family. He had no idea what to expect from Rafael, or how he would react to their intrusion.

As Mark led them into the room, a very thin old man glanced up at them and turned his head away. "What do you want?" he asked. "I don't have time for chit-chat."

"We only want to visit with you," Trey replied. He decided to stretch the truth as much as he needed to as he continued. "We met an old friend of yours, and she asked us to check in on you to see how you were getting along."

Rafael continued to look away from his visitors. "I don't have any old friends." After a few seconds' pause, he added, "so y'all can go back to Kansas now."

Trey caught Mark's eye. Mark nodded at him and motioned for him to ignore Rafael's remark and keep on talking. "Mr. Torres, I'm Trey Robbins, and this is my wife, Zoe," Trey said. He gently pulled Skye in front of him and held her protectively up against his thighs. "And this is our daughter, whose name is Skylar."

"That's nice. Good to meet y'all. So glad we could have this little visit," Rafael said sarcastically. "Now if you don't mind, I'd like you folks to leave so I can eat my lunch in private."

Trey looked over and noticed the full tray of food beside the bed. He raised his eyebrows at Mark. Mark shook his head and hastily moved the rolling cart with Rafael's lunch tray on it out into the hallway. "Don't need any projectiles handy," Trey heard Mark mutter to himself. He wasn't sure what to think about the nurse's remark and didn't have much time to contemplate it. Skye moved away from his grasp and walked toward Rafael's bed. The movement distracted him.

"Rafael?" Skye asked in a shy, hesitant voice as she approached the elderly man's bedside.

"What?" Rafael spat out in disgust, obviously taken aback by her approach.

Trey was even more surprised by Skye's movement toward the grumpy old man, who was sitting upright against a stack of stout pillows. Before he could react, Skye had crawled up on the side of the bed and lifted up Rafael's frail left hand with her own. She tenderly placed her other small hand over the top of Rafael's.

Rafael looked down at their entwined hands and then slowly looked up at Skye. He opened his mouth as if to speak, but nothing came out. Zoe lurched forward toward their daughter. Trey put his arm out to block her motion. He shook his head at Zoe, without taking his eyes off of Rafael and Skye. He wanted to see what unfolded between them. He'd expected Skye to be terrified at the sight of the withered old man, not rush to be next to him. Could she have forgotten what Rafael did to her when she was a young Indian woman named Radha? Was her soul trying to forgive him so it could get on with its current incarnation as Skylar Robbins? Trey stood still, anxious to see what happened next.

Finally, Skye spoke. "We just want to make sure you are doing okay. Please don't be afraid," Skye told Rafael as she began to stroke the top of his hand softly with her much smaller one. "You know I would never hurt you, never ever, not in this life or the next. Nor will I ever forget you, not in this life or the next."

Is that our daughter talking? Trey wondered.

Rafael swallowed deeply, with a look of intense concentration as he stared into Skye's eyes. To Trey, time seemed to stand still for many moments. Rafael's response came in such a soft whisper, Trey had to strain to hear it. "I know you wouldn't. I'm not afraid, little one. We'll be together again one day, I promise you."

Rafael then shook his head sharply as if to clear his mind and focus his attention on the little girl beside him. "Uh—er— what'd you say your name was again?" he asked, still staring searchingly into Skye's light blue eyes.

"It's Skylar now, but you can call me Skye."

"Skye," he said slowly, as though testing the name out on his tongue. "Skye . . . such a pretty name for a little girl."

Skye smiled broadly in response. As she did, Rafael flinched, with a look of utter shock in his eyes. He looked up at Trey in bewilderment, as if he'd forgotten anyone else was in the room other than himself and Skye. He clearly didn't understand the intensity of his feelings for this young blond-haired stranger. Trey was shocked as well, having expected any kind of reaction from Skye but the one he'd just witnessed. He had expected a completely different reaction from Rafael, too, for that matter. Zoe stood in stunned silence at his side, as rigid as a tree in the Petrified Forest.

"Who exactly is this friend you mentioned?" Rafael asked, directing his question at Trey without taking his eyes off of Skye.

"It's er—uh—it's uh," Trey stuttered. "Asha. It's uh, Asha Joshi from Bombay. She told us she was once engaged to your brother, many years ago."

Rafael's eyes opened wide, a look of recognition flashing across his face. "Asha?" he choked out.

Trey nodded. Rafael gently but firmly nudged Skye off the side of his bed. "Run along now, missy. I'm through visiting with y'all. Mark, I'm through visiting now," he emphasized as he motioned to the nurse to clear his room.

Trey leaned over and whispered to Zoe to take Skye back to the lobby. "I'll be along shortly," he said softly. He stood back as Zoe led Skye toward the door.

"Goodbye, Rafael," Skye said, waving shyly as she exited the room with her mother.

Rafael sheepishly returned the wave. As the door swung closed, he turned back to Trey and scowled. "Why are you still here? I told you I'm through visiting."

Trey inched closer toward the door, but then turned back toward Rafael. He didn't come all of the way out here to slink out of the room like a coward. He wanted answers, and he wouldn't leave until he got them, he told himself. "I'll only stay a minute, Rafael. Before I leave I need to ask you if you remember Asha's daughter, Radha?"

Rafael suddenly looked as if he'd been slapped across the

face. He winced but did not respond. Trey noticed a look of remorse skitter across the old man's face, his expression indicating that, indeed, he did remember Radha.

"Do you remember what happened to her?" Trey asked. He paused but, again, Rafael didn't reply. Trey was getting increasingly impatient.

"What happened to her, Rafael? What'd you do to her? We know you abducted her from her family's cotton factory." Trey's voice was getting louder and louder, resonating around the compact room. "Tell me! Tell me what you know about Radha's disappearance!"

Rafael was shaking his head violently back and forth. He placed a hand over each ear and yelled, "Get out! Get out of my room!" He turned toward his nurse and yelled, "Mark, I mean it! Get this man out of my room. Now!" With that, Rafael thrust his arm out and swept everything off the nightstand beside his bed, sending it all crashing to the floor. Trey watched the base of Rafael's bedside lamp shatter into a multitude of pieces.

Mark grabbed Trey's sleeve and escorted him out the door. "I've seen him erupt before," the nurse said in an apologetic tone to Trey. "When he gets like that, it's best to just leave him alone. I speak from experience. Rafael won't talk unless he wants to, which is seldom. Who is Radha, by the way? How's she connected to Rafael?"

"I'm not sure, Mark," Trey answered. "That's what we had hoped to find out. Radha was a fifteen-year-old girl who was abducted from India in 1966, and we've reason to believe Rafael was the man who snatched her away from her family. Asha was Radha's mother, and a friend of ours. I'm certain Rafael knows the truth about Radha's disappearance."

"Well, if he does, he isn't apt to tell you," Mark said, his brows knitting.

Jeanne Glidewell

Trey made no comment; he wasn't anxious or willing to elaborate on Skye's connection to Radha. He might end up looking like a candidate for the Wallingford Institute himself.

Mark shuffled his feet a few times and then looked up at Trey and said, "It's obvious to me this is a personal investigation, and not a legal one, so I'm going to tell you what I know about Rafael's past."

"Thank you, Mark. I'd appreciate whatever you can tell me."

"Rafael is extremely tight-lipped and temperamental," Mark began. "He's always been very moody, but has never been considered a serious threat to anyone here at the Institute. Rafael's done something in his past he has trouble living with. But he's never indicated to anyone, as far as I know, what it was he did. It's assumed by most of us it involved the death of a young girl, quite possibly the Radha you referred to."

"And why is that?" Trey asked, wiping his sleeve across his forehead. He took a step back, wanting to lean against the wall for support. He knew his worst fears could be confirmed with the nurse's next comments.

Mark continued, "There was a highly publicized, but brief, investigation not long after Rafael was admitted to this facility. According to his file, he was admitted to the local hospital at first, with bad lacerations to his left leg, but he would never tell anyone how the injuries occurred. A hunter discovered the decomposed body of a young woman on his family's ranch a few months later. The body was never identified. No one fitting the coroner's description of the corpse had been reported missing anywhere in the vicinity, and the dental records didn't match any missing person report anywhere else in the country either. Although Rafael was the most obvious suspect, the woman's death couldn't be pinned directly to him. And since the body couldn't be identified, the pressure was off the authorities to find the killer."

"I see," Trey muttered. He didn't really see or understand, but he felt obliged to respond to the nurse.

Mark went on to say, "I've only worked here for a few years, but since Rafael's on my floor I've studied his files, and I'm just relating to you what I know from reading them, you understand."

At Trey's nod, he continued, "The local hospital then transferred him here for an evaluation and treatment, and because his condition continued to deteriorate over time, he became a permanent resident. At the time the murder investigation took place, Rafael was probably too wacky . . . uh, excuse me, I meant to say he was too mentally unbalanced to provide any details or information to the homicide detectives. After they made a few visits to interrogate him, the whole thing finally just blew over. The case got put on the back burner and eventually was forgotten."

"Do you remember what year this all happened?" Trey asked, even though he felt quite sure he knew the answer without hearing it from the nurse.

"I believe it was the same year you mentioned. Late in 1966. The hospital had performed an operation to repair some severed tendons in Rafael's injured leg. When he came out from under the anesthesia, Rafael seemed to have lost all touch with reality. Frankly, I've never seen him react to anyone the way he did to your daughter. That whole scene astonished me. They both acted like they had met each other before."

They had, Trey said to himself. But out loud he said, "Zoe and I didn't expect Skye to react to him that way either, or for Rafael to react to her at all. I'm still not sure what to make of it."

"I'm not sure if you should make anything at all of it. Like I said before, Rafael can be very unpredictable. But anyway, I hope this has helped in some small way toward finding out whatever it is you needed to know," Mark said with sincerity.

"Yeah, it has. Thanks, Mark. We appreciate your help."

Rafael, now alone in his room, was trembling as drops of sweat formed on his upper lip. Lying back with his eyes fixed on the ceiling, he roughly wiped a tear off his cheek with the back of his hand, a hand still tingling from the little girl's touch.

Who was this little girl? Rafael wondered, and why did she make him feel so tempted to enfold her in his arms and hold on to her with whatever strength he had left? *How could she make me feel so cherished, so protected?*

Asha, Radha. He repeated the names to himself several times in thoughtful contemplation. The memories those names evoked began to play in his mind like a movie. Skylar had brought forth emotions he had forgotten he had. Remembering the little girl's crooked little smile, his thoughts went back to the first time he'd seen a lop-sided grin like Skylar's . . .

NINETEEN

Bombay, India, 1966

"Hey there, short timer, get that blasted thing fixed yet?"

"Yeah, it was just a bad bearing, nothing too challenging," Rafael hollered back over the roar of the ship's engines.

"That's good. Oh, Rafael, the captain wants to see you when you get a chance. No hurry. He says it'll be another three or four hours before we dock in Bombay."

"Okay. I'm about done here anyway," Rafael shouted. "Thanks, Cletus!"

Rafael had worked alongside Cletus since he'd joined the crew of the *Nighthawk*, a freighter that transported cotton and other goods to and from ports around the world. Cletus had been a good friend and a close comrade. Rafael was going to miss him and the rest of the crew. He would miss a lot of things, he knew, but it was time to move on.

It was 1966 and Rafael was thirty-seven years old. After eighteen years as a deckhand, and later as an engineman on the *Nighthawk*, he'd be resigning his position at the end of this next voyage when the freighter docked in Corpus Christi, Texas. From there he'd head north to Wyoming to try and fulfill his father's dream of rebuilding the cattle ranch. Remembering Eduardo's last words, Rafael knew it was time to go home. The time was right.

Rafael had kept the taxes paid on the property since his

171

father's death, knowing Juan would turn over in his grave if the ranch was ever allowed to slip out of the Torres family's hands. He owed this much to his father, Juan.

Having spent the majority of his time on the sea for nearly two decades, Rafael had been able to save most of his pay. He had built up a substantial nest egg, which he would dip into now to buy a bull and some breeding stock. Even after building a modest but adequate home, he should have enough left over to see him through the first few years, which were bound to be lean.

Once the ranch was back up on solid ground, Rafael hoped to find a good woman, settle down, and raise a family. He wanted a lady of his own, not the type of female like the ones whose affections he'd occasionally bought in port towns. *I want somebody to love, somebody who'll love me in return,* Rafael realized. The sea had been his lady for eighteen years, but the sea didn't warm his bed at night. The sea couldn't sit on the front porch with him and watch the sun set over the mountains, or feed and nurture his babies at its breast. He wanted a woman who was everything his own mother couldn't be: a woman who would stick by him through good times and bad. He'd find that woman and make sure she never found a reason to leave him or their children. They'd grow old together on the ranch and one day turn their productive business over to the next generation of the Torres family. This had been his father's dream—and now Rafael was making it his own.

"Engine okay now?"

"Yes, sir," Rafael replied to Captain Pietro. "Cletus told me you wanted to see me about something."

"Yeah, I do. I need you to pick up a small shipment for me while we're in port. The *Nighthawk* will only be docked in Bombay for about eight hours, just long enough to refuel and load up. Harley's in sickbay, and I'll have my hands full with a large load of manganese we're taking on. The shipment I need you to pick up is a special textile order, only a dozen crates or so, which will be ready for you in the front office of the factory. There'll be a cargo van waiting for you to use near the refueling dock. Okay? Any problem helping me out?"

"Aye, captain, no problem," Rafael said. "Which factory's it at?"

"Are you familiar with the Deshpande Cotton Factory?"

Rafael looked up at his captain as the weight of an anvil seemed to slam him in the chest. "Aye. Very familiar, sir. I helped build it."

His palms sweating and his breaths coming in quick, shallow gasps, Rafael stepped out of the van and stared reflectively at the front facade of the imposing building he'd helped design many years before. He hadn't stepped foot on the property since his last day on the cotton factory's payroll. Other than a few minor aesthetic improvements, not much appeared to have changed. The parking lot had been paved, and an amateurish attempt at landscaping now flanked a concrete sidewalk leading up to the front entrance. Mango and olive trees had been planted sporadically around the building, giving it a less austere appearance. Rafael had to admit he liked the new look. He would have bet his last year's salary the landscaping had been Asha's idea, and he could visualize her on her hands and knees, lovingly patting soil around the roots of each tree and flower. The potential of seeing her again had butterflies doing cartwheels in his stomach.

He stood outside the entryway for several minutes, taking deep breaths in an attempt to calm his nerves. What would he say to Asha if by chance he did encounter her? The disturbing thought made him consider turning around and leaving, but he couldn't return to the ship empty-handed.

It was the lunch hour, and there was no one else entering or exiting the front office. He ran his fingers through his hair several times, eased open the door, and froze at the sight of the young woman standing before him.

He was suddenly fifteen years old again, gazing into the eyes of a young woman whose likeness mirrored that of one that had haunted him for years. Her hair was a little thicker and a little longer, and her nose was sharper, more refined. But her eyes and her smile were a perfect match to the image he had carried around in his mind since the day he'd walked out the very door he now clung to.

Rafael couldn't move, couldn't blink, and couldn't speak. He had to remind himself to breathe. He was momentarily stunned by the impact this vision of beauty was having on his ability to function.

The young woman behind the desk smiled in greeting with the same crooked smile he remembered so well. The effect of the memory almost knocked the breath out of him. He stared at her, his mouth opened in shock.

"May I help you?" she asked him at length.

When he didn't respond, the woman repeated the question. He was tongue-tied, still staring at her as he stood rigidly in the doorway. With concern in her voice, the woman asked, "Sir? Are you all right?"

"Uh, yeah, uh, I'm Rafael Torres from the *Nighthawk*," he finally replied. "I'm, uh, I'm here to pick up a shipment for Captain Pietro."

"Oh, yes, there's a pallet of crates right here against the wall for the *Nighthawk*. The loading crew is at lunch, but there's a dolly behind the door if you'd rather not wait."

"That'd be fine. Uh, I can get it. It's just a small order."

"Could you please sign for pick-up on the bottom line of this form?" At his nod, she handed him a clipboard and pen. He grasped the clipboard with a spastic, uncoordinated motion.

Rafael scribbled his signature quickly and laid the clipboard down on the desk beside the young woman. His signature was totally undecipherable, but signing the form was only a formality anyway.

"Are you sure you wouldn't like me to try and get some help for you? The boxes are quite heavy."

"I can get them myself, Miss—"

"Joshi, Radha Joshi," she said. "It's nice to meet you, Mr. Torres. Let me know if you decide you'd like some help."

Radha Joshi, she'd said to him. Radha must be the daughter of Asha and Nirav, Rafael thought. *Asha, the woman I would've laid my life down for, and Nirav, the man who stole her from me.* After all the blood, sweat, and tears Rafael had expended on helping Asha rebuild the factory, Nirav had come out of nowhere to supplant him in every way. *Not only did Nirav claim Asha as his wife and sire this beautiful daughter, but he's also enjoying the fruits of my labor here at this factory.*

Rafael clenched his fists, suddenly overwhelmed with a desire for retribution for an injustice he'd suffered so long ago. He felt the rage vividly, as if it were a tangible object boiling out around his collar from the very depths of his soul.

"I don't need your help, Radha Joshi," he spat derisively. "I don't need anybody's help!"

Radha was obviously startled by his sudden vehemence. "I'm sorry, Mr. Torres, but I don't know what I've said to provoke you. I'm only trying to help."

Rafael knew he was being unreasonable and making Radha very uncomfortable, but he could do nothing more than glare at Nirav and Asha's young daughter.

"Have I met you before somewhere?" she asked him, with a flustered expression on her face.

"No, you haven't!" With that, he snagged the dolly from behind the door and began loading crates on it to take out to the van. His movements were jerky and deliberate as he tried, unsuccessfully, to get his emotions under control. Back outside, he violently flung crates into the rear of the van. Fortunately, the contents of the crates were not fragile.

After he'd pitched the final crate into the van, Rafael placed the dolly back where he'd gotten it. "I guess that's it," he said, reaching for the doorknob and stepping over the threshold to leave.

"Thank you, Mr. Torres," Radha said coolly, but cordially. "Have a nice day, sir."

Rafael stopped and turned around, his eyes locking with Radha's as he stepped back into the small foyer. He knew this lovely young lady, who looked and sounded so much like her mother, must be Nirav's pride and joy. This was Rafael's chance, his only chance, for revenge against the man who'd taken what he felt was rightfully his eighteen years prior.

Without a second thought, he reached out and snatched Radha's wrist and yanked her toward him. "You're coming with me!" he snarled.

He wrapped his arm around her small waist as she screamed, feeling her ribs through the thin material of her blouse. He quickly placed his free hand across her mouth to silence her, but just as quickly removed it, realizing it would take both arms to contain her as she fought against him. Fear was etched across her face as she kicked his shins repeatedly and tried to bring a knee up into his groin. Rafael felt triumphant, and despite himself, he felt aroused. He tightened his grip on her as she struggled to free herself from his grasp. The harder she fought, the tighter he squeezed.

"Help!" Radha screamed futilely, the din of the textile-producing machinery drowning out any noise emitting from the front office. "Somebody, please help me!"

Rafael covered her mouth again with his rough hand as he dragged her out the front door and pulled her hastily up the sidewalk to the rear of the cargo van. He was strong from many years of hard labor, but Radha was tougher than she appeared. It was all he could do to hold onto her with one arm. He finally reached the van, as nervous sweat poured down his entire body.

On the floor of the vehicle was a large roll of strapping tape, which he used to tape over Radha's mouth, and bind her arms and legs. She continued to struggle in earnest, but she was no match for Rafael's strength, which had increased with the adrenaline now coursing through his veins.

When he was convinced Radha was securely bound, he slammed the rear door and looked around the parking lot. There was still no one in sight. He jumped into the driver's seat and sped out of the lot onto the street. Heading north on Marine Drive, he wasn't sure where to go or what to do next. He was shocked by his own actions, suddenly afraid of what the outcome might entail. He briefly considered taking her back and dumping her out in the factory's parking lot, but he knew it wasn't a viable option. Radha knew his name and the name of the ship he worked for. The authorities would be on him before the *Nighthawk* had left the port. He had to think, which was hard to do with Radha groaning and thrashing about in the rear of the van. She was petrified, he knew, and no doubt wondering what it was he planned to do with her. It was exactly what he was wondering, too.

Rafael looked back at Radha every few minutes, wishing now that the entire incident had just been a bad dream. *Why couldn't it be me lying in the sick bay with dysentery, instead of Harley?* he wondered. But it wasn't a bad dream, and he wasn't in sickbay, so he'd better come up with a plan and come up with it fast! The *Nighthawk* was due to sail in less than six hours. That didn't give him much time, he thought. Or maybe, it gave him too much time. Time to get caught and arrested by the authorities.

Once Radha's disappearance was discovered, it wouldn't take long for someone to notice the shipment for Captain Pietro's ship had been picked up, and the papers alluding to this fact lay on top of Radha's desk. A lot of shipments went out of the factory every day though, so with any luck at all, no one would put two and two together, at least not until after the freighter had left port. Even then, it wouldn't take long for the Port Authority to catch up with the slow-moving cargo ship.

Rafael concluded he needed to think of a way to divert attention in another direction. He eased the van into an alley and parked. Reaching into the glove compartment of the van, he came up with a pen and a blank pad of paper. He thought carefully before printing in bold, black letters.

I have your daughter, Radha, in my possession. I have taken her in an effort to make you see the error of your ways. Do not attempt to involve the authorities or she dies! In exchange for the safe return of your daughter, put two million rupees in a satchel and leave the bag in the green trash bin at the N.E. corner of Victoria Station. You have three days to meet this demand. Come alone if you want your daughter left unharmed.

Rafael folded the note, checked to make sure Radha was still restrained, locked the van, and ran around the corner to a pharmacy. There he purchased a stamped envelope, filled in the factory's address, which he'd committed to memory years ago, and then posted the ransom note. Rafael didn't plan to be around to collect the ransom; the money was of no significance to him. He only hoped to cause enough of a distraction to give him a little time before the *Nighthawk* was linked to the kidnapping.

He was thankful now he had not signed the pick-up form

with a legible signature; he was fully aware his name would've raised a red flag with Asha and Nirav. On his way out of the pharmacy, Rafael dropped the pen he'd used and what remained of the pad of paper into a trash bin. He didn't want to leave any evidence behind in the cargo van Captain Pietro had rented for him to use to pick up the textile order. The odds were against him as it was. There was no sense in making the odds even worse.

Hurrying back to the van, Rafael noticed a pile of extra large burlap bags next to a dumpster in the alley. They were smelly and heavily soiled, but they would serve his purpose. He picked up a couple of the bags and pitched them into the back of the van. He then unlocked the front door of the van and crawled back to where Radha was sprawled out between the haphazardly arranged crates of fabric. Rafael noticed a rip in the bodice of her dress, a result of her earlier struggle in his arms. He felt bad he had damaged her garment. She'd done nothing to him but offer to help. And now she was being punished for it.

Radha looked up at him with sheer terror in her eyes, and at that moment he felt intense regret. "I won't hurt you, little one. Just do as you're told, and you won't be harmed," he said to her. "This really has nothing to do with you personally."

He then shoved one of the burlap bags down inside the other one to double the strength, and slid the opening over Radha's head. He was glad to not have to look at the accusation in her eyes any longer. "I'm going to have to put you in this bag for now," he said. "I'll let you out of it as soon as I can. I promise."

Rafael drove back to the harbor, passing several of his crewmates who were on shore leave for a few hours. Most of them he knew were either soaking up suds in taverns scattered along the harbor, visiting the red light district, or helping the captain with the large manganese shipment that was scheduled to be transported to south Texas.

Rafael parked the van close to the ship and, trying to look as nonchalant as he could, unlocked the rear door of the van. He shoved Radha's feet into the bag, twisted the end of the bag, and knotted it. Throwing the bulky bag over his shoulder like a bag of potatoes, he kicked the door shut with his foot.

All of the activity was centered at the aft of the ship, so he hurried up the gangway at the bow and, unnoticed, slipped down to the engine room in the hull. He slid his hand across the top of the frame of a small storage room door until he located the key. He unlocked the door and rushed in to deposit his squirming bundle. He was the only one who used the tiny room containing nothing but a large oily trunk where he kept his tools locked up so he could find them when he needed them. This would be the perfect place to stow Radha, he decided. He didn't think anyone could hear her over the engines, no matter how loudly she might yell.

Rafael carefully untied the knot to free the young girl. He didn't want to destroy the burlap bags, which he would most likely need to get her off the ship once they reached Corpus Christi in the same manner as he'd brought her on. He didn't even want to think about how he was going to accomplish getting Radha off the ship without being detected. He had enough to worry about at the time.

"You okay?" he asked inanely, after tearing off the tape that had restricted her speech. He had pulled the tape off carefully, not wanting to cause her any more discomfort than necessary.

"No, I'm not okay, you brute! You get this tape off my arms and legs this minute and let me out of here! My father will hunt you down and destroy you if anything happens to me. Do you hear me?" she asked. Rafael knew she was speaking with as much bravado as she could muster while fighting hysteria.

He was tempted to put the tape back over her mouth, but instead began to free her legs from the tape that bound them. "I told you I wouldn't hurt you, Radha, and I meant it. It's your father I have an issue with, not you. And I don't intend to give him the opportunity to hunt me down and destroy me, as you put it."

"And just what do you intend to do with me?"

"I'm taking you to the United States with me, so try to think of this as a vacation," he told her in a sarcastic tone. "Until then, make yourself comfortable. This will be your home until we reach Corpus Christi, Texas."

"Wait! Don't leave me in here!" she cried as he turned to leave. All signs of her earlier defiance had vanished. He shut the door, locked it, and slipped the key into his pocket. He couldn't take the chance someone might find the key and open the storeroom now. Losing his tools was one thing; this was something else entirely!

Using the front stairwell, Rafael raced up to the crew's sleeping quarters. Searching through a linen closet, he found a pillow and several blankets. As hot as the engine room was, Radha wasn't apt to need them for warmth, but they'd serve as a cushion for her on the hard floor. Inside the blankets, he hastily stuffed a packet of toilet tissue, a couple of towels and washcloths, a comb, and a bar of soap.

Back down in the engine room he found two metal buckets. He filled both of them half full of water. Radha could use one bucket of water to take a sponge bath, which she'd no doubt want to do after being confined inside the offensive burlap bags. The other bucket would have to suffice as a chamber pot. She wouldn't be too thrilled about that, he was certain. Somehow Rafael knew she wouldn't appreciate his attention to her personal needs, but he wasn't a cruel man as a rule. He didn't want her to suffer if he could help it. She had suffered enough at his hands already.

"You expect me to use that damned bucket as a toilet?" she

railed at him when he explained its purpose a few minutes later. It was uncharacteristic of Radha to curse, but she was beyond incensed. "You've got to be kidding! What kind of fool are you?"

A complete fool, he thought. What in Hades was he thinking when he abducted this young girl? Well, he was committed now. "Sorry, but it's the best I can do. This is not the Taj Mahal I have brought you to, if you hadn't noticed. I'll bring you down some food later, after we sail out of the port."

"Oh, thank you, kind sir," she said, sarcastically. "Don't forget the champagne."

Two hours later the *Nighthawk* had left the harbor and was sailing at fifteen knots an hour across the Arabian Sea. Rafael had gotten the textile shipment unloaded from the cargo van just minutes before the ship had weighed anchor. He was now in the galley searching for food to take down to Radha to go with the tankard he'd already filled with water.

"Hungry?"

Rafael jumped in alarm at the sound of the captain's voice behind him. "Uh . . . er, aye, sir. I didn't get a chance to eat today." He hadn't eaten a bite all day, but hunger was the last thing on his mind at the moment.

Captain Pietro laughed and said, "Me neither. I'm here to find some grub myself. Did the pickup at the factory go okay?"

"Oh, aye, sir. No problems."

"Good. Thanks for helping me out. I'm going to hate to see you leave the crew. You've been a real asset to this operation. And say, Rafael, when you get a chance, could you go down and see what all that thumping's about in the engine room?"

Rafael swallowed hard. He nodded, and after filling the tray with food, he made his way back down to the hull. He heard the thumping as he neared the storeroom.

"What do you think you're doing?" he asked as he entered

the storeroom. Right away he saw she had poured the water from one bucket into the other, and had been using the empty bucket to pound on the door of the storeroom.

"Trying to alert somebody to rescue me, you idiot! What did you think I was doing? Polishing my fingernails?" Radha replied. "I can't stay in this teeny closet, and you know it! It's stiflingly hot and claustrophobic in here."

"Bang the door with the bucket one more time, and you'll be spending the duration of this voyage in that trunk. Would you like that better? Then you can really see what hot and claustrophobic feels like."

Rafael could tell the severity of her situation had just hit her like a slap in the face. She had the look of a wild animal trapped in a cage. At that very moment, Rafael would have given anything to be able to turn back time and rethink his hasty, reckless actions. Even the thought of Nirav's anguish did not bring Rafael any pleasure now. He felt like the worse type of human being imaginable, and he was so very ashamed of himself.

"Please don't do that to me. I'd die in that slimy thing," she pleaded with him.

Rafael knew he could never follow up on his threat, but he couldn't let Radha know of his weakness. Radha's cooperation would make the situation easier for him. He would have to make her think he was a nastier, meaner individual than he really was. As it was, he had just committed a nastier, meaner act than he had ever thought he was capable of, and he wasn't proud of the fact. He turned back toward Radha, forcing an intimidating look on his face.

"Then keep that in mind if you plan on using the bucket again for anything other than relieving yourself. Not that anyone's going to hear you over the engines anyway," Rafael told her. He didn't want her to know the captain had already heard the racket she'd been making, just in case she tried it again and Pietro decided to check it out for himself. "I don't think you'd like having to relieve yourself on the floor, or having me haul the bucket in for you to use once or twice a day. Do you?"

"No," she responded, shivering despite the heat. Her face flushed bright pink, and Rafael knew she was envisioning the embarrassment of having to use the bucket while he stood by and watched.

She poured half of the water from the full bucket into the empty bucket. *She's showing submission without having to admit defeat. That's what Asha would have done in this situation. There's no mistaking that Radha is her mother's child,* Rafael thought. His respect for Radha's pluckiness went up another notch. He had his hands full with this spirited little lass.

"Okay then, here's some food and water. I'll check on you later, when I can get away from my duties," Rafael promised.

Rafael tracked down the captain and assured him the thumping had stopped. "Must've been the sound of the water hitting the prop and reverberating down the drive shaft," he fibbed to Pietro. "In any event, it has stopped and the engine is running smoothly. If you should hear it again, let me know and I'll take care of it."

When Rafael entered the storeroom a few hours later, he found Radha curled up in the corner of the room, clutching her stomach in distress. Her face was ashen, her expression, pitiful. She had the same look about her his brother, Eduardo, had had many years ago aboard a ship very similar to this one. Rafael stood there in silence as Radha pulled a bucket in front of her and retched violently. She was experiencing a severe case of seasickness. *It's going to be a long, long voyage to Texas—for both of us,* Rafael thought.

Over the next few days, Rafael found himself spending more time tending to his sick hostage than he did to the engines of the *Nighthawk.* He carried buckets of alternately clean and soiled water in and out of the storeroom. He took extra pains in procuring appetizing meals for Radha, but stopped taking them down to her when he realized the mere sight of food made her queasy and light-headed. The nausea had continued long after her stomach had emptied.

Rafael held Radha's head as each bout of the dry heaves racked her slim body, and cooled her down with a damp rag whenever beads of sweat formed across her forehead. She didn't ask for his help, or thank him for it, but Rafael didn't expect any gratitude. If it weren't for him, she wouldn't be in this condition to begin with, he told himself. He felt almost as miserable as Radha did, just knowing he was responsible for the agony she was suffering.

When Radha complained about her hot, dirty, and smelly clothes, Rafael came up with a pair of shorts and a clean shirt for her to wear. She was relieved to find they were very comfortable, despite being much too large for her. Radha wasn't at all concerned about her appearance, just thankful to have something cool and clean to wear.

She couldn't remember ever feeling so miserable as she did during the first few days on the rough, sometimes turbulent, sea. During the very first day on the sea, Radha was afraid she would die. After that, she was afraid she wouldn't. She'd always loved life, cherished every minute of it, but now death looked much more inviting. One evening as Rafael ran a cool, wet rag over the back of her neck she asked him to kill her and put her out of her misery. She had no desire to have her agony prolonged.

"Don't be silly, Radha. You'll feel better as soon as your body gets accustomed to the movement of the ship. It shouldn't take much longer than another day or two."

"Have I told you what a scummy, slimy, disgusting human being I think you are?" she asked him.

Rafael hung his head, and replied, "I know you have every reason to hate me, Radha, but it was never my intention to make you suffer. I'm not enjoying this any more than you are," he assured her.

"Then let me go, Rafael. Please, I beg of you. I'm homesick. I miss my family and I know they're worried sick about me. I promise not to tell them what happened or even mention your name." Radha's eyes filled with tears as she begged for mercy. She didn't know what was going to happen to her at the hands of this crazy sailor who had imprisoned her. She couldn't imagine it would be a pleasant experience, and the possibilities that flitted through her mind made her shudder.

"I know your family is worried, and I'm sorry I can't undo what I've done. Taking you away from your family was a mistake, one I'm not particularly proud of. I really don't know what possessed me to do such a thing. But I can't let you go now. It's far too late for that. I'm afraid you are stuck with me, little one. I will try to take care of you as best I can. I'll go to the galley now and round up some crackers and soda for you. If you can keep them down, they should help settle your stomach and bring you some relief."

"All right, Rafael," Radha said wearily, too weak to persist in her attempt to persuade him to release her. She eased back down on the blankets, tears beginning to stream down her cheeks. She watched as Rafael left the room, almost positive she'd seen tears in his eyes, as well.

Radha was confused by the tenderness her captor had shown her on numerous occasions. She couldn't understand what could bring a man capable of such compassion and gentleness to snatch her away from her family the way he had. Rafael had told her he had a score to settle with her father. What could her father have done to Rafael to make him capable of such evil? She was afraid to ask him.

As Rafael had said, the crackers had helped alleviate her nausea to some degree. The soda eased her stomach cramps and moistened her dry mouth. Her body was beginning to grow accustomed to the pitching and rolling of the vessel, as Rafael had assured her it would. She still didn't feel good by any stretch of the imagination, but at least she no longer wanted to die.

She was now more in danger of dying of boredom, she was sure, as the long hours ticked away slowly in the tiny, cramped room. The next time Rafael came in to check on her, she complained to him about having nothing to do. Within minutes, he brought her several books he'd found somewhere aboard the ship. The first book about the navigation of shipping lanes didn't hold much interest for her, but the other two regarding marine life she found full of interesting material. Reading was better than staring at a blank wall for hours and hours.

Later the same afternoon, Rafael showed up with a deck of cards. He taught her the game of poker, and dropped in several times throughout the remainder of the day to play a few hands with her. On his final visit of the day, he showed her how to play solitaire, for those times when he couldn't get free to join her. She was thankful for the single light bulb that swung from a wire above her head.

Radha found herself looking forward to Rafael's company, which irritated her immensely. Radha didn't want to feel for him or care anything about Rafael at all. She wanted to hate him with every fiber of her being, and she was finding such hate impossible. And the fact he wasn't hard to look at didn't help matters either. *I must be an even bigger fool than he is,* she thought.

TWENTY

"I see your nickel and raise you a nickel," Radha said, adding another raw pinto bean to the growing pile between herself and Rafael.

Radha's face lit up as Rafael let out a dramatic groan. She'd beaten him the last five hands in a row. She was really getting good at this game, she thought smugly.

"I fold," Rafael said, laying down a pair of aces.

"Ha!" Radha said, gloating. She counted out the beans in front of her, did some mental calculations, and said, "You now owe me a grand total of a hundred ninety-six dollars and fifty cents."

"So what'd you have in your hand?" Rafael asked her out of curiosity.

"Nothing."

"Nothing?"

"Nope, not even a face card," she replied, laughing.

"Curses!" Rafael said, charmed by Radha's good-natured ribbing. "I knew I shouldn't have taught you to bluff so well."

"Seven card stud, jacks or better, deuces and jokers are wild," she said as she began to deal the next hand.

"You're getting much too familiar with this game," Rafael teased her. "I'm going to have to keep an eye on you after we get off the ship, aren't I?"

189

"Oh, you can count on it, sailor!" she replied in a flash. She was in high spirits today. Rafael had told her they'd be docking in Corpus Christi early the following day. Even now the cargo ship was anchored in the bay, waiting for its appointed time to enter the ship channel into the Port of Corpus Christi.

Radha didn't know what was going to happen to her, and although she still didn't trust Rafael completely, she felt sure he wouldn't harm her physically. She sensed the entire abduction incident had been out of character for him. Radha found she rather enjoyed his company. A much more unpleasant and unsavory character could have kidnapped her, she thought; so, in an ironic way, she considered herself fortunate. Radha always was the type to look at the bright side of every situation, and now was no exception.

She had lost a few pounds on the long voyage, and though she wasn't unhappy about trimming down a bit, it hadn't been the most appealing way to achieve weight loss. Although the seasickness had eased up a bit, it hadn't disappeared. But she felt like her old self today as the ship lay anchored idly off the coast, rocking gently in the low swells on the calm sea.

Still not confident enough to eat a full meal, she had been consuming a steady diet of soda and crackers. She would be very relieved to get off of the ship and feel solid ground under her feet. She never wanted to step foot on a ship again. And she never wanted to eat another dry, tasteless cracker either!

Rafael told her they were going to go to Wyoming, where he wanted to rebuild the cattle ranch that was still owned by his family. He and his father and brother had left the ranch to go to India when Rafael was eight years old. They had all three worked for her mother's father at the cotton factory. But his father and brother had both been killed in the same explosion that had taken her grandfather's life back in 1944, well before her parents had even met. Radha had heard very few flattering remarks about her grandfather. From the few comments her mother, Asha, had made about him, her grandfather had been an intolerable tyrant. Even Rafael had referred to him as "uncompromising." And although he hadn't elaborated any further on his connection to her family, she knew there was more to it than he'd told her. She hoped, in time, he'd feel comfortable enough to tell her the rest of the story.

"Penny for your thoughts," Rafael said.

"Just thinking about my family and missing them," she lied. "They must be really upset, fearing the worst and not knowing what happened to me."

"Yes, I'm sure they're very upset," Rafael replied. Then he made an obvious attempt to change the subject. "So, Radha, what would you buy with a hundred ninety-six dollars and fifty cents if those beans were real money, and you could have anything you wanted?"

Radha thought for a moment before answering. "Other than a plane ticket to Bombay?"

"Yes," he said with a sigh, "other than that."

"A horse then."

"A horse?" he asked, laughing. "Why in the world would you want to buy a horse?"

"I don't know. Horses just fascinate me. They always have. I've never actually been on a horse, but I think being able to ride across an open field on one would be so thrilling, so exhilarating. I guess it's just a silly dream of mine." Radha averted her eyes, blushing in her embarrassment at having voiced her secret dream.

Rafael was once again struck by how much this young lady before him reminded him of his brother, Eduardo. The mere thought of Eduardo flooded him with guilt over his recent actions. He reached out and lifted Radha's chin up with his index finger, encouraging her to look at him as he responded.

"It's not a silly dream, Radha. I haven't been on a horse in years, but I remember the feeling of freedom it gave me when Eduardo and I rode horses across the ranch as young boys. I guess a feeling of freedom is something you haven't felt in recent days, huh?" Rafael asked in an apologetic voice.

"No, I've just had feelings of nausea and despair in recent days," she said. It was the truth, but she felt bad about saying it when she noticed sadness and remorse on Rafael's face. She forced a lighter tone into her voice and continued. "Although the last couple of days haven't been all that bad. You've helped make them a lot more bearable for me."

"I'll try to make it up to you, little one. Once we get to Wyoming, I'll work on making your dream of riding a horse come true. I owe it to you. Now I'd better get back to work. I'll be back in an hour or so with—"

"Soda and crackers, right?" she finished for him.

Rafael chuckled. "Yes. Sorry about that. You're being a good sport about it though, Radha. I promise the night after tomorrow you'll eat like a queen. And what's more, all soda and crackers will be banned from our ranch. If I see one little cracker trying to sneak onto our property, I'll blow it to smithereens with my shotgun."

"Hmmm . . ." she said, cocking an eyebrow at him in a teasing gesture, and wondered about the way he'd described the ranch as their property.

"On second thought," Rafael said, misinterpreting her response, Radha was certain, "I think I'd better ban all shotguns from the property too!"

They were both laughing as he closed and locked the door.

Rafael had about eight hours to get everything taken care of in town before he needed to be back aboard the *Nighthawk*. The cargo ship would be docked at the Port of Corpus Christi overnight, and he wanted to sneak Radha off the vessel in the wee hours of the morning. Very few of his crewmates would be spending the night on the ship, and those that were would be fast asleep at that time, many of them almost unconscious from over-imbibing in local taverns. The majority of the crewmembers would end up at one of the handful of flophouses near the harbor, as was usually the case.

Rafael's first order of business was to secure transportation. They needed a way to get to Wyoming, and most likely, something to live in, once they got there. He hitched a ride into town and was dropped off at a large used car lot. Luck was with him. At the far end of the lot was a newer-model Ford pickup with an older, but well-maintained, camper attached to the bed of the truck. It had just been taken in that very morning as a trade-in, he was told. Rafael was able to convince the salesman to let him purchase it, foregoing the customary mechanical inspection and detailing in order to take immediate possession.

The next stop on his list was a large farm and ranch supply store where he bought a lock, numerous packs of vegetable seeds, onion sets, asparagus roots, a few yards of nylon rope, and several six-gallon gasoline cans.

He drove down the street to a service station, where he had the attendant check the oil and the air pressure in the tires, and then fill the truck and gas cans with fuel. He lashed the cans to the back bumper with the nylon rope, and then installed the sliding bolt lock to the outside of the camper door to enable him to lock Radha inside the camper whenever he deemed it necessary. He couldn't afford to take any needless risks at this point in the venture.

Next on his agenda was the general store. Rafael walked with brisk steps down each aisle, filling his basket with cookware, bedclothes, toiletries, and anything else he thought they might need to set up housekeeping in the small camper. He browsed through the ladies' apparel department, selecting a new wardrobe for Radha, smiling as he tried to visualize her attired in each outfit he selected. The western garments he chose were so vastly different from those she was accustomed to wearing.

He'd already selected some jeans, shirts, socks, and undershorts for himself; his wardrobe was almost as limited as Radha's. As an afterthought, he included leather hats, jackets, and gloves for both of them, as well as footwear. He knew instinctively that Radha would enjoy owning her own leather boots and cowboy hat. Just as she'd appreciate the western outfits he'd purchased for her. He couldn't wait to see her in the new clothes.

Before proceeding to checkout, he added several books, a sewing kit, first aid kit, several colorful hair ribbons and a scarf for Radha, and a new deck of cards to replace the deck they'd worn out on the ship.

To top off his already overflowing basket, he added a bright plastic flower arrangement to use as a centerpiece on the tiny dinette table, and a new pair of curtains with a floral design to hang over the miniature sink. The pattern featured daisies, which Radha had told him were her favorite flowers. He knew she'd want to add a feminine touch to the camper, and Rafael wanted her to be as comfortable in her new environment as possible. It'd be easier for both of them if she were at least somewhat content in her new life with him on the cattle ranch. Radha's happiness was becoming of greater and greater importance to him, he realized with some anguish.

Rafael's last stop before returning to the ship was a grocery store, where he stocked up on canned goods, coffee, and standard miscellaneous food items. He was careful to only buy enough meat, produce, and perishables as he thought they could consume before the food spoiled.

With all his chores taken care of, Rafael went back to the

Nighthawk to rest and stay out of sight until the early morning hours. Before he could relax, though, he'd have to ascertain Radha's cooperation. It would require an acting job Rafael wasn't sure he could pull off.

"You have two options, Radha. You can walk with me up the stairs and down the gangplank to the pier, not making a sound. Or you can exit the ship the same way you boarded it, taped up inside a burlap bag," Rafael told her. He hated having to speak in such harsh terms to her but knew her cooperation was crucial. "If you choose the first option and then decide to draw attention to yourself, you'll be silenced and transferred to the bag. Understood?"

At Radha's stilted nod, he continued, "I don't want to have to put you through that again, but I can't, and I won't, take any chances of being detected as we disembark this vessel. So which will it be?"

"I promise to not make a sound, Rafael. I couldn't endure another episode in that disgusting burlap bag," she said. "I promise you if you'll allow me to walk off this ship, I will do so without making a sound. At this point, my main concern is just getting off this ship and back on to solid ground as quickly as possible."

"Okay, then. I will hold you to that promise," Rafael said. "In the meantime, get some rest, and I will be back for you in a few hours. I have some loose ends to tie up between now and then."

He unlocked the old trunk and removed his tool kit to load into the Ford truck as Radha watched in apprehension. Rafael knew she was trying to appear brave and confident, but she couldn't hide the uneasiness she must be feeling, not knowing what was in store for her once they departed the ship. *I have put her through enough already. I must try to put her mind at ease—as much as possible anyway,* he thought.

Before exiting the little storage room, Rafael cupped her chin in his hand and tried to comfort her. "It will be okay, little one. I would never intentionally hurt you, not in this life or the next."

"Radha!" Rafael yelled out in panic. "Radha, where are you?"

He raced around in a frenzied, frantic fashion, looking for her in every direction. The bolt was slid shut on the outside of the camper door, he noted. It was impossible for her to have locked it from inside the camper.

Rafael realized he shouldn't have risked leaving Radha alone in the truck when he went inside the gas station to pay for the fuel, but he hadn't wanted to disturb the companionable atmosphere they'd been sharing. Other than the attendant who'd filled the tank, and who was now standing behind the counter inside the station, there wasn't another soul in sight. Wanting to conserve the spare gasoline he carried in cans lashed to the bumper, Rafael had purposely chosen this fuel station along a desolate stretch of highway south of Abilene in central Texas to take on more fuel. There wasn't apt to be an overabundance of people around this out-of-the-way station.

Up until now, the day had gone without a hitch. No one else had been stirring aboard the *Nighthawk* at three o'clock that morning when he and Radha had made their way stealthily up from the hull and down the gangplank with only a sliver of moon lighting the sky.

Radha had been true to her word, moving about as quietly as a cat stalking a field mouse. She had seemed even more reluctant to be caught sneaking off the ship than he had. After a successful exit off the ship, Rafael had helped her into the camper and handed her a new change of clothes before he slid the bolt home on the exterior lock and climbed into the truck's cab.

Just north of San Antonio, Rafael had pulled into a deserted rest area. After allowing Radha to utilize the restroom and stretch her legs, he invited her to sit up front in the cab with him. Tired of being locked in cramped quarters, no doubt, she'd been quick to accept his offer. Radha had rattled on in an effusive manner about the picturesque landscape. In the light of the cool, crisp morning, she was getting her first view of the wide-open spaces of Texas, something she was unaccustomed to, having lived in the crowded confines of Bombay.

And now, Radha was gone! She'd vacated the passenger seat of the blue Ford pickup and vanished into thin air. Rafael was beside himself. He was more concerned about Radha's welfare than his own. *A lot can happen to a pretty, young lady who's as unfamiliar with her surroundings as Radha must be,* he thought.

Radha wasn't inside the station, nor was she walking along the road. She couldn't have gone far, Rafael realized as he raced around to the rear of the small station, almost colliding with Radha as he rounded the corner. Rafael's face was shrouded in alarm, as Radha asked him, "What's wrong?"

"Where have you been?" he asked.

"Using the restroom in the rear of the station."

"Don't ever do that again without asking me first," he said, distraught, but very relieved.

"I'm sorry, but I had to go—"

"Ask me next time," he cut in, a sharp edge to his voice, "or I'll have to leave you locked up in the camper until we reach our destination."

"Oh no, please don't make me ride back in the camper. I would miss out on all the scenery," she pleaded. "I'll ask next time, I promise. I just wasn't thinking, and I really had to go—urgently."

"Well, all right," Rafael replied as he held onto her elbow and led her back to the cab of the truck. "No harm done. Just don't let it happen again. It startled me. I was afraid something had happened to you. There are a lot of crazy people out there who prey on innocents like you."

"No kidding?" Radha asked with a shy grin.

Touché, Rafael told himself, stung by Radha's unspoken accusation. Talk about the pot calling the kettle black! Once again he was reminded of the callous act he'd perpetrated against the young woman, whose mother, Asha, had long ago told him he and she both should continue to live in a way that would have made Eduardo proud. Well, Eduardo wouldn't be too proud of him now, any more than he was proud of himself for the crime he'd committed in kidnapping Radha.

For the next several hours, they rode in silence while Rafael ruminated over the enormity of his actions, and Radha sulked, huddled in the far corner of the bench seat of the truck. Rafael missed her animated chatter. Finally, he spoke, "Are you hungry?"

"Very."

"Me too," he said. "I believe I promised you a grand meal once we were off the ship. We'll stop soon, eat dinner, and call it a day. We're not far from the Texas/New Mexico border."

Radha was thankful a short time later when Rafael pulled the truck up alongside a small, enchanting lake in Sugarite Canyon, just outside Raton, New Mexico. Other than her and Rafael, the entire area appeared to be deserted. They got out and wandered around, checking out the campsite and stretching their legs. Radha was stiff from many hours of riding and was sure Rafael was too.

"I noticed a shallow area in this little cove, behind the row of pine trees, Radha," Rafael said to her as he pointed to a spot just beyond the front of the truck. "Would you like to bathe and freshen up a bit while I prepare dinner? The water will be cool, but clean."

"I'd love to. I've never felt so filthy in all my life," she replied. She was finding it impossible to maintain her mutinous behavior in the face of such unmolested beauty, so she gave up trying. She reached for the towel and soap Rafael held out to her. "Thank you, Rafael. I won't be long."

As if to assure her of her privacy, Rafael said, "Dinner won't be ready for about forty-five minutes, so take your time. I'll be in the camper, out of view but within earshot, if you need any assistance. Stay alert. There are bears and cougars in this region."

Bears and cougars aside, she was anxious to immerse herself in the water. After stripping off her clothes behind the wall of trees, she waded out from the bank. She found the water much chillier than she'd expected, and couldn't believe its clarity as she watched her toes wiggling, two feet below the surface.

Radha had always had an adventuresome nature, and although she loved and missed her family, she was amazed to feel no particular desire to be back in Bombay at the moment. Rafael was old enough to be her father, only eight years younger than her Papa, but for some reason she didn't notice the age difference when she was with him. He was protective of her in an almost obsessive way, but he was thoughtful and sensitive to her needs and desires. Rafael made her feel more alive, more complete than she'd ever felt. It was as though they were two halves of a whole, predestined to be together. Radha had always trusted her instincts, and she now accepted her current situation as something that was meant to be.

Replete after a feast of chicken, potatoes, and corn, Radha leaned back, patted her stomach, and said, "I feel like I could burst at the seams. Thank you, Rafael. That was delicious."

"I'm glad you enjoyed it, but please don't explode on me," he said, laughing. "I've made a big enough mess in here as it is."

She looked around, noticing for the first time the array of dirty pans and utensils covering nearly every square inch of the stove and meager counter space. "Yes, you did, didn't you? Why don't you go clean up in the lake while I attempt to put the kitchen back in order? You won't believe how clear and cool the water is."

"Actually, I will. That's one thing I've always remembered and missed about my childhood in Wyoming. Just wait until you see the crystal clear creek that flows through the cattle ranch."

Rafael scraped off his plate and placed it in the sink. "Use the water as sparingly as you can," he advised Radha. "This camper's water tank has a very limited capacity. I'm glad I remembered to fill it at the roadside park in Amarillo. A little fresh water is better than none at all."

"I'll be conservative with the water, Rafael. Now get out of my way for a while so I'll have room to work."

"Okay. Thanks for volunteering to clean up this disaster zone I've created. When I get back from washing up, I have a surprise for you."

"A surprise? Really? Tell me, what is it?" Patience had never been one of her virtues. Even Rafael was already aware of that character flaw in Radha. He laughed at her childlike exuberance.

"Well. Let's put it this way," he replied, removing a tall, thin bottle from the propane-powered refrigerator, and holding it up for her inspection. "I didn't forget your champagne!"

Early the following morning, Rafael and Radha headed north through Colorado. Radha's excitement increased the closer they came to Wyoming. She was intrigued as Rafael pointed out numerous herds of antelope grazing in fields of sagebrush, and a deer with her twin fawns drinking from a farm pond. She spoke infrequently, not because she was sulking this time, but because she was enthralled by the magnificence of the Rocky Mountains, the spectacular range that paralleled the road they were traveling. "This is incredible, Rafael. Is Wyoming anywhere near as beautiful as Colorado?" Radha asked.

"As far as I'm concerned, Wyoming's the most beautiful place on this planet. I'll take you to see the Grand Tetons someday, a mountain range on the western edge of the state. A more majestic sight is hard to imagine."

"I can't wait to see that," Radha said, surprised to realize it was the truth.

Rafael smiled at her enthusiastic reply, and said, "And I can't wait to show it to you."

Slipping back into a comfortable silence, Rafael began to whistle cheerfully. After a few minutes he turned on the radio, grinning as the sound of Jefferson Airplane's new hit single, "Somebody to Love," filled the cab of the truck.

Rafael had no trouble locating the Torres Cattle Ranch, even though it was almost unrecognizable. The old log cabin was much smaller than he remembered it, and was now useless and uninhabitable. The windows had all been broken out, and the roof was caving in. Human scavengers had looted the home. Very few possessions they'd left behind still remained, other than the huge table in the front room of the three-room cabin. His father, Juan, had handcrafted the table out of rough-hewn pine logs, and it was much too large to fit through the door or it would, no doubt, have been stolen also. Everything else worth salvaging had been removed.

Evidence also indicated the cabin had become a haven for numerous varmints. An opossum and her brood had taken up residence in a kitchen cabinet, the mother snarling and gnashing her teeth as Rafael approached. Not anxious to tangle with the ill-tempered critter, Rafael kicked the cabinet door closed, a door that hung on one rusted hinge.

Outside, weeds and scrub brush surrounded the cabin, reaching up to the roofline. The outbuildings were in an even greater state of disrepair, Rafael noticed. The cattle barn had all but collapsed, and the chicken coop threatened to suffer the same fate at any moment. Rafael was surprised to find a shovel, hand-operated garden tiller, pick ax, and other small tools inside an old tool shed behind the cabin. They were worn and rusty, but serviceable. It was apparent they weren't good enough for looters, but they were good enough for Rafael.

Next to the tool shed, the outdoor latrine stood proud, unaffected by time. Nearly thirty years had passed, and yet the outhouse was just as Rafael remembered it from the last time he'd seen it in 1937. *I'll give the weeds around it a few whacks with the machete I spotted in the tool shed, and it will be functional again within a few minutes,* he thought. With a little assistance from Radha, they could remove the camper from the bed of the truck and set it up on its jacks near the outhouse. The living arrangements would suffice, he felt, until he could raze the cabin and build a new home in its place, complete this time with electricity and indoor plumbing.

The table inside the camper made down into a bed. Radha, being slim and petite, reported to Rafael she'd slept quite soundly on it the previous night. Over the cab of the truck was a larger bed, ample enough for Rafael's heftier frame. Despite his growing attraction for the much younger woman, Rafael vowed to never ask Radha to share a mattress with him. It wasn't in his nature to force himself on any woman, and he had no respect for those men who did. But should Radha ever express a desire for his affections, he'd be more than willing to oblige her. For now, he was willing to let their relationship run its natural course. Rafael was pleased with its progress so far.

"Rafael, come quick!" he heard Radha yell out to him. The urgency in her voice instantly brought Rafael out of his reverie. He strode outside the cabin where she'd been waiting while he'd surveyed the interior.

"Look!" she exclaimed, pointing toward a section of toppled fencing at the crest of a rocky outcropping.

Just beyond a stack of bent, rusty posts, in a haphazard pile on the ground, two small but stout and solid black horses grazed on the abundant vegetation. The markings on the free-roaming stallions were almost identical, except for a jagged white slash bisecting the forehead of the somewhat larger stallion. Both had white front forelegs, long untamed tails, and scraggly manes. Alerted by Radha's voice, the skittish animals scampered off, moving out of sight behind a grassy knoll.

"Wild mustangs," Rafael said, his left hand shadowing his eyes, which hadn't quite adjusted to the bright sunshine outside the cabin.

"They're beautiful, Rafael," Radha commented in awe.

"They are indeed," he agreed. "The mustangs are descendants of the horses that were brought to America by sixteenth-century Spanish explorers. They're strong and make excellent pack-horses, which made them valuable assets. The sturdy breed adapted well to living off the land," he explained.

"Are there a lot of wild mustangs in Wyoming?" Radha asked him.

"Yes, many thousands of them are still roaming the western states. Not too long ago, I read there are statutes being considered to protect them now from slaughter and mistreatment."

"That's good. They're too beautiful to destroy, wild and free. I hope we have an opportunity to see them again."

"Oh, I'm sure we'll see them around here once in a while.

They tend to roam a specific territory where there are good grazing grounds and watering holes. Both can be found all over our ranch. I imagine they've grown quite accustomed to frequenting this property, since it's been vacant for so long."

"Beautiful," Radha repeated, scanning the horizon as if looking for signs of additional wild mustangs. "This is so exciting. The wide-open spaces here are so incredible. I've never seen anything like them. It sure makes a person realize how small and insignificant he is in comparison, but it gives one a feeling of such freedom. I hate to admit this to you, Rafael, but I think I'm really going to like it here."

"I hope so, little one. I truly hope so."

TWENTY-ONE

Kansas, 2001

"Hi, Mommy," Skye said, bounding down the steps of the school bus that always dropped her off at the top of the driveway when her four-hour school day ended.

"Hi, punkin. How was the field trip today?" Zoe asked, placing a tender kiss on her daughter's forehead. Skye's kindergarten class had spent the afternoon at the Zarda farm. Like the Robbins' property, the Zarda farm was located just outside the city limits. But unlike the Robbins', the Zardas owned a vast menagerie of farm animals. Some, like their ostriches, were more unusual than the others.

"It was cool, Mommy," Skye told her. "We had lots of fun at the farm. We got to watch them milk the cows and feed the pigs. They have chickens and goats and everything. They even have a llama and a couple of ostriches. Mr. Zarda let us pet the llama, but not the ostriches. He showed us a scar on his hand where one of them bit him last year."

Skye told Zoe all about her day as they strolled hand-in-hand down the long driveway toward the house. Skye talked about how the farmer's wife had let her and the other children gather eggs in the chicken coop.

"It was just like an Easter egg hunt. They have a bunch of horses too, but none of them look like Thunder," Skye said matter-of-factly. Zoe was relieved the reference to Thunder seemed to cause no distress to Skye. Perhaps, she thought, her daughter was comparing the Zardas' horses to the statue Victoria had given her for her birthday, also dubbed Thunder, and not the horse she had ridden in Wyoming when she was Radha.

"Miss Johnston told us the horses are all apple—er—apple loosies."

"Appaloosas?"

"Yeah, that's it," Skye said. "Their cat, Dolly, had a bunch of kittens in the barn, and we all got to play with them. They are sooooooo cute, Mommy. Mrs. Zarda said cats help keep the mice and snakes out of the barn. Do you think we need some kittens to keep mice and snakes out of our barn? I promise I'd take care of them. Oh yeah, and Mr. Zarda took us all on a ride on their hay wagon, too!"

Skye was excited about all the day's events. Zoe knew Skye loved school and was having fun with all the new friends she'd made. Zoe had adjusted well to the new schedule also, finding she now cherished the few hours each day Skye was in school. They gave her a chance to rest and relax. She'd even rekindled an interest in photography, a hobby she hadn't had time to involve herself with since the birth of her daughter.

Trey took a break from his work each afternoon to share a glass of iced tea and chat with her on the front porch. Zoe knew this was his way of trying to make the adjustment easier for her, and she appreciated his thoughtfulness.

Trey had been busy working with his father, harvesting the wheat and milo crops the last few weeks. He hadn't touched the barn, but Zoe knew he simply hadn't had the time to devote to a project of that magnitude. She wouldn't have brought it up anyway. The two of them had been getting along so well since the whole reincarnation thing had sprung up with Skye, she didn't want to do anything that might shatter this peaceful period in their marriage. In the scheme of life, she realized once again, some things are just not important enough to squabble over—and the deteriorating relic of a barn fell firmly into that category.

"Mommy?" Skye's voice broke in to Zoe's wandering thoughts.

"Yes, punkin?" she responded. Zoe and Skye had reached the house and were climbing up the front steps to the porch.

"Can we get some chickens?"

Twenty-Two

Wyoming, 1966

With so much to do to get the ranch up and running again, Rafael didn't know where to begin first. It was too early in the season to plant a garden. Although it was late April, the frost-free date was still over a month away. In Wyoming, the Easter lilies didn't bloom until early August, and the growing season in this climate was a short one. Even the warmest days were followed by cool evenings. Rafael hoped Radha wouldn't mind learning to can and preserve fruits and vegetables to help keep their produce available throughout the long winter ahead. *There are two seasons in Wyoming,* he thought, *winter and July.* And even then, he could remember a time or two as a young boy on the ranch, nearly freezing his butt off in July.

It was imperative he didn't waste any time in getting the house rebuilt. He and Radha couldn't endure a Wyoming winter in the camper. They needed to be in the new home by first snowfall with at least three cords of firewood at their disposal. He'd have to invest in a new chainsaw, as well as power tools to construct the new log home. Whatever logs he cut that were not straight and true enough to use in framing the house, he could saw into smaller lengths to use for heating it. Nothing would go to waste.

Before he could begin on that endeavor, however, his first priorities were to repair the fences and build a shelter for the cattle he wanted to buy to start building a herd. He'd need fence posts, spools of barbed wire, a post-hole digger, a sledgehammer, and numerous other things. The list grew as he considered the necessities for getting the ranch up to par and ready for livestock. Also, as a means to protect Radha's future, he wanted to secure life and long-term-care insurance policies, just in case something happened to him.

He'd have to look into purchasing a rifle so he could take advantage of the plentiful wild game populating the property, and also a large freezer chest to preserve the venison, antelope, and elk meat.

But before Rafael did anything, he needed to arrange to have electricity run to the ranch, and a 300-gallon tank of propane brought out too. The compact propane tank in the camper didn't hold more than a few days' worth of fuel, and he couldn't be running back and forth to town every week to have the canister refilled. He didn't have the luxury of spare time. As it was, he'd have to utilize his time wisely, and accomplish as much each day as possible. He had a long list of tasks to accomplish.

Rafael considered other matters that would need attention. He didn't want to have phone service on the ranch; there was no need to present a temptation for Radha to make a telling call back to Bombay, or to local authorities, for that matter. But he probably should rent a post office box, not for personal correspondence, but for receiving the bills he was apt to incur. It was just another one of the many details he'd have to attend to in a short amount of time.

By the latter part of May, Rafael had made substantial progress on the ranch. The fences were up and secure, with all new metal posts replacing those that were bent or rusted through, and a gate had been ordered to contain the cattle he hoped to purchase soon. After he removed the old posts he threw them into a deep ravine in the east pasture. The huge pit also served as a receptacle for the scraps from the torn-down old cabin. Its wood, and that of the collapsed barn, could be used in lieu of firewood. Still, there was material that couldn't be burned and would need to be discarded. Eventually, he'd fill in the ravine to eliminate its hazardous potential. Fearing she'd stumble into the broad and irregular ditch, Rafael warned Radha to keep away from the east field when she was out and about on the property.

While he labored on restoring the ranch, Radha toiled in the new garden she had planted. Earlier, Rafael had tilled up a large patch of ground near the creek, and devised a watering system, using a gas-powered generator to pump water from the creek for irrigating the garden. Radha could take care of watering and could tend to the garden from that point on, if she wasn't opposed to the task.

To Rafael's relief, Radha seemed to enjoy working in the garden. She spent many hours hoeing weeds and loosening clods of dirt from around the tiny sprouts emerging from the sown seeds. She told Rafael she loved to watch the plants grow and flourish. It amused him to see her race out early each morning to check on their progress. One morning, to her dismay, she found over half of the garden had been trampled overnight. A large majority of her tender seedlings were destroyed. She wanted to sit right down in the dirt and sob, but that wouldn't be a very productive use of her time. Instead, she ran back to the camper to discuss the latest development with Rafael.

Rafael tried, but failed, to suppress his laughter. He surveyed the damage with Radha. "From the looks of these hoof prints, I'd say your wild mustangs made a nocturnal visit," he said. He took the next day off from his tasks to erect a fence around the garden plot, and Radha began with renewed energy to replant more seeds.

The following week, Radha convinced Rafael to take time off again to teach her to fish for trout in the creek. She was familiar with a deep-sea rod and reel, but manipulating the fly rod took some practice. Radha soon became proficient enough to cast a fly within a ten-inch radius of her targeted site. Rafael was impressed with her perseverance, and amused by her reaction when she landed her first fish.

"That's it?" she asked in disgust.

"Yep! That's what's known as a cutthroat trout."

"Why, it's no bigger than what we used for bait when Papa and I fished out on the Arabian Sea."

Laughing, Rafael replied, "Well, dear, that's why it's so sporting. It's a challenge to catch enough of them to make a meal. And you will love the way they taste!"

Radha was soon catching enough to make a meal, and there was plenty left over to freeze for future meals. She experienced a thrill each time she felt the tap of a fish on the end of her line, and an even greater thrill when, on occasion, she hooked a larger brown or rainbow trout.

One sunny afternoon, as she walked across the field hauling a stringer of fish back to the camper to clean, she stopped abruptly, struck by a feeling of guilt and remorse. It had just occurred to her she hadn't thought of her family in days.

Meanwhile, back in Bombay, the search for Radha had all but been abandoned. The first few weeks, Asha and Nirav had been successful in their desperate attempt to keep the investigation alive. But to Asha's dismay, the Indian authorities soon turned their attention to other cases they felt had more hope of being solved. When Radha's kidnapper failed to retrieve the satchel full of ransom money, the investigators lost interest in the sensational case involving one of the most affluent families in the city.

Asha was listless and despondent, having suffered a loss of this caliber before when Eduardo was killed. Nirav was in far worse condition. He lost all interest in the cotton factory. He stopped communicating with the other members of his family. Shrouded in guilt and wallowing in the depths of despair, he was unable to offer comfort to Asha or Mohandas. Asha understood his grief and didn't look to her husband for emotional support, but rather drew on her own internal strength to keep going.

Two months later, Nirav contracted a particularly virulent strain of influenza. He lost all desire to go on living and succumbed to the virus late one evening.

Asha, already numb with grief, stepped back into her former role, and took control of the factory. Due to the policies and procedures put into place by Nirav in the preceding years, the cotton mill ran like a well-oiled machine. This was the company's saving grace, because Asha was capable of being little more than a figurehead. It was all she could do to put one foot in front of the other and get through each day. Sometimes it was a struggle just to get out of bed and dress herself in the morning.

Her son, Mohandas, was only eleven years old at the time, but Asha knew he'd have to begin learning the cotton business if the factory was to have any hope of long-term survival. It could only operate on autopilot for so long; someone with authority had to be at the helm to guide it along a successful path. And Asha just didn't have the heart to do it much longer. She prayed the business could sustain itself on the strong foundation on which it was built until Mohandas was of an age to take over.

Even after Asha had accepted the fact that Radha was

temporarily lost to her, she refused to accept the idea her daughter could be dead. One day she would hold her in her arms again, she vowed.

TWENTY-THREE

Wyoming, 1966

The fierce Wyoming wind whistled though the windows, and rocked the camper on its jacks. Large droplets of rain and pea-sized hail pelted the tin roof, making a deafening sound inside the camper. Looking down from his bed above, Rafael could see Radha was restless, tossing and turning under her thick wool blanket. Although she was accustomed to the torrential downpours of Bombay's monsoon season, he knew she'd never experienced a storm of this magnitude while inside a camper. But then, neither had he—and it was unnerving.

Radha gasped in alarm when Rafael shook her shoulder gently. "Radha?" he whispered. "Are you awake?"

"Yes, Rafael, I can't sleep. The storm's too loud."

"I can't sleep either. I think we should go to the barn and wait it out. I don't trust the sturdiness of the jacks on this camper. And I don't like feeling like a lightning rod either."

"I'd like to go to the barn, too. This thing swaying back and forth makes me feel like I'm back on the ship. It's making me queasy."

"Come on, then. Let's go. There are a couple of rain slickers in the storage compartment under your bed. They should keep us from getting too drenched while we make a dash for the barn."

Rafael had been spending long days constructing the new

barn. He rose before sunrise and dragged in close to nine o'clock in the evening for a late supper. Each night he placed a tender kiss on Radha's forehead and thanked her for having a hot meal waiting for him. He was relieved she didn't seem appalled at his subtle displays of affection. He longed to take their relationship to the next level, but he wouldn't press her into something he felt she wasn't ready for. Rafael had to keep reminding himself that Radha wasn't much more than a child. She was young enough to be his child, in fact, despite her mature personality.

Rafael was also grateful for the help she rendered by freeing him to work on other, more pressing things. Radha kept the camper immaculate and their clothes laundered. She hand washed them in the creek, and hung them out to dry on a line she'd strung between two large cottonwood trees. She seemed happiest when she was busy. Maybe it kept her mind off other matters, Rafael surmised. In any event, he was thankful for all she did. Her industry allowed him to work without distractions.

Radha was also amassing an impressive stock of canned vegetables for the upcoming winter. On one of Rafael's trips to Wamsutter, he purchased numerous cases of canning jars, a pressure cooker, canning salt, a jar lifter, and an instructional manual about canning and preserving produce. He'd salvaged the cast iron wood stove from the old cabin and set it up in the tool shed for Radha. After studying the instruction manual Rafael had bought, Radha began canning all the excess bounty from her garden. Colorful jars of corn, beans, squash, carrots, tomatoes, and pickles lined the shelves Rafael had made for her in the shed. She even canned a bushel of plums she'd found on a wild plum tree on the property. Preserving food was a labor of love for her. Radha was determined to do whatever she could to contribute to their success in rebuilding the ranch.

It amused Rafael when she said, "Everything on the supper

table, except the antelope steaks of course, was grown in my garden," and "I put up another fourteen quarts and eighteen pints of green beans today." There was undisguised pride in her voice as she made an accounting of each day's accomplishments.

Rafael also felt pleased about all his accomplishments. Other than the construction of some individual stalls, and the double doors, which only needed to be hung on their hinges, the barn was ready for livestock. He'd drawn up blueprints for both the barn and the new home. For the last several years his spare time had been devoted to collecting and studying "do it yourself" construction manuals. His experience in helping Asha rebuild the cotton factory had also been beneficial. It gave him a good base of knowledge on which to expand. Now he was putting the knowledge to good use.

With the barn project completed, he could soon begin in earnest to build their new home. It would be a three-bedroom, two-bath ranch home, with a covered wraparound porch, an open country kitchen, and a massive rock fireplace. The logs would be cut from the many thousands of lodge pole pines that densely populated the north section of the property. The fireplace would be hand laid with rocks from the creek bed. Radha had already begun collecting rocks and piling them up for Rafael, so they'd be handy when he reached that stage of the project.

It was mid-August 1966, and Rafael figured he could have the roof and exterior walls finished by the end of September, if all went as planned. Heavy equipment had been leased for lifting and maneuvering the heavy logs, which would speed up the process considerably. Hopefully, they could move into the house in early October, and he could work on the interior throughout the winter. Come spring, he would work at restoring the old chicken coop. Then Radha could have the chickens she'd expressed a desire for. Fresh eggs and poultry would be welcome additions to their diet.

Tonight, however, they'd have to seek shelter in the modern new barn. At least they'd be safe there.

"The rain has slacked off a bit. Let's make a run for it, little one," Rafael suggested.

"Race you!" Radha challenged. "Last one to the barn is a one-eyed polecat."

Now where did she get that expression? Rafael wondered in amusement. Radha had such a compelling personality. He wished Eduardo could have met her. Rafael grinned at the thought. *What am I thinking? If Eduardo were still alive, Radha could have been his daughter, which would've made her my niece!*

Before Rafael could respond to Radha's good-natured dare, she'd bolted from the camper in a dead run.

"No fair," Rafael panted, ducking into the front opening of the barn a few seconds behind Radha. "You're a lot younger than I am."

"Yeah, but you're . . . hey, what's that noise?" She asked as they both turned toward a racket coming from the far corner of the barn.

"I don't know. Stay right here," Rafael insisted. He switched on his high-powered flashlight and panned the rear wall with its beam. Blinded by the light, two black stallions stood at attention, snickering at the intruders. Like Rafael and Radha, the wild mustangs had sought shelter from the raging storm.

"Looks like they had the same idea," Rafael commented. "Here, Radha. Hold this beam on them for me for a minute. If they look like they're going to rush this way, just jump back and get out of their way."

Radha held the light while Rafael lifted the twin doors up on their hinges and secured the latch. Resting a hand on each hip, Rafael exclaimed with pride, "There now, little one. You have your very own horse!"

"Really? Oh, Rafael, my very own horse?"

"Yep! There's one for each of us."

Radha swung the light away from the stallions in her excitement. She moved toward Rafael and hugged him. He knew it must have been an impulsive reaction, but it pleased him. No longer blinded, the mustangs raced toward the opening they'd earlier entered, but the newly hung doors now blocked the opening. "Up the stairs! Quickly!" Rafael hollered over the clamor of the storm.

They scampered up the stairs to the loft Rafael had designed as storage space. "They look healthy, but they're wild and green. Once I manage to break them, you'll be able to realize your dream of riding across an open field on the back of a horse," Rafael told Radha.

"Oh, I can hardly wait, Rafael. That'll be so exciting," she said breathlessly, as she pushed her long brown hair back from where it had fallen around her face in her hasty ascent up the ladder. She wore her hair tied back during the day, but released it and gave it a hundred full strokes before bedtime, using the hairbrush Rafael had bought for her. It was Rafael's favorite time of the entire day, watching Radha brush her long, thick mane of lustrous hair. Years ago he'd watched her mother do the same thing every evening before she went to bed.

"What is involved in *breaking* a horse?" Radha asked, running her fingers through her tangled tresses once more.

Rafael finger-combed his hair, too, aware it must look even wilder than usual. "A lot of bruises mainly," he joked, "and an occasional fractured bone."

"I'll do it," Radha volunteered, after Rafael had explained the process of breaking horses. "Just show me how, and let me do it. I can break the one that will be mine, at least."

"No!"

"But I'm younger, remember? I'll heal faster."

"Regardless, I don't want you injured. These stallions are stout and powerful. They could inflict a lot of damage on a little thing like you. I don't even want you near them until I'm sure they're subdued enough for you to be safe around them. Promise you'll stay away from them for now?"

"We'll see . . ."

"Radha, I mean it! Riding them too soon would be much too dangerous."

Radha nodded, as if to humor him, and Rafael continued, "I'll take the larger of the two. He appears to be more domineering and aggressive."

"The one with the lightning bolt down his forehead?"

"Yeah—hey, I think you just named him for me. I'll call him Lightning. What are you going to name yours?"

"Why—Thunder, of course," she replied without pause. "On a night like this, could it be anything else?"

The two mustangs whimpered and pranced with nervous energy around the barn. Huddled together in the loft, Rafael and Radha looked down at the stallions from their perch above. Rafael enfolded Radha in his arms to keep her warm, and she rested her head on his shoulder. With a contented smile on her face, she drifted off to sleep while Rafael listened to the sounds of thunder and lightning, both inside and outside the barn.

"I'm okay. Really," Radha told Rafael. "Nothing's hurt so far but my pride." Gamely, she hopped back onto her feet after having been thrown off the back of Thunder for the fourth time. A hard worker, Rafael had quickly constructed a corral to contain the wild horses, and that's where they were now.

"Are you sure you don't want me to take over?"

"No, I can handle it, Rafael. I'm going to keep getting back on Thunder until he knows I'm the boss. I refuse to let him get the best of me."

"Good girl," he said. He was worried but full of admiration as he watched Radha slap her hat against her leg and put it back on her head. *How can anyone look so adorable in a cowboy hat and boots?* Rafael wondered. *I think she'd sleep in those boots, if she could.* He watched as she dusted the dirt off the back of her jeans and approached the indignant stallion again.

Radha had insisted on breaking Thunder herself, and badgered Rafael until he gave in. He was beginning to regret having relented. It was clear to Rafael that Radha inherited her mother's independent nature, her determination, and her perseverance. He knew it was important to her to conquer the stallion on her own, and he didn't want to break her spirit the way she was attempting to break Thunder's. He sighed and told himself, *I only hope she can succeed before Thunder succeeds in breaking her neck!* It was difficult for him to watch Radha as she flew through the air, landing with a resounding thud for the fifth time.

"I have him right where I want him now," she yelled, picking herself up from the ground again. He knew she'd be sporting plenty of bruises tomorrow.

"I can see that," Rafael yelled back, shaking his head and sighing heavily. Despite his fears, he laughed softly as he walked away from the scene.

Rafael and Radha were brushing down the horses in the barn on a sunny afternoon in late September. They'd just returned from their first horseback ride around the ranch on Thunder and Lightning. It'd been a delightful afternoon for Rafael, and a much-needed break from the construction project. It gave the blisters on his palms a chance to callus over.

"Thank you, Rafael. That was the most wonderful experience of my life," Radha said, smiling happily.

Rafael wholeheartedly agreed. Any time spent with Radha was wonderful, but knowing he'd helped her realize a dream made their time together even more special. As long as he lived he would never forget the sight of her racing across the field atop Thunder, waving her hat at him with her left hand, and hanging on for dear life with her right.

Lightning was still prone to unpredictable behavior. Thunder, on the other hand, was almost as docile now as a plow horse, eager to please his new master. Like Rafael, Thunder behaved as if he were entranced with the slender young woman.

But then who could blame him? Rafael wondered. Even now, as Radha ran a currycomb through Thunder's newly trimmed and more manageable mane, the stallion was nuzzling Radha's side, slightly under her left breast. *Lucky devil,* he thought. Just then Lightning reached back and nipped him, breaking the skin and leaving an ugly, red welt on his forearm.

I love her, Rafael admitted to himself that evening as they sat under the stars roasting hotdogs over an open campfire. He'd gone and fallen deeply in love with the enchanting young woman. His whole world now revolved around the daughter of a woman who had once meant the world to him.

Radha now meant more to him than anyone ever had in his entire life, including her mother, Asha. Feeling the way he did about Radha, he knew he had to put her best interests before his own, or he wouldn't be able to live with his own conscience. Whatever happened to him was immaterial. It was only her welfare he was concerned with at this point.

Once again he was reminded of his late brother. Like Eduardo, Radha made him want to be a better person. He'd gladly pay the price for his sins if the end result was happiness for Radha.

As he studied her now, she looked comfortable and relaxed.

But was that because she was happy here on the ranch with him? Or had she merely given up hope of seeing her family again, and was just trying to make the best of a bad situation? As if she felt him looking at her, she turned her gaze toward him and smiled. Her almost black irises glittered with the reflection of the campfire between them. *She's a beautiful person, inside and out.* He'd finally found somebody to love, and he was quite sure he was going to have to give her up. Sadness overwhelmed him.

Radha was like a butterfly, whose beauty was enhanced by its freedom of flight. Capture the butterfly, pin its wings to a board, and it would wither and die. He'd have to unpin Radha's wings and set her free. If she loved him, as he loved her, she'd eventually fly back to him. Granted, it was unlikely she'd ever do that, but it was a chance he'd have to take. *Love sure does make a man behave stupidly,* he jokingly told himself.

Yet Rafael loved Radha enough to grant her the freedom she deserved, despite the agony it was sure to cause him. *I owe her that much,* he thought. Just as he owed her the truth of why he'd abducted her in the first place. He needed to have a serious talk with Radha, and there was no time like the present, he decided.

Radha listened as Rafael related his entire life story to her. The truth behind the kidnapping incident came as a great relief to her. She knew he was a kind man by nature, and there had to have been something traumatic happen to him to cause him to abduct her the way he had.

"So you see," Rafael continued, "it was all in retribution for an injustice that was never even imposed on me. Your father didn't steal your mother from me. She was never mine to begin with. A lot of things are much clearer to me now," Rafael explained to her. "At the time that I abducted you, I was in shock at the sight of what seemed to be a mirror image of my memory of your mother. I wasn't thinking clearly. No, I wasn't thinking at all, I was only feeling. Feeling the long-ago heartache of losing something I thought I needed to go on living. I was wrong, but I didn't know it at the time."

"Oh, you poor, poor man. Your childhood was so much harsher than my own." Radha's voice was filled with compassion. "Forced to become a wage earner at nine, and then on your own at fifteen, the same age I am now," she continued. "Why, it would've only been natural for you to gravitate toward my mother. A drowning man, whether he's drowning in the ocean or in his own grief, will latch on to anything that floats. I read that somewhere," Radha said. She looked at Rafael's troubled expression and felt a sudden need to comfort him. He'd somehow come to mean more to her than life itself.

Radha reached over and stroked Rafael's forearm several times before she continued. "My mother has always had a way of making everyone around her feel special. To a homeless, vulnerable fifteen-year-old young man, suddenly alone and adrift, she would've been a welcome port in a storm. No one could blame you for wanting to be loved by her or for latching on to her the way you did. That would have been a normal reaction."

"How did you get to be so wise at such a young age?" Rafael asked.

"I am my mother's daughter."

Rafael sighed. "You are at that, and fortunate to be so," he said. "I should've been more appreciative of what she did for me, instead of wanting something more from her than I had a right to want."

"You were young, Rafael," Radha defended. "Not to mention you had just lost your entire family. I think you're being too hard on yourself. You need to give yourself more credit." She patted Rafael's hand, then lifted it up over her shoulder and snuggled against him.

"After losing Eduardo and my father, your mother was the only one in my life who really cared what happened to me. I thought I was in love with her, and managed to convince myself she surely felt the same way about me," he said, looking into Radha's warm brown eyes. He was surprised to see tears pooling in them. "Not that she ever gave me any reason to think that way. I realize now my idea of love was distorted. What I felt for her then could not even come close to what I feel for you now, Radha."

"Oh?" Radha asked with a curious expression on her face.

"I only hope you can find it in your heart to forgive me. I wronged your mother by not standing by her when she did find love again with your father. But I've wronged you far more significantly by taking you away from your family, and away from your hopes and dreams."

"But . . ." She shifted abruptly to face him.

Rafael ignored her interjection as he continued, "You have told me several times that you wanted to go to medical school. I think it's time to follow your dreams, little one. It's not too late, and it's what has to be done."

"Rafael," Radha began as she picked up his left hand in her own and covered it with her other hand. She stroked his hand absentmindedly as she said, "You have given me new hopes and dreams, and I love you, Rafael. Believe it or not, I want to stay with you now, not attend medical school."

"Please don't say that, Radha. It only makes it harder for me to do what I must."

"And what's that? What must you do?" she asked.

"Return you to your family. Take you home to Bombay so that you can have the kind of life you deserve. The life you planned for. You told me yourself you dreamed of being a cardiologist."

"Well, I've changed my mind!" she declared adamantly. She slapped him roughly on the shoulder. "And you will never get me on another blasted ship! Never, ever!"

"No, I wouldn't do that to you," he said, laughing softly. "I'll take you home on a plane, and then turn myself over to the authorities once we reach Bombay. I can afford the plane fares. I won't be needing any money where I'll be going once this is all said and done."

"Oh, no, you won't!" Radha declared. "It's true you changed my life when you took me away from my family. But don't ruin my life now by taking me away from yours and forcing me to go back to Bombay. You and I were meant to be together. This is my home now, Rafael," she said. Rafael's head was bent and he looked down into his lap. Radha used her forefinger to tilt his chin up to look her in the eye.

He returned her smile as she continued. "I feel as though I have known you forever, throughout eternity. I don't want to leave you or this ranch I've grown to love. I've a garden to tend to, a horse to take care of, and soon, a new home to decorate." She looked down at her hands, now clasped tightly in her lap, and finished in a shy whisper, "And most importantly, I have a man I hope will warm my bed one day, and give me lots of babies to love and raise."

Rafael was amazed. He considered pinching himself to make sure he wasn't dreaming. He couldn't possibly have heard her right.

"Do you mean that, Radha? Do you know what you're saying?" he asked, hope mingling with disbelief.

"Yes, I know exactly what I'm saying and I mean every word of it. I want to stay here with you. I need you in my life. You are my life now, Rafael."

"But you're so young, so much younger than me."

"I'm old enough to know what I want, old enough to make my own decisions," Radha argued. "Besides, to one's heart, age is irrelevant."

Rafael kneeled before her, grateful beyond belief. "Radha, my beautiful darling," he whispered. "You've made me the happiest man in the world. I know I'm not worthy of a bride like you, but will you honor me by marrying me?" His voice was hoarse with emotion.

"Yes, I'd be very proud to be your wife," Radha whispered back without hesitation.

"I love you, little one." He clasped both her hands in his, kissed them gently, and sat beside her.

"I love you too," Radha said, leaving her head on his shoulder. "If it's all right, I'll call my family after we're married to let them know where I am and tell them I'm okay. I do hate that they must be suffering, not knowing what has happened to me."

Rafael blanched at the thought of Asha being told he, Rafael, her old partner and confidante, had abducted her only daughter. He breathed a sigh of relief at Radha's next words.

"But I will simply tell them I ran off with you because I loved you and wanted to marry you. It won't be stretching the truth too much, will it? I'll say that I insisted on eloping, despite your objections. It will be the best solution all the way around. And I don't want any more mention of you turning yourself over to the authorities. You do that, and I will lie through my teeth, deny every charge you make against yourself. Do you hear?"

Rafael pulled her into his arms and kissed her very soundly. "I hear, little one. Thank you." He kissed her again and said, "Next Thursday I'm going to Rawlins to pick up a stock trailer and haul home a dozen head of cattle to start our herd. What do you say we go together and exchange vows before the Justice of the Peace that day? We can move into our new house the following week. It is liveable now. I'll give you a generous allowance to decorate it in anyway you wish. I want you to be comfortable in the home we will share together with all the children our love will bear."

"Oh Rafael, just imagine. That sounds so wonderful to me! I'd like nothing better than a house full of children, our children." Radha danced around him, slapping her hands together over and over.

Rafael was amused by her animated display of excitement. "I'd like nothing better either," he said. "I'm sorry you won't be able to have the lavish wedding you deserve, with a long white gown, three-tiered cakes, attendants, and all that."

"Oh, Rafael," Radha said. She sighed in frustration. "I don't want any of that. All I want is you—to spend the rest of my life with. Besides, I think a brand-new log home is a pretty wonderful wedding present. Don't you?" she asked in delight.

"But you deserve so much more, and I wish I could give it all to you," he said.

"Don't you know it's not what you have in life, but whom you share it with that matters?"

"You are teaching me that right now, Radha."

"You've also taught me a lot. Among other things, you've taught me to garden, play cards, fly fish, and to break and ride a horse. Now will you teach me one more thing? Something I'm very anxious to learn."

"What's that?" Rafael asked.

"Teach me how to please you. Make love to me tonight," Radha whispered shyly. She blushed at her own forwardness.

"Are you certain that's what you want? Wouldn't you rather wait until next Thursday night after we've taken our vows?"

Rafael had dreamed of this for months, but now that it was becoming a reality, the thought disturbed him. Radha was an innocent. He wasn't sure if he could hold back from ravishing her like a starving man tearing into a juicy steak. He'd have to show great restraint and gentleness, make sure he didn't hurt her any more than necessary. He grinned broadly in anticipation. Radha began to tremble in her own excitement.

"I'm absolutely certain, Rafael. As I'm sure you have noticed, patience is not one of my strong points. And being a virgin on my wedding night is not important to me whatsoever, unless it is to you."

"No, it's of no consequence to me. Only your happiness and well-being is important. But, you see," he explained, "there may be a little discomfort the first time, and I'm reluctant to cause you any further pain."

"I'm not afraid of a little pain, Rafael. Just ask Thunder," she said wryly. "I know you wouldn't deliberately cause me pain. You've proved that. The pain you can't prevent will be worth it."

Two hours later, Radha and Rafael lay spent and sated on Rafael's small, but adequate-sized mattress. Radha had insisted Rafael not treat her with kid gloves. So he complied, and Radha graduated from a girl to a young woman in his arms that night. He prayed he had not hurt her and that she was as deliriously in love as he was.

"I stand corrected," Radha whispered to Rafael.

"Huh?" he asked, concern etched in his voice.

"*That* was the most wonderful experience I've ever had! Horseback riding now pales in comparison."

Rafael laughed in relief, and soon fell into a relaxed sleep. The love of his life was curled up in his embrace, with a most blissful smile on her lips.

Twenty-Four

Rawlins, Wyoming, 2001

"Oscar?"

"Yeah, Mark?"

"Got a minute?" Oscar asked, leaning back in his chair watching George W. Bush on the desk TV. The President was addressing the nation regarding the war on terrorism following the September 11th attack.

"Sure, what's up?"

"Rafael in fourteen is not doing too good," Mark said.

"Yeah, I know. I talked to Dr. Wheeler this morning, and he said the cancer had spread to the bone and to the liver. You know, Rafael can barely stand to be touched now; yet, despite his agony, he won't submit to pain medication."

"I've tried to sneak the morphine patches on to his back, but he finds them and rips them off," Mark told Oscar. "I've never seen anyone so determined to suffer, have you? He won't eat much of anything, and he won't allow us to feed him intravenously."

Oscar nodded. "I know. He's so weak now he hasn't flung any food at me for weeks. To tell you the truth, I kind of miss the spunkiness the old feller had."

Oscar's remark surprised him. But Mark had noticed a change in Oscar; like so many others, he seemed to be feeling more compassionate toward his fellow Americans these days.

"Yeah, me too. I'm going to hate to see him go. He's been around here longer than most of the furniture. In fact, he's been here longer than I've been alive. Oh, and Oscar, he told me he wants to have a will drawn up—and he wants to have it witnessed."

"Arrange it then," the head nurse at the Wallingford Institute instructed him. "I don't think he will be with us much longer, so get right on it. And do whatever you can to make him comfortable."

"I will, Oscar. Rafael also wants to see the Robbins family again. He told me he needs to tell them what happened to their friend's daughter. Said he won't be able to rest in peace until he gets it all off his chest. This attack on our nation has affected everyone, maybe even Rafael. What do you think I should do about it, Oscar?"

"Call the Robbins, Mark. Get them out here, somehow, ASAP. Everyone deserves one last chance at redemption, you know. Well—almost everyone, that is." His implied exception did not need to be verbalized, as he glanced back at the television where Bin Laden's face filled the screen.

TWENTY-FIVE

Wyoming, 1966

Progress on the home construction project slowed down considerably the next few days. Radha enjoyed having Rafael spend a lot of time with her in the camper. "We're going to have to get out of bed more, so we can get some rest," he had jokingly told her. "I'm getting a bit too fond of the cute little birthmark on your right hip."

"I always knew it was good for something," Radha quipped. After spending the mornings frolicking in bed with her, Rafael worked on the electrical wiring of the new home in the afternoons. It was a challenging task; a log home didn't have sheet-rocked walls to hide wiring behind, Rafael explained to Radha.

While Rafael struggled with the wiring, Radha spent the afternoons riding Thunder. A hard frost brought an end to her gardening; nothing but a few turnips remained to be harvested. As much as she enjoyed gardening and canning, Radha wasn't disappointed to see the growing season come to an end. It allowed her more time to spend with Thunder, and riding horseback around the ranch never ceased to excite her. It was as exhilarating as she had dreamed it would be. Thunder was a kindred spirit, and she loved him with her whole heart.

Rafael had directed her to avoid the east field, and the forest and vegetation was too dense in the north field for her and

Thunder to transit safely, but they still had over six hundred acres to roam in the south and west sections.

"Be extra careful when you are out riding alone, Radha," Rafael said. "Thunder still has wild instincts, no matter how domesticated he behaves. Something could spook him and cause him to bolt on you." He winked and added, "And you do realize you could have already conceived our first child, don't you?"

The thought had not occurred to Radha, but the very idea of it thrilled her. Her thoughts centered on the possibility one chilly afternoon as she and Thunder made their way across the west field.

A child, Rafael's child, was the only thing Radha could imagine that could make her life any happier or fuller than it already was. She wanted a whole passel of children and knew Rafael felt the same. They both dreamed of having a thriving cattle business to hand down to their offspring one day, and were anxious to begin producing their heirs right away.

Radha was also anxious to speak to her parents in Bombay, and planned to do so on Thursday, after she and Rafael exchanged vows in Rawlins. She wanted to relieve the anxiety she knew they must be enduring, and attempt to pave the path for Rafael to be accepted as their new son-in-law. She knew they wouldn't be pleased to hear she eloped with him to America. And that was exactly the story she'd have to tell them.

Asha and Nirav wouldn't understand how she could have put them through the pain and suffering of letting them believe she'd been abducted. They'd be hurt when she told them the ensuing ransom note had been her idea, but she had no other choice but to lie to them. If she told them the truth, they'd never welcome Rafael into the family. As it was, their relationship with him would be a tenuous one at best. She'd be lucky if her father did not opt to fly to Wyoming, demand an annulment, and force her to return to Bombay with him.

Nirav might also elect to have Rafael charged with statutory rape, she suddenly realized. Even though she'd be lying about her age on the marriage license, it would be easy to prove fifteen was her actual age.

Radha was aware Rafael and her father hadn't been the best of friends all those years ago, and their relationship had been controversial. She had no way to predict how her father would react to the news of her marriage to Rafael, but she could assume his reaction wouldn't be favorable. It was sure to be a bittersweet confrontation with her parents when the time came. *They'll be ecstatic that I'm alive and well,* she thought. And they'd be livid she had not contacted them to let them know that.

The more Radha thought about the potential consequences of communicating with her parents, the more she considered postponing the phone call to India.

As Thunder trotted along the fence line into the south field, Radha gave the situation serious deliberation and wasn't proud of herself for coming to the conclusion she didn't have the courage or confidence to contact her parents at this time. She decided it'd be best to wait until after her eighteenth birthday. As a legal adult, they wouldn't be able to enforce their will on her. And with any luck at all, by then, she and Rafael would have produced a baby to help soften the blow. She knew her parents well enough to know they could never turn their back on their own flesh and blood grandchild, despite their displeasure with Radha and Rafael.

Radha sighed, relieved to have made a decision on the matter, even if her decision made her feel a little uneasy and *a lot* guilty.

"Tomorrow's the big day, my dear," Rafael told Radha as he placed a kiss on the side of her neck. "Are you having any second thoughts?"

"None at all."

"Good. I don't want you to enter this commitment with any reservations at all."

"I have no reservations, Rafael. I promise."

It was Wednesday evening and the two of them were enjoying a glass of wine after dinner. Donning heavy leather jackets and knit hats, they were relaxing on the pine swing Rafael had constructed and hung on the front porch of their new home. Although there was still a lot of work to be done on the interior of the new log house, they would be moving into it after they returned home from Rawlins as newlyweds.

Rafael draped his arm over Radha's shoulder as they swayed idly on the porch swing. "I think it would be best for us to get married tomorrow afternoon. We can go out for a nice supper to celebrate, and then spend the night at the Stagecoach Inn in Rawlins. It appears to me to be the nicest hotel in town. It's clean and well kept."

"That sounds nice," Radha said. "Any place is fine with me as long as we are together."

Rafael squeezed Radha's shoulder lovingly. "We can pick up the stock trailer and cattle on Friday morning as we are heading home."

"*Heading home* has a really nice ring to it," Radha said, nodding with a contented smile on her face. She pushed her feet against the porch deck to move the swing again. "I look forward to growing old with you here on our ranch, surrounded by our children and grandchildren."

"So do I, little one. Our future looks bright and promising. But I don't want us to feel rushed on our wedding day. It's an important day for both of us, and I want it to be enjoyable, a very special occasion," Rafael said as he held her hand up against his and entwined her fingers with his own.

"It will be, Rafael. It will be unforgettable, I'm sure."

They finished off another glass of wine before Rafael stood up, grasped Radha's hand again and pulled her up to her feet. "I need to get you tucked in. I noticed an oil leak under the truck this afternoon, and I want to get up early to check it out before we head off to Rawlins."

"Okay, I need to get some beauty sleep anyway."

"You fishing?" Rafael asked.

"Excuse me?"

"For compliments," he clarified, laughing at her look of confusion. "You know you couldn't be any more beautiful to me than you already are."

Radha swatted him playfully. "No, I am not fishing! But I do need to get some rest. Tomorrow will be a long day."

At Rafael's nod of agreement she added, "And the most wonderful day of my life."

TWENTY-SIX

Kansas, 2001

"I don't think we should take Skye out of school or subject her to anything that might bring on more anxiety or nightmares. Do you, Zoe?" Trey asked, after she had repeated to him her phone conversation with the nurse from the Wallingford Institute.

"No, she hasn't mentioned Radha or anything to do with all that in a long time. There's no sense stirring it all up again now. I don't think it would be of any benefit for her to hear what Rafael has to say, especially now that her memories of that lifetime seem to be fading. But even though I don't want Skye involved, I do think you and I should go out there."

Skye's nightmares might have ceased, but Zoe's had not. She was now waking up almost every night, shaken from dreams that involved a variety of frightening scenarios of how Radha had died. But it was Skye's face she saw in her dreams, not a fifteen-year-old Indian girl. Zoe hadn't mentioned these dreams to Trey. She didn't want him to be concerned about her. He'd gone out of his way in recent days to be more thoughtful, less temperamental, and certainly more affectionate. He was becoming more involved with both his wife and his daughter, spending quality time with his family in the evenings. Zoe had come to the realization their marital problems had been as much her fault as his, and she was willing to meet him halfway in their attempt at a reconciliation. The least she could do was to quit acting like some kind of spoiled prima donna.

"Zoe, I'm not too sure we should go out to Wyoming either," Trey said, breaking into her thoughts.

"Why not?"

"What can be gained by it? We know Rafael killed Radha. We don't know how or why, but knowing the details might be more distressing than not knowing. I've given it some thought, and I think when Skye met Rafael in August, she forgave him for whatever he did to Radha. Probably in an effort to relieve herself of the painful memories, so she could get on with her present life as Skylar Robbins. Maybe we should just leave it at that."

"I can't leave it at that, Trey. I have to know what happened so I can get on with *my* life. I just can't leave the loose ends untied like that. I'm not sure I can explain why, but it's important to me to have this whole thing resolved. And my gut feeling is you also need to know the truth—as does the Joshi family."

"Well, you may be right. I'll admit I'm curious to find out the whole story, even if I find it distasteful. And if it will bring any degree of relief to you, I guess I agree we should go. I'll call my folks and see if they can keep Skye for a few days while we're gone. I don't think Mom will mind taking her back and forth to school."

"No, I'm sure she won't," Zoe agreed. Trey's mother had just complained to Zoe a few days before that she and Joe Junior didn't get to spend enough time with their granddaughter. This would be an ideal opportunity for them to have Skye to themselves for a couple of days.

"Do you think Jutta would want to go? I'd feel better if she were with us for some reason," Trey said.

"Me, too. And I imagine she'll be as interested to hear Rafael's story as we are. I'll give her a call. Now that she's only practicing a few days a week, she should be able to clear her schedule easily enough," Zoe said. She reached for the phone. She no longer had to look up Jutta's number because she'd utilized the phone's speed dial function.

"When she called to tell us about her engagement to Dr. Azzam the other day, she said she's considering writing a novel about reincarnation and this whole experience with Skye. I'm sure she'll welcome the chance to accompany us to Wyoming, just to see how the story ends, if nothing else!"

Zoe dialed the phone, and then replaced the handset when she heard a busy signal. "I'm almost afraid to hear what Rafael has to tell us. Mark said it was important for him to get it off his chest, so he could die in peace," she said. "Mark seems real fond of the grumpy old coot for some reason."

"Hard to imagine, isn't it?" Trey asked. "The past sure must be eating at Rafael, huh? I wonder what's made him decide to open up. Could it be an effect of the September 11th terrorist attack?"

"It's possible," she agreed, as she hung up the phone again after another unsuccessful attempt to reach Jutta. "I guess we'll find out soon enough. When should I tell Jutta we're leaving? Is tomorrow morning all right? Mark said it was imperative we get out there soon. He said Rafael is fading fast."

"Yes, if Mom and Dad are available to take care of Skye, which I'm sure they will be, we'll leave first thing tomorrow morning," Trey said. He winked at Zoe as she hit the speed dial button once again. He continued, "Boy, am I glad Wyoming is close enough that we don't have to fly there. This experience will be stressful enough as it is. You never liked to fly, even before nine-eleven, and now it will really be tough to get you on an airplane."

"I know that's right!" Zoe agreed, a moment before she heard Jutta's gravelly voice say, "Hello."

★　★　★　★　★

"Rafael is awake. He's alert and restless, and ready to talk to you all," Mark told Zoe, Trey, and Jutta when they approached him at the nurses' station of the Wallingford Institute in Rawlins. "I have to warn you his condition has deteriorated a lot since you last saw him. Like I told you on the phone, he's eaten up with cancer now. Dr. Wheeler is amazed he's lasted this long. He said Rafael is living on borrowed time. That's why we were so adamant about getting you out here as soon as we could. Rafael won't be with us much longer."

Despite the nurse's warning, Zoe was shocked at the appearance of the shrunken old man in room fourteen. Rafael looked like he'd aged ten years since August. He was wasting away; his frail body looked as if the bedclothes that surrounded him were swallowing him up. His sallow skin and gaunt cheeks made his eyes look like they were too large for his face. His lips were dry and pasty; his sunken eyes were red and puffy.

"Come on in, folks," Rafael said. His voice was loud and clear, despite his body's weakened condition. "Please have a seat. The story I have to tell you is a long one, I'm afraid, but it's one that I want and need to tell someone who can pass it on to Asha for me."

"You want us to pass your story on to Asha?" Trey asked, disbelief evident in his voice.

"Yes, it's very important to me she knows the truth about what happened to her beloved daughter, Radha. But before I begin, please introduce me to your companion."

Trey introduced Jutta as requested. "Rafael, this is Jutta Meyer, a dear friend of ours. She would like to tape-record your story, if it's agreeable with you. We'll see that a copy of it gets to Asha."

Zoe noticed Trey didn't mention that Asha wasn't sound enough in mind and body to comprehend what the recording entailed. There seemed to be no point in informing Rafael about Asha's dementia, her inability to assimilate and comprehend whatever it was he felt compelled to have relayed to her.

Rafael nodded his assent, and then looked around the room searchingly. "Where's your little girl—Skylar?"

Trey explained Skye was in kindergarten now and staying with her grandparents while they were in Wyoming. It was clear Rafael was disappointed, and he said as much. "I was hoping to get to see her again. I can't explain why, but I feel like I've known Skylar forever, even though I only spent a few minutes with her. It was meeting her that convinced me I needed to clear my conscience before I die. I believe in karma and don't want to have to pay for my sins in my next life. I've paid for them enough in this lifetime already. But I've asked the Lord for forgiveness and placed my soul in his hands."

At his chilling words, Zoe briefly wondered about the wisdom of her decision to come to Wyoming to hear Rafael's story. She twisted the ends of her hair as she thought of the possibility she wouldn't be able to handle what Rafael told them today. Maybe they should've done as Trey suggested and left well enough alone.

Rafael glanced at them and began. "I'd like to begin by apologizing for the way I behaved at our first meeting," he said. "I was overwhelmed by the memories that Skye evoked in me, memories I had buried in my subconscious for many years. She reminded me so strongly of Radha."

Zoe looked up in surprise.

"You see—I do remember Radha, like we were together just yesterday. I loved her," Rafael continued.

"You loved Radha?" Zoe and Trey echoed, bewildered at Rafael's admission. Zoe was beginning to suspect they'd all misjudged Rafael and his relationship with Radha. *This promises to be an even more poignant story than we'd anticipated,* Zoe thought.

"Yes, I loved her with all my heart and soul, but I failed to protect her as I should have. Her death was an accident, a tragic, unfortunate accident; but I've always held myself responsible for it, as I still do. I have a lot to atone for." Rafael stopped talking long enough to blow his nose and readjust his position on the bed. He explained the events that had preceded his thirty-odd years at the Wallingford Institute. Zoe, Trey, and Jutta sat entranced as they listened to him relate his detailed life story, starting at the very beginning with his childhood on the cattle ranch, and culminating with his and Radha's final day there.

TWENTY-SEVEN

"Radha, honey, can you hand me that oil filter wrench?" Rafael asked, as he lay on his back under the truck. She and Rafael had both awakened early on their wedding day, anxious to get the truck repaired and get on their way to Rawlins. Rafael was impatient now as he worked underneath the engine.

With the sun just peeking up over the horizon, Rafael had gone outside to check out the problem with the Ford pickup, while she packed a bag to take with them on their trip. After Radha had finished packing, she went outside to see how Rafael was coming along on the repair. He told her he'd discovered the oil leak was due to a filter not having been tightened sufficiently, an oversight he said would've been detected in a mechanical inspection, had there been time to let the Texas dealership perform one. She watched as he jacked up the front end of the truck to gain access to the filter. He assured her it would just take a few minutes to correct the problem, and then they'd be ready to go. They would get an oil change on the truck while in Rawlins, as one was long overdue.

His first attempt to tighten the gummed-up filter failed. With a firm grip on the wrench, Rafael slipped it around the oil filter again and gave it another forceful yank. As the filter rotated slightly, the frame of the truck shuddered, tilting the large jack up on its edge. Rafael saw the jack sway out of the corner of his eye and panicked. Radha watched as he thrust himself out from under the truck. In his haste, Rafael made just enough contact with the jack to upset it and cause it to topple out from beneath the bumper.

Rafael yelled both in surprise and anguish as the truck crashed down on the jack, trapping his left leg under it as it fell. Radha gasped in terror. She watched Rafael try in vain to pull his leg out from under the fallen jack. But it was wedged tight. She knew he couldn't move it without doing further damage to his already severely crushed limb. She paled as she saw the first signs of blood begin to seep through the fabric of Rafael's denim jeans just above where the jack had punctured his flesh.

"Oh, my God! Rafael, what can I do? Tell me what to do to help you," she pleaded. "I'll do anything, Rafael, anything I possibly can."

Radha scurried around, frantic, as Rafael moaned and writhed in agony. She tried to hoist up the bumper, but found she couldn't budge it. As Rafael struggled to retain consciousness, Radha was in turmoil. She had to get someone to help her, but how? And who? There was no phone service on the ranch, and the nearest neighbors were the Goodmans, who lived about two miles to the east of the Torres' property. She'd never met them, but knew Rafael had talked with the sheep ranchers on several occasions and had found them to be friendly, pleasant neighbors. She knew they would help her if she were fortunate enough to find them at home.

Radha's only option was to take Thunder and ride across the east field to the Goodman's. She'd ask them to drive back and help her lift the truck off Rafael. If no one was home at the sheep ranch, she'd break into their house and use their phone to call for help. Radha would do whatever it took to bring help to Rafael.

"I'm going to the Goodman ranch for help, Rafael. I'll be

right back with people who can lift the truck up," she assured him, forcing as much calmness into her tone and demeanor as she could manage.

"Stay out of the east field, Radha! You'll have to go the long way around," he ordered in a trembling, pain-filled voice. "Crossing the east field is too dangerous."

"I'm sorry to have to disobey you, Rafael. But I have to do what I have to do to help you. I can't worry about my own safety right now. It is critical I bring help back as quickly as I can."

Radha ran to the barn, telling herself that as much as she hated to disobey Rafael, she had no choice; she had to put his well-being ahead of her own. She would deal with his displeasure with her later. She couldn't afford to take the extra time to go the long way around. Radha leapt onto Thunder's back and directed him past Rafael, who was lying helpless, trapped under the bumper jack. She veered Thunder toward the east field, ignoring Rafael's pleas as he begged for her to stop.

"No!" Rafael cried out in a futile effort. His voice was weak and ragged. "Radha, stop! Please, stop! I can free the leg myself! Please, please stop!"

He knew Radha was determined to risk all she had to help him. Her devotion to him was touching, but he was not willing to let her risk injury on his behalf if he could help it. He'd sacrifice his leg before allowing her to do that for him. He didn't deserve someone as goodhearted and unselfish as Radha Joshi. He had to protect her!

With all the strength he could muster, he jerked his leg out from under the bumper jack, and gritted his teeth as a deep, gaping gash ripped through his thigh. Shaking off the excruciating pain and the light-headedness that followed, he hobbled to the barn, dragging his mutilated leg behind him. Awkwardly,

Rafael climbed onto the top of Lightning's back, and with blood seeping through the jagged tear in his jeans, he spurred the stallion into action. Together, they raced across the east field. Each jolt stemming from the horse's motions sent ripples of fire coursing through his entire body. He fought back nausea brought on by the pain.

"Thunder, whoa!" he yelled over and over again, striving to make his voice heard over the pounding of the horses' hooves. He was closing the gap, but Radha was too intent on her mission. Rafael could see she had no clue she was being pursued.

Just before Thunder and Radha reached the outer perimeter of the huge ravine, Rafael screamed as loudly as he was able. Thunder appeared to eye the ravine too, and at the last moment, the horse came to an abrupt halt. Thunder's sudden stop from full speed propelled Radha forward into the deep pit. Her small body flew through the air in what seemed like slow motion to Rafael. He felt his heart skip several beats. He watched in horror as her body came to rest on a pile of metal debris.

Rafael's senses reeled as he slid off of Lightning's back, landing in an ungraceful heap on the ground. He crawled down into the imposing ditch as fast as his mangled leg would allow him, hoping against hope that the scene he'd just witnessed had been a pain-induced figment of his imagination. He was horrified to discover it hadn't been a figment at all, but a harsh reality.

Radha lay sprawled out before him, with two inches of rusty metal protruding from where she'd been impaled through the throat. Her arm and leg muscles were twitching in convulsive spasms, her chest heaving as she attempted to fill her lungs with air through a punctured windpipe. She looked up at Rafael with a plea for forgiveness on her face. There was no fear in her eyes, only regret. Regret and unconditional love.

Rafael grasped her trembling hands with his larger, callused hands, which were shaking even more violently than hers.

"Radha, my love, what have I done to you? I'm so sorry. So terribly sorry," Rafael whispered, tears streaming from his eyes.

Radha tried to respond, but was unsuccessful. She opened her mouth to speak but no words, only blood, bubbled out. Rafael read her lips as she tried with a valiant effort to get her message out to him. "My fault, not yours, not Thunder's. I'm sorry. I love you," she mouthed. "I will love you forever, Rafael."

Rafael knew she was dying. He prayed he would die too. He couldn't imagine a life without her. He only wanted to live long enough to see she got a proper burial. He couldn't leave her body in this ravine filled with rubbish. It would be a sacrilege.

"I love you too, little one, with every fiber of my being," Rafael whispered, choking on his tears. "I'm so sorry I brought you to Wyoming, only to have it end this way. Thank you for bringing me such love and happiness. You know I would never have intentionally hurt you, not in this life or the next. And I'll never forget you, not in this life or the next. Wait for me, my love. I promise I'll be with you again someday."

The pain etched on Radha's face dissolved into a peaceful smile as her eyes glazed over and her writhing body stilled. With great care, Rafael lifted her body off the metal post and laid it down on a nearby grassy mound. He buried his face in his hands, as he sobbed and prayed.

Two hours later, Rafael was found by passing motorists, on the road near the driveway of his property. Draped over Lightning's back, he was unconscious from the loss of blood. Emergency technicians were summoned, and he was transported to the nearest hospital where surgeons fought to save his life. To Rafael's dismay, they succeeded. He never returned to the Torres Cattle Ranch, but he left his heart and his sanity there at the bottom of the deep ravine in the east field.

Zoe wiped tears from her own cheeks, unaware she'd been cry-ing. Who was this compassionate, thoughtful individual who had replaced the gruff, moody, and temperamental man they'd met in August? He seemed an entirely different Rafael Torres than the one they had encountered before.

"Oh, Rafael, I'm so sorry," Zoe said softly. "How heartbreak-ing for you." She could hear Jutta sniffle beside her, and Trey's face held a thoughtful expression.

"It was," Rafael agreed in a choked whisper. "It still is, for I mourn for her as much today as I did back then." He sighed. "Thank you all for letting me get this off my chest. I'm not only asking for forgiveness, but also for understanding."

Rafael blew his nose, and then offered fresh tissues to Zoe and Jutta. After they each pulled a tissue from the box, he continued. "Please let Asha and her family know I would have given my life for Radha. I take full responsibility for her death, and if it is any consolation to her family, I've been consumed with guilt and remorse for over three decades. Had it not been for my unforgivable actions, Radha would probably still be alive and well today, with her family in Bombay. She could've been a world-renowned cardiologist now," he stated. With sincere sad-ness in his voice he said, "Radha had the drive and determina-tion to be whatever she wanted to be."

Zoe wiped her eyes, patted Rafael's bony shoulder, and said, "Rafael, we also have a story to tell you. A story that should explain the familiarity you and our daughter seemed to feel with one another. And it's a story that may bring you some comfort. You see, Radha is alive and well. She is alive in our daughter, Skylar. Please, Rafael. Settle back, get comfortable, and rest while we tell you all about it. You'll see that while

Radha's body didn't survive that fateful day in 1966, her soul did."

TWENTY-EIGHT

Rawlins, Wyoming, 2001

"Wow, what a story!" Jutta exclaimed from the rear of the mini-van. Zoe nodded her agreement.

As Trey maneuvered the vehicle out of the Wallingford Institute's parking lot, Zoe thought about all they'd learned from Rafael that day. She was so thankful she'd been able to convince Trey to make the trip to Wyoming. She could put her fears to rest now and get on with her life.

Zoe listened as Jutta continued, "That's so kind and thoughtful of Rafael to leave his family's cattle ranch to Skye in his will. I guess in an odd way, she's the closest thing to a relative he has left. What are you going to do with the ranch?"

Jutta had directed the question to Trey, who answered, "Well, I thought we'd drive out there now to have a look at it. Zoe wants to take some photos of it to show to Skye someday. It will be an eerie feeling to see it, knowing now the events that unfolded there all those years ago."

"And then?" Jutta asked, still seeking an answer to her question.

"Zoe and I discussed that while you were on the phone with Karem. We decided since it'll belong to Skye, it should ultimately be her decision. We'll have to wait until she is older, maybe in her late teens or early twenties, to tell her everything we know about the whole situation. Then she can decide what she wants to do with the ranch. It's better to wait until she is old enough to make a mature decision."

Jutta nodded. "By then, all of Skye's memories of past lives should have faded away. It'll be less of an emotional strain on her."

"That's what we figured," Zoe cut in. "The ranch has sat vacant for many years, so a few more shouldn't matter. We'll keep the taxes paid on it for her in the meantime. Jutta, I'm glad you thought to bring a tape recorder. I called Mohandas from the pay phone and promised him we'd get a copy off to him soon. He can choose how or what to tell Asha. He's not sure if he should tell her anything at all. The story is so incredible, it might just confuse her more. Mohandas said since Asha met Skye, she seems so much more content that he hesitates to tell her anything that would upset her."

"At least Mohandas will have the closure he has longed for," Trey said. "And waited many, many years for."

"Yes, he was very relieved to hear the story and finally know the truth," Zoe said. Then, remembering what else Mohandas had told her, "Oh, and Mohandas had some news too," she added. "He and Sitha are adopting a nine-year-old boy named Levi. Levi's parents were killed in an auto accident a few days ago. His father worked for Mohandas at the cotton factory for years, and was a good friend of his. Mohandas was, in fact, the boy's godfather. He and Sitha are sad and upset about the death of Levi's father, but thrilled at the prospect of being parents."

"That is exciting news, although it's sad the boy's parents were killed," Trey said.

"They will be wonderful parents to Levi, though," Jutta chimed in. "And, by the way, thanks for letting me tag along. I can't wait to get started on my novel. Hearing Rafael's story, I think one thing I've been curious about has become very clear."

"What's that?" Zoe asked.

"Skye's emotional reaction to her memories involving Rafael were not due to any abuse she suffered at his hands, but rather to the heartache of being separated in such a terrible accident, from someone with whom she shared a deep, intense love. I'd say the two of them are what we would call soul mates in my business. It's a sad but romantic story, don't you think?"

Zoe agreed. The tale she heard wasn't what she'd expected to hear from Rafael. She was relieved the truth of Radha's disappearance had been disclosed, and the young girl had found love and joy with her captor, instead of pain and torture. Her death had been a tragic accident, as Rafael had proclaimed. But it had been just an accident, not a homicide. Rafael was guilty of kidnapping, but not murder.

"It also explains another thing," Jutta said to her new friends. "The birthmark you showed me on the back of Skye's neck. In past-life regressions it's often discovered that my patients' birthmarks correspond to fatal wounds they've suffered in previous lifetimes. For example, someone who has a birthmark on their chest might recall a past-life memory of having been shot or stabbed in the exact location. It's amazing how often this occurs. It happens too often to be coincidental. It doesn't explain the birthmark on Skye's right hip, but the one on her neck sure fits with the manner in which Radha died. I had wondered if a correlation to one or both of Skye's birthmarks might surface in Rafael's story,"

Zoe was intrigued. "Now that you mention it, I do remember reading about the significance of birthmarks in several of the books I read about reincarnation. I'm so happy Rafael decided to share his story with us before it was too late. He won't live much longer, I'm afraid, and the truth would have died with him."

"I'm just happy to have the whole thing behind us," Trey said.

Several months later, Zoe was lounging on a wicker chair on the front porch of the farmhouse, reading the latest bestseller, and enjoying an unseasonably warm spring day. In the background she could hear the rhythmic tapping of a hammer, as Trey put the final touches on the new barn.

Zoe sighed. She was thankful she and Trey had been able to resolve their differences and rekindle the flame that had brought them together years before. Their marriage was stronger than it had ever been. They'd learned to communicate and compromise.

Things are going so well for our family, Zoe thought. *Next year Skye will be a first-grader, and I'll be teaching third grade at the same school. I can still be close to Skye without smothering her.* The school board had approved Zoe's application in March. She looked forward to putting her elementary-education degree to use and having a rewarding career as a teacher.

And she had to admit Trey had been right all along. Skye was blossoming with the addition of friends her own age to play and interact with. It was nice to see her daughter acting like a normal, rambunctious six-year-old, no longer haunted by memories of a life in India. When the news of Rafael's death arrived just before Christmas, Skye had shown very little reaction. "I will never forget him," she had simply said. But, of course, Skye would forget him soon enough, Jutta had said.

Today was Saturday and Skye was dressed in her favorite faded denim overalls. As Zoe sipped iced tea, Skye sat with her back up against the front door, daydreaming as she stared out toward the front yard. Suddenly, with a very determined look on her face, she picked up a crayon and her Pocahontas notebook. She flipped to a page near the center of the notebook and began to print carefully.

"What are you doing, punkin?" Zoe asked her.

"Writing my name."

"Oh?" Zoe replied. Her mind flashed back to a similar conversation nearly a year before. "So you're writing 'Skylar Robbins'?"

"No, Mommy. I'm writing my old name," Skye answered. "When I was eighteen, they called me White Flower."

ABOUT THE AUTHOR

Jeanne Glidewell, and her husband, Robert, live in the small Kansas town of Bonner Springs. Besides writing, Jeanne loves fishing, traveling, and wildlife photography. As a 2006 pancreas and kidney transplant recipient, Jeanne volunteers her time as a Life Mentor for the Gift of Life Program in Kansas City, mentoring future transplant recipients. It's her way of giving back.

Jeanne has published many magazine articles, being a former staff writer for a locally based publication. She has had two Lexie Starr cozy mysteries published in recent years, *Leave No Stone Unturned,* and *The Extinguished Guest,* and has the third, *Haunted,* ready for publication. She is a member of Sisters-in-Crime and Mystery Writers of America and is currently working on another Lexie Starr mystery novel and considering a sequel to *Soul Survivor.* To contact Jeanne, go to her Web site at http://www.jeanneglidewell.com.